THE
BULLHORN
REUKUS

To Ruthie and Leslie

Nelson P. Bard

The Bullhorn Reukus

By

NELSON P. BARD

VANTAGE PRESS

NEW YORK WASHINGTON HOLLYWOOD

FIRST EDITION

Copyright, © 1964, by Nelson P. Bard

Published by Vantage Press, Inc.
120 West 31st Street, New York 1, N. Y.

Manufactured in the United States of Ameirca

To Tom Lewis
who made me do it.

FOREWORD

This is a story about Cleveland, Ohio and a real family, the Stones. It is then biographical, but not entirely so, for many of the characters are fictitious. Much of the story is based on fact, but fact handled so carelessly that it is a safe assumption that the story is more fiction than not.

CONTENTS

THE
BULLHORN
REUKUS

CHAPTER I

THE STONE FAMILY IN 1864

The dew had gone off the hay, cut yesterday and raked into long rows across the field. The sun promised a blistering heat for the next few hours, and already the sweat was wetting the shirt of the boy who gingerly put his bare feet on any bare ground he could find among the sharp timothy stubble. He was doodling the hay into cocks, being careful to fold in the ends so that the cocks would lift clean onto the hay rack, when the hired man pitched them up.

As the boy worked his way down the windrow, he seemed to be immensely happy about something for he chuckled and talked to himself. His hair, long and tousled, was blonde, but there was enough red mixed in to make it seem a delicate pink. When the light shone on it at just the right angle, it was red and no doubt about it. A high forehead, prominent cheek bones, ample nose and jaw, all promised a handsome man would come from this boy in another year or two. The eyes were deep set, blue and shaded by heavy white eyebrows. As they squinted now in the sunlight, they seemed to be closed. He was listening for the dinner bell.

A stranger would have guessed his age at sixteen to eighteen. He had never shaved. The hair on his face was at least a half inch long and maybe longer on his chin. His arms and legs were long and thin, but his shoulders were the shoulders of a man. He stood five feet ten inches tall in his bare feet, weighed one hundred and sixty odd pounds and was not a day over thirteen years old.

That was the way with old man Stone's boys. Twenty-five or thirty children he had, born in three different batches, and all the boys had grown to be men years before their age, and they lived to be old men, too. The eldest still lived and he was in his eighties, and young Jim was the youngest.

13

The folks in the Valley had laughed when Old Mr. Stone was married for the third time, at the age of seventy, to a woman less than half his age, but children came of the union in rapid succession. Six there had been and the oldest two of these were grown and married, and the third learning to be a blacksmith when James was born.

There was many a ribald suggestion that the hired man had sired the youngest, but as the baby grew and the features shaped themselves in the mold they would carry through life, Old Man Stone was there in his face.

The Stones lived on a rich and rolling farm in the Licking Valley of Ohio. It was clear of debt, all that remained of three fortunes made and lost in one lifetime. One had been made on the construction of a canal that had started at Cleveland and ran off to the south somewhere. The members of his present family had never seen the canal. Another fortune had been made by buying a worthless swamp near Columbus and damming it here, dredging it there and selling the whole kit and kaboodle for enough to live on forever. How the third fortune had been made is now forgotten, and how all three were lost is also forgotten. But if the loss of these fortunes bothered anyone, it was some one other than Old Man Stone.

The farm was rich and well cared for. Because the boys were gone, except young Jim, and help scarce with all the young men in the Army, Mr. Stone decided to raise no row crops. He raised his cattle in the pastures, green and well watered, and wintered them on timothy and clover that came from the meadows. His only plowing was to plant oats and the garden. Folks said he was crazy to plant no corn, but he did as well as they.

When at last the dinner bell rang, Jim shouldered his fork and carefully picked his way out of the stubble. Once in the wheel tracks with their soft dust, he made fast time and in short order was at the back steps.

"For land o' Goshen, Lyde," he called to his sister, "gimme a dipper of water."

"I'll give you the bucket," she said, "it's about empty and warm."

"Don't you never draw water?" he chided her. Picking up the bucket he went to the stone-sided well, and quickly dropped the wooden bucket to the water. The wheel screeched as the cotton line ran through it. "Reckon I'll have to put some soap on the exle up there," he said aloud, "it sets a fellow's teeth on edge and a shiver on the spine." Then he pulled up the full bucket of cold clear water. He poured most of it in the house bucket, and hoisted the well bucket to his lips and gulped the cold water down greedily. Some ran past the corners of his mouth and down his blue shirt front and inside his pants, but it did not make much different, because he was already sweat wet.

Jim carried the water back to the house, with his left arm extended sideways to shoulder height. Tough as his feet were, the pebbles on the path hurt them and the dog fennel on either side was scant improvement. However, with some slopping of water and scraping of the calves of his legs, he reached the steps, climbed them and entered the dark kitchen.

Seated at the table before the window sat the father. On his left with his back to the door was the hired man. A place was set at the end of the table opposite Mr. Stone for the mother. Jim and Lyde would sit with backs to the range facing the hired man. On the sill two potted flowers peered out the opened window. The range, black and hot, gave off little orange lights through the cracks in the lid and doors, while a tea kettle rattled on the back. From the oven came the strong, good smell of baking bread.

"Come and sit, Jim," said the father.

"Got to wash, Pop," answered Jim.

"Quick then, because I'm hungry and your Mom is about to kill me with smells."

"It's not me," said the mother with pride glowing on her moist face. "It's Lyde. She made the lightbread and the rolls. All I did was help."

"You'll make Burr a good wife, Lyde," said the father. "When is it to be?"

"He hasn't asked me yet," she admitted, "but if he doesn't pretty soon, I'll throw a rope around him and hog-tie him till I get a preacher."

What kind of talk was this wondered the hired man, but he said nothing. Not another woman in the whole of Licking Valley would have admitted so much as a nickel's worth of interest in any man, but here was a girl not yet twenty talking of hog-tieing a man and getting a preacher. As he looked at Lyde he noted the

15

lovely swelling of her chest, the mature broadness of her hips and the clear white skin and light blond hair, whipped back and knotted at the base of her skull. He wished Lyde had wanted to hog-tie him, because he wouldn't have so much as lifted a finger to stop her. He looked at his plate before him, bottom up, waiting for the blessing before he could turn the plate over and help himself to the potatoes, new peas, meat and gravy, and rhubarb sauce.

While Lyde squealed and burned herself on the hot tins, and Jim bubbled and blew water on the back porch, the mother quietly supplied the odds and ends that made a good table. Pickles, cottage cheese, jam and onions were put there. It was easy to see that the mother was not one to force her will upon her family, and it was also easy to see that she was proud of her children and not easily shocked by them. At least Lyde's remark brought no remonstrance.

In a way life had been good to this third Mother Stone. Of course, she had borne children late in life and worked hard, but she had not gone to barren spinsterhood, a fate she had considered inevitable when she was thirty and still unmarried. If she wondered what it might have been like to have been married to a younger man, she covered her thoughts well, and devoted herself to her family and Mr. Stone—she called him that to the day he died. If there were disadvantages to the match, there were advantages to offset them. Mr. Stone was lavish with money when he had it and her lot was an easier one by far than it might have been.

Then there was the home. It was large, built of brick, and had a good roof. Set far back from the road on the crest of a knoll it was almost free of dust. It had a good basement and four chimneys and three fireplaces. There were twelve rooms, some so small that a bed and commode left scarcely room to open the door. On the ground floor was the kitchen to the back, the dining room, the sitting room and the parlor. The parlor was for weddings, funerals, and Christmas parties. In between times it was cleaned weekly, but kept dark with paper over the windows.

The family spent most of its time in the kitchen, but on Saturday nights when everyone had his bath, the unwashed members sat in the living room, waiting their turn. In clean night clothes the children would scurry upstairs to bed.

16

If Mrs. Stone's contemporaries had pitied her for being an old maid at thirty and then for throwing herself away on a man old enough to be her grandfather, they also saw the practical side of the match. Where else in the Valley was there a farm as good, paid for, and an old man waiting to die? But Mr. Stone lived to eighty, ninety and then a hundred years of age and still no sign of failing, with youngsters still in the house.

Jim came through the door with his face pink from a lavish use of the towel, his hair a shambles.

"Comb your hair, Jim," said the father.

"Damn," said Jim, going back outside.

"How much dirt did you wash off and how much did you wipe on the towel?" drily asked the mother.

" 'Bout half 'n half," replied Jim as he re-entered, his hair plastered back, the ends dripping water down his neck. A big grin showed an even set of large teeth.

"Sit down," urged Lyde, pushing Jim toward his chair, "before the whole dinner is ruined."

"Touchy as hell, ain't she, Pop?"

"Let us pray," said the father. "Sit down, Lyde. Take your elbows off the table, Jim." He waited for his instructions to be obeyed, and then looked at his plate bottom side up before him. "Lord who giveth and who taketh away, bless us this day that we may carry out Thy will. Don't do anything for us that we can do ourselves, but if there is something we ought to be doing and ain't, just show it to us, Lord, and say, 'Git to work and do it.' We don't aim to overlook anything, but there seems to be a heap a man don't think about. Keep a lookout on Taylor down there in Georgey, who ain't got sense enough to look out for himself. And, Lord, keep this family of ourn happy and busy. I reckon if You keep 'em busy that'll be enough. Thank ye kindly for this food. Take care that we know what needs our help, Amen."

The plates were turned right side up and the food was taken hot and steaming from the oven and placed on the red checked table cloth. The father helped himself liberally and passed the food along. Jim and the hired man seemed in a mood to eat 'til they burst, and heaven help them, if they hadn't. This was Lyde's meal and she carefully noted each mouthful that was put away and the expressions on the faces of the eaters.

Her father had shaved this morning and his face was white

and pink and healthy looking. His hair was snow white and so were his eyebrows, and he looked to be scarcely seventy. His Adam's apple worked slowly up and down as he carefully chewed his food with his few remaining teeth.

There was not a word spoken during the meal. It was a sort of a rule. When you talked and ate, too, your wind cooled your food and blew the good out of it. So no one said anything. At last, Mr. Stone wiped his face with his napkin, took a drink of water and polished off his lips again. Then he spoke.

"What's the matter with Burr's tongue, Lyde?"

"Nothing," she replied and she was not embarrassed or shy about talking about her lover before the family, "he wants to learn him a trade, before we marry. He says he loves me and he sparks me romantic, but wants to wait."

"What's he aim to learn?"

"To be a cabinet maker."

"Well now, I guess," said Mr. Stone. He thoughtfully worked this over in his mind as he ate his blackberry pie. Then, "Lyde, did you ever see anything he made?"

"Yes," she replied, "I saw a hayrack and a wheelbarrow and a wagon box, he made, and they were made good and strong, and painted red. He wants to make tables and chairs and highboys out of oak and walnut and maple. He wants to make high class furniture."

"What is he doing to learn him this trade? Last I heard he was working for his pa same as ever."

"His pa needs him," said Lyde.

"Hell, with three sons still at home besides Burr? Why does his pa need him?"

"He says he does," weakly replied Lyde.

"Lyde."

"Yes, Pop."

"Do you love him?"

"Yes."

The hired man got up, flushed red and mumbled something about feeding the horses and left. Scarcely anyone saw him go, or paid him the slightest mind.

"Do you burn when you see him and eetch where you can't scratch?"

"Mr. Stone!" cried the mother alarmed.

18

"Yes, Pop."

"Git you a rope."

Jim lay in the shade of a big elm that spread its branches over the eaves of the house. In the yard were locust trees and maples giving good solid shade. Under them were beds of myrtle, bunches of orchard grass and twigs that had fallen during the winter and not been raked up. Chickens dusted themselves in the loose dirt between the roots. A gander stretched his wings full and rose on tiptoe and stretched his neck. A bee added his voice, but Jim scarcely heard it. Life was good. His belly was full and he was sleepy.

Mr. Stone was stretched out on the sofa in the living room taking his hour's nap, just as he had done for years. A few flies buzzed around. Lyde and her mother were busy washing the dishes and cleaning up. The hired man was slopping the two or three pigs with garbage from the kitchen. Having finished, he put his left foot on the middle slab of the pigsty fence, put his chin in his hand and watched the hogs scramble for their dinner. A young cockerel tried his voice, but his crow was off key and weak, so he lifted his wings in the shade of a grape arbor to let the air reach his warm body. A hawk circled slowly overhead. In the barn, the horses had been fed and watered. Now they, too, dozed and switched at flies with their long tails.

This was the part of the day Jim liked best. It was made sweet by the morning's work and the midday dinner, but made sweeter with the realization that he must soon be back to work with the hay. He would sweat this afternoon, he knew, because the sun was melting the wax out of him right here in the shade. A big white cloud crossed the sun.

"Maybe I better get after that hay," he thought. "It's prime hay now, just green enough and just dry enough. I'd hate to get it wet. Sure would." So he sat up and put the tattered straw hat on his head, rolled over on his knees and stood up. The rattle of the wagon told the women that Jim and the hired man were on their way to the hayfield.

Summer turned into autumn. The oats were in a stack by the barn, cut and cradled and tied by straw as they had been for years. The barn was stuffed to the rafters with hay and more in a stack just outside. The horses were sleek and fat and the cattle filled their hides so that not a rib showed. The first hickory nuts were dropping out of their shells and next week school would start.

Jim's career in school had been uneventful enough. Each year he had attended in blue shirt and overalls, barefoot when possible, in cowhide boots when not. He had gone from grade to grade each year, and this year would be the biggest boy in the school. He wasn't the oldest by far, but he had grown up while the others had not. It was that fact that bothered him. If he only knew enough to graduate this year instead of next he would have liked it better.

It had been the same way with Taylor before him. The teacher had been young and small, and when the boys had needed smacking, she wasn't big enough to do it, so she had said sternly to Taylor, "Take that boy in the woodshed and hide him good for having no manners." And Taylor had taken a boy, a little boy but still the same age, out back and spanked him with a shingle. Taylor hadn't minded it. In fact, he had enjoyed it, but Jim hoped he wouldn't have to do it. That was the trouble with being man-sized at thirteen.

Jim got a handful of soft soap from Lyde and took a walk down to the creek. He intended to take a bath in the creek and put on clean clothes he brought with him. As he walked along his mind was turning over the possibility that the teacher might decide to tan his hide. Would he bend his bottom up to her to smack? He wondered and laughed. The teacher this year was a new one from another township. If anyone in the neighborhood had seen her, they had not known it.

Preoccupied as he walked, he came to the creek unobserved, and unobserving. There was a tremendous flurry and splashing and then quiet. Clinging close to the bank, completely naked and neck deep in water were Burr and Henry Fuller.

"Gosh a'mighty, Jim," said Burr, "you give us a scare. We thought that shirt you was a-carrying was a woman's skirt and us naked as jay birds. You coming in?"

"I aim to," said Jim and in fact was already half out of his clothes. He deposited the soap on a stone and was soon splashing and hopping in the now slightly soiled water of the creek.

"Colder'n hell, ain't it?" he remarked.

20

"It's cold all right, but it'll get you clean," said Henry, "but I'm clean enough now to last me." Jim applied the soap liberally and jumped in to wash off. Once clean the three boys sat naked on the bank to dry.

"How old are you?" Jim asked Burr pointedly.

"Nineteen," said Burr.

"'N you?" queried Jim of Henry.

"Eighteen."

"I got more hair on my chest than both of you put together. I'm only thirteen."

"Are you sure of your age?" asked Henry.

"Yup."

"Maybe it's cuz your pop is oldern ours that you got hair young. Maybe you was born a couple years older," Henry suggested.

"Nope," said Jim, "I was born a baby just like you, but I took to growing fast."

"You're bigger than we are," said Burr, "but you ain't as strong most likely, but you will be some day."

Jim thought this over for a while in silence and suggested they lift rocks or wrestle to see if he was as strong, but Burr said he wouldn't want to set on a future brother-in-law. That nettled Jim and he decided to probe this new subject.

"I don't know's you'll be my brother-in-law or not, Burr," he said quietly.

"Why not?" asked Burr alarmed and rising to his feet. "Lyde likes me."

"Sure, but she ain't going to wait for a man forever."

"What do you mean?"

"I mean just this. No girl is going to fancy a feller and then sit around forever waiting for him to take her to the parson. Hear you are wanting to be a cabinet maker."

"Yes," said Burr.

"And you're going to marry her when you are one."

"Yes."

"But you're still a-farming. Next year you won't be no nearer to a cabinet maker than this. Every year Lyde is getting closer to being an old maid and you still sitting by. Why don't you be a cabinet maker if you're so set on it?"

"Does Lyde ever talk about me?"

21

"Yes."

"What does she say?" begged Burr. Henry was listening wide eyed and his mouth had dropped open.

"She says you're a likable feller. You spark her good and she says she'd marry you, but the trouble is you ain't got no gumption."

"Lyde says that!" said Henry.

"You heard him, Brother," said Burr, "but I got gumption. I'm going to Newark to make me into a cabinet maker this week."

"What you going to do with Lyde?" asked Jim.

"Why, nothing," slowly answered Burr.

"You are dumber than most. Take Lyde along."

"Now?"

Jim gave Burr a slow exasperated look and started to dress. "Them ain't man hairs you got. Them is milkweed down you ain't brushed off."

"I ought to tear you up for being so aggravating," said Burr, "but I won't. I wonder would Lydy-girl go with me?"

"D'j'ever ask her?"

"No."

"You're dumb, Burr."

"Where are you going, Brother?" asked Henry, for Burr was pulling on clothes and heading up the road toward the Stone place. When Burr made no answer Henry hollered that his pa would have his hide, but Burr was gone.

22

CHAPTER II

JIM ATTENDS SCHOOL

"I don't reckon you'll be needing me today," said Jim to his father the day before school opened.

"Don't suppose I will," answered the father smiling, "but what are you up to?"

"I'm the biggest boy in the school," Jim stopped as though that explained everything. His father was plainly mystified, but did not speak, so Jim continued, "I'll have to clean the stove and black it. It be the surest thing you know, so I'm going over to the schoolhouse today in my old overalls and keep my new ones clean tomorrow."

"That ain't no rock you got on them shoulders, boy," the old man beamed a scant-toothed smile and repeated, "no rock."

So with a bucket, a rag, a can of stove blacking and his lunch Jim hiked down the road to the school. He kept a sharp lookout for stones that might hurt his feet, but his mind was way ahead of him. He imagined that the teacher was at the school when he got there. She was pretty and she was small enough she had to look up to him, way up. He talked to her about the children she'd have in class and how she could count on him. Everybody depended on him because he was older than most. But when he reached the school yard no one was there.

The schoolhouse was made of brick and had been whitewashed once long ago. During the summer the grass in the yard had grown into hay and only the packed clay around the door and on the path to the two privies had resisted it. Jim looked at the hay, and remembered there was a scythe and a whetstone in the woodshed, but that would come later, after the stove was cleaned.

He had a time opening the door. It had not been locked, but had swelled and Jim had to climb in through a window and throw his weight against it from the inside, but it gave way. Once

23

the door was opened, Jim set to work in earnest and was soon showing the effects of soot, rust, dirt and blacking.

He ate his lunch and continued with his work. He wondered if he wasn't a fathead to be doing work until he was asked. But hell, he was always asked. He wondered why. He swept the floor, broke down the mud daubers nests and scrubbed as clean as he could where they had been. He scrubbed the blackboard and wrote his name with soggy chalk. He washed where he had written. Then he sat down by the well and rested. He wondered if he ought to cut the hay, and knew he would. He'd have to to-morrow anyway.

As he rested a horse and buggy slowly came down the road, and stopped. The driver, probably the new teacher, backed the horse and cramped the wheels to give her room to alight. Then she came in the gate and right up to him.

"Good afternoon," she said primly.

"Howdy, Ma'am," he replied.

"I'm the new teacher."

"I reckoned as much."

"What have you been doing?" she asked.

"Cleaning house."

"Well, let me see it."

Jim followed her in and watched her look around. He could see she was disappointed and vaguely wondered what she'd have been, if he hadn't cleaned up or even opened the door. By her clothes, he could see she was used to class. Her clothes were well made and they swished when she walked, and barely cleared the floor. Her hair was dark and her eyes were brown and she did have to look up to him.

"If you'll 'scuse me," he told her, "I'll cut the hay out here in front. I ain't got time to do the whole shebang before chore time." He left her looking at the books on the teacher's desk.

By the time he finished the front, it was time to leave, so he entered the schoolhouse to tell the new teacher so-long. Her head was laying on her arm and she had been crying, but she looked up and wiped away the tears and blew her nose. "What a small nose she has," he thought, "even Lyde has one twice as big and Lyde is pretty."

"I'm just a bawl baby," she said, "I was expecting a school-house all painted white with a flagpole with a gold knob on top and a green grass lawn in front. I expected desks instead of benches and books instead of this old sawdust."

"I see," said Jim, not seeing.

"How can I teach my little ones from books like this," she groaned and read from the First Reader, " 'Black is the gate to hell and fiery are the furnaces?' That," she said, "to teach little children to love to read."

"Don't appear right," Jim agreed, "but I did it."

"How long have they used these books?"

"Let's see, now. Taylor and Lyde used them and Harry, my oldest brother did. I guess maybe twenty or twenty-five years."

"Oh heavens!"

There seemed nothing more to say, so gently Jim said he had to go home. Together they closed the door and Jim helped her into her buggy and untied the horse. With a wave of the hand she went up the road and Jim went down.

The next morning, the morning that school was to open, dawned bright and frosty. Jim had risen earlier this morning and had fed the stock, milked the two cows and turned them out to pasture. Then he joined the family in the kitchen. Everyone was eating except Jim's mother, and she was frying pancakes. Jim sat down without a word, and breakfast went on as usual in silence.

After breakfast, Mr. Stone usually told the hired man what he wanted done. He never addressed Jim, but it was understood by all that Jim was included in the instructions. As the old man cleared his throat and adjusted his thoughts in an orderly manner, Jim spoke, completely upsetting Mr. Stone's thoughts.

"Papa."

"Yes, Jim."

"Can I use your razor?"

There was a silence, and a real silence it was. Lyde finally giggled and the hired man hid behind his saucer of coffee.

"Growing up are you, son?" asked the father.

"Yes, sir."

"Do you know how to shave?"

"I've seen you do it."

"Then I'll shave you myself this morning."

The father departed to get his razor and Jim dipped a basin

25

of hot water from the reservoir of the range. Somewhere deep
inside he felt a purr rise, and he enjoyed the feeling. Soon the
old man returned and began to strop the razor while Jim lathered himself to the eyes. And then Mr. Stone began to shave him.

"Jim."

"Yes, Pop."

"Is she pretty?"

Jim opened his eyes and looked at his father, but with over a
century's practice in looking blank, the old man's face showed
nothing.

"Who, Pop?"

"Your new teacher."

"Yes."

"I thought so," said the father, "I thought so. Maybe you will
learn something that hadn't in the books this year." The razor
slid smoothly over Jim's face and there was none of the scraping
that goes with the shaving of a mature beard. When the soap was
scraped off, the fuzz was with it. "Son, there's a heap of things a
woman can teach you, but common sense ain't one of them. You
won't have to wait for your beard to turn gray to find it out,
neither. I wan't never a hand to run from a woman, but unless
you know what you're doing, you had best do it."

Jim said nothing, but he grinned and squirmed a little. Maybe,
thought Jim, there was something this father of his could do—
read what was on a fellow's mind. Well, she was pretty and only
about five years older than he was. Then the old man spoke
again.

"Women will hurt hell out of you with their mouths. It ain't
what they say always that hurts, its the way they can turn the
corners of their mouths. And the more you think of them, the
harder they can hurt."

"Pop."

"Yes."

"I ain't in love."

"Not really you ain't, but you'll think you are."

Jim washed himself and took special pains to see that his ears
were clean. Lyde came over to inspect them and could find no
fault. Soon he was off for school in new pants and shirt, and barefoot, because it wasn't cold enough for shoes.

When Jim reached the school he saw the boys and girls he

knew from last year, getting acquainted and comparing heights to see how much they had grown during the summer. There were a few buggies and surreys in which had come the little boys and girls who were new in the community or just starting. Invariably, mother or an older sister brought them, and Jim knew some would cry when their folks left. If the new teacher was there, she must have been in the schoolhouse for she was nowhere to be seen outside.

At nine o'clock one of the older girls rang a bell and the schoolhouse filled. There was a great deal of commotion as seats were sought. Boys shoved one another and tried to all get on the same bench, but Jim was very quiet and took a seat in the last row. It took nearly forty-five minutes to get the new Primer Class inducted, to dry their tears and to usher the relatives out. When at last she was alone with her pupils, she looked out at the bunch of clean pink faces before her and in a low voice began to talk. Instantly, it was quiet.

"I am Miss Virginia Lippincott," she said. "This is my first year of teaching. I don't expect to be a perfect teacher or even too good of a teacher, but how good I am, or how bad depends in a large way on you. If you try to learn and work with me, we will all have a happy time, and we will all learn a lot." She smiled and then went on, "I want to know your names and to get to know you right away. So let's start over here in the second row. Each of you stand up, tell me your name and what grade you are in this year."

The girls told their names primly and precisely and sat down, but there was something about the boys' names that elicited a lot of giggling. In fact, it became apparent that unless something was done, they would never get through. The teacher was annoyed but said nothing. Jim at last could stand no more of it. Standing in the back row, he spoke.

"You small fry hush your giggling this minute." Silence settled over them as all the pupils turned to look at Jim. "Joel Smith, stand up." Joel stood. "Miss Virginia, this is Joel Smith. Last year he was in the Third Reader, but he was awful poor. He has a twin brother Harold over there. Stand up, Harold. They look alike, but Joel has a big brown freckle on his jaw. Just remember 'j' as in Joel and jaw and you can keep them separated. Harold ain't very smart either.

"The next boy is Irwin Potter. He ain't very healthy, but he's right smart. Probably the best reader for his size in school. He's in the Fourth—no Fifth Reader this year." So it went as he introduced the eight boys who had not done the job themselves. Then he came to himself.

"My name is James Franklin Stone. I'm not the oldest here in school, but I took to growing young and I'm the oldest acting. I've got one or two years more to go, depending on who is teaching and whether they want me around. Last year I tended the stove and took care there were no bad fights." Then he sat down.

"James."

"Yes, ma'am," he said, standing.

"Why didn't you tell me yesterday you were coming to school here as a pupil?"

"You didn't ask me."

"No, I didn't. How old are you?"

"I'm thirteen years old last July 5th."

"Is that so?" She sounded astonished. She wondered how the conversation had become so personal, and was in the process of changing the subject when Jim spoke again.

"Miss Virginia, you know about us now—we most all were born here in the Valley and growed up here, but you came from somewheres else. Won't you tell us where you went to school and where you came from and if it ain't no secret, how old you are and how much you weigh?"

Miss Virginia laughed nervously, then she stopped and looked into the eyes in front of her and then at the rafters and really laughed. Even the little tots in the front bench laughed, although only a minute before they had been sniffling.

"Yes, Jim," she said, her brown eyes smiling and a dampness in the corners, "I will tell you about myself. I was born in Boston and went to school there and my folks are there. I left because I wanted to see the west and I got this school through the minister of my church. I'm nineteen years old."

"The last teacher we had was nineteen last year, but she got married. She lives over to Mt. Vernon now. But about this Boston—" Jim paused and looked puzzled.

"Yes, Jim, what about Boston?"

"Well," said he smiling apologetically, "when I see you yesterday I thought you come from a high class place like Cleveland, or maybe Columbus."

28

CHAPTER III

ABOUT A MARRIAGE AND A DEATH

School that fall was a positive pleasure to Jim. There were only three others his age and with no certain books to read, it was rather indefinite as to what they were supposed to learn. Miss Virginia spent a great deal of time trying to teach them to write letters, to spell and to use correct grammar.

In December, Burr came home from Newark. When he walked up the lane to the Stone home through a six-inch fall of snow one Saturday morning, his face red from the cold and his feet nearly frozen to stumps, it did not require a Nostradamus to prophesy what was on his mind. Jim opened the gate and knew at once what Burr had come for.

"Hello, Burr," he hailed, "kind of cool for a city feller out here in the country."

"Howdy, Jim," answered Burr, "how's everybody?"

"Folks are all fine," replied Jim, and then he felt an urge he was to feel again and again through life. It was an urge to have a little fun. Perhaps the world does love a lover, but at the same time it is willing to make fun if it can, so with a sober face Jim continued, "That is, except Lyde. I ain't seen her since the morning she left. She 'peared all right then."

"Left?" asked Burr, "My God, when? Where did she go?"

"I really don't know," replied Jim, and he looked so sad that tears appeared to be on the verge of falling. His lower lip trembled ever so slightly.

Burr was aghast. "Who did she go with?"

"Do you remember the hired man we had—a middle-aged man about thirty or so? He was getting bald—a little. She ran off to Mt. Vernon with him. I guess they got married, but I ain't never heard."

"Oh God," moaned Burr, "she should have waited. I have only

29

been gone six weeks. What did your folks think about it?"

"They hated it," admitted Jim, and he wondered if he was not going a little too far with his joke. After all, he had not thought Burr would fall for it so hard. Maybe if he made it really wild Burr would smell a rat. So Jim began again, and a sob seemed to be stuck in his throat, "Of course, there's no understanding grown folks. Mama blamed the hired man and Papa blamed you. Didn't either of them blame Lyde, because she was a girl and girls ain't got much sense anyhow.

"Papa figured you was to blame, because you sparked Lyde and got her to thinking thoughts about young'uns and such, and then ran off to the city. He figured if you was going to upset her so, the least you could do was finish the job, but no, you leave the hired man to do that. So far's Pop could tell, he didn't have one penny to rub against another."

Burr seemed to sag in his boots. Out of the corner of his eye Jim watched him and regretted the whole impulse, so he decided to set the matter straight. He sat up brightly "Say, I got an idee. Our new maid! She's a lot prettier than Lyde and she's making fritters now. Come on up to the house!"

"There's no one prettier than Lyde," said Burr.

"She's got the Stone nose," simply said Jim.

"I don't care if she has. It's just right on her. There is no better looking girl in Ohio than Lydey Girl."

"I guess there ain't no harm in thinking another man's wife is good looking," said Jim over his shoulder, leading the way to the house. There was no answer from Burr.

Opening the door to the kitchen and stomping snow off his shoes at the same time, Jim called, "Deliah! Oh, Deliah! We got company." Burr stomped and followed him into the kitchen.

In the dimly lighted kitchen Jim got the feeling quite suddenly that something was wrong. He had expected Lyde to be there, but instead his eyes made out a familiar form and face.

When she turned full toward him, Jim saw Miss Virginia, and his knees suddenly felt very limp. Burr was miserably holding his fur cap in front of him.

Clearing his throat Jim said in a voice so fierce, it seemed to come from someone else, "Deliah, this is Burr Fuller. Burr, this is Deliah Jones our new maid, since Lyde run off with the hired man."

30

"Why Jim!" exclaimed Miss Virginia.

"No need to hide it," said Jim, "she ran off and everybody knows about it except Burr who has been to Newark."

Miss Virginia looked Burr over and Burr stared back. Jim wondered if he should run out now, or wait to see what happened when Lyde showed up. He decided to stay for another minute or two, and then he caught sight of the churn.

An old fashioned dasher churn with its loose fitting lid and hole where the dasher handle comes through is certain to splash, especially if worked energetically. It not only splashes everything within a five foot radius, but the churner usually gets his share. Jim now knew that Lyde had been churning, that some one had told her Burr was in the yard, and that she had gone to get a clean apron, or to remove the splashings from the one she was wearing. Also she was probably just inside the dining room door, listening right this minute.

"Deliah, Burr thought Lyde was pretty. I told him you was prettier, especially in the nose, but Burr said he liked girls with big noses. So I brung him in to look you over. I've got some chores now, so I'll be trotting."

Jim made for the hay mow as fast as his legs could carry him. Once there he almost died in laughter. If he worried about the outcome of his joke, it was not readily seen. "Deliah Jones, this is Burr Fuller," and then he laughed all the harder. Then he wondered how the hell Miss Virginia had managed to get in without him seeing her.

After Jim left the house, Burr shuffled his feet and tried to think of an excuse to leave. Lyde wiped away the last spot of cream from her apron, and with her lips drawn into two straight lines, she marched into the kitchen. Before the astonished suitor could say anything, Lyde spoke and there was acid in her voice.

"So, Mr. Burr Fuller, you think my nose is big, do you? Why don't you tell me so, rather than to go around telling the neighbors?"

"I didn't say your nose was big, Lyde. Honest! I said I thought you were beautiful even if it was big." Seeing that he was getting nowhere fast, he decided to explain, "Jim said you had the Stone nose."

"And what may I ask is wrong with the Stone nose?" Ice was never so sharp, so cold, or so brittle.

31

"Oh Lyde! There's nothing wrong with the Stone nose," he said desperately.

Lyde walked right up to Burr, slowly and majestically. Both had forgotten that Miss Virginia, or Deliah Jones, existed. "You have insulted the Stone nose," she said, "now kiss it." She held her face up to him and smiled a smile to melt the heart of the devil.

"My God, Lyde, you are as bad as that lying little polecat of a brother of yours." He kissed her on the bridge of the nose and then held her tight and kissed her on the lips.

Miss Virginia looked on. She had been a spectator at the oddest little drama she had ever seen. That big Jim had lied to his sister's fellow, and when caught up by circumstance, had lied on so beautifully that she could not restrain her admiration. He had even included her in his lie and made her follow his lead. But when Lyde followed the same line, Miss Virginia knew Boston had no jokesters like this family, or from the looks of it, lovers either.

At length, Lyde remembered, and with a quick look over her shoulder, turned toward Miss Virginia. She had her arm around Burr's waist. He tucked her under his arm, and held her close.

"Burr, this is Miss Virginia Lippincott, the new teacher at the school." He grinned sheepishly at her and said, "We met, but seems her name is different sort of."

"Yes, Burr," said Miss Virginia, "I seem to be several people today."

There is an old adage that two are company, but three are a crowd. Somehow that did not hold good here, because there seemed no restraint and no shyness on Burr's or Lyde's part. They talked of his work, where he lived and how he was getting along. He figured that if they were careful they could be married and live on what he earned. It was all very exciting and so very indefinite until Lyde brought things to earth with a crash.

"I am going to marry you Christmas, Burr, right here in this house."

"Christmas," he echoed, "that's less than two weeks off." There was a silence as the young folks let the matter sink in. "I haven't even asked your pa yet."

From the living room which was beyond the dining room and a long way off, judged by the cozy standards of the younger set, came a voice strong and full of impatience, but with a humor

32

aplenty in it. "Keerist A'Mighty, Burr Fuller, take her and she's your'n. She ain't been worth a tinker's dam to no one, ever since you came a feedaddling around her."

"Thank you, Pa," said Lyde.

Women like to talk. It is their very nature, so give them a reason to talk and stand clear. Lyde, Miss Virginia and the mother now settled into such earnest conversation that Burr, who was the cause of it all, was forgotten. Like a lost soul he wandered to the living room and sank down in a chair by the fireplace.

"Son, what do you know about women?" asked the father.

"Not a damn thing," said Burr.

"A'ready you show signs o' getting along in the world," said Mr. Stone. He closed his eyes and rocked slowly and seemed to get a quiet music from the squeak of the rocker.

The fire crept up the back wall of the fireplace and fell back. Occasionally there was a crackle as the fire gnawed on the log, dry and brittle. In the corner of the room stood a rag carpet loom with a half finished rug on it. Upon the floor were several small throw rugs. A few sturdy chairs and a small table, on which stood a tall lamp with a large blue bowl, completed the room's furnishings. The room was papered with a design consisting of a rose as big as a cabbage, and a bowl of grapes the same size. Both the rose and the grapes were burgundy red.

In the kitchen the talk was still going strong on the subject of clothes and bridesmaids. To Burr it sounded alarming and he felt scared. It seemed like such a tremendous step he was taking. He wondered if he ought to stay or go. Then the old man began to talk.

"Son, I been married longer than most men live. Eighty-six years off and on is a long time, and all I know about being married is that it can be heaven or it can be hell. I been lucky and haven't seen much of the hell part, but you won't know your wife and you won't know yourself, until your children start to die and your crops fail, or your work fails. Then you'll pray to the Lord God A'Mighty and you'll look at your wife for the first time. Like as not she won't be pretty nor young no more, and you will see her as she is. She'll be looking at you, too, and if she is one of God's women, you'll find peace and strength in her face and your own strength will come back and you'll pull out of your trouble.

"Men are strong in the body. They got big hands and strong

legs and big shoulders. But when a baby dies and a son dies a man ain't strong."

The old man rocked on. He closed his eyes and covered them with the tips of his fingers, and Burr knew that what this old man had said had sprung from the memory of other times and other places. He felt that truth had been told, but he wanted no more of it. Rising quietly he left the room, for here was a man who gave his daughter away in marriage with a jest, and lost several fortunes without a memory, but was still mourning the loss of children dead these many years.

"Lydey Girl, I got to go now," he said quietly.

"Must you?" she asked.

"Yes, but I'm coming back whenever you say."

"Come back with your cutter this afternoon," she said simply, "and take me over to see your ma."

"All right," he said, "you know what Ma will be like. I'm the oldest and she thinks I'm pretty young."

"Hush, boy," said Lyde, "all mothers think their boys marry too young."

The remaining time before Christmas fairly flew past. Burr finally caught Jim in the orchard and washed his face with snow and stuffed some down his neck, but it was a job Burr had a terrific struggle to do, and he knew that in two more years Jim would have been too big for him—maybe sooner. The whole struggle was one of friendliness and, indeed, Burr could not find it in him to be cross to anyone.

He had expected the sparks to fly when Lyde and his Ma met, but no such thing occurred. They had known one another all their lives, but that did not mean there could not have been trouble. Lyde had walked into the kitchen as his Ma was mixing bread dough and had simply said, "Well, Ma Fuller, I finally caught Burr, but he was a slippery one," and his Ma had puddled up and said, "Lyde, I'm glad he's got you as long as he has to have some one." When it was over Lyde had gotten herself covered with flour, and Henry complained the bread was made of flour and tears, and as a consequence was too salty.

A letter had come from Taylor, who was camped with the Union Army at Dalton, Georgia. He told of the mud, the heat, the flies and the sickness during the past summer, and the terrible battles at Chattanooga, Missionary Ridge and Tunnel Moun-

34

tain. Of the battles themselves, he said little except to say they were bloody and that he was in them and weary of the war. The letter left him well and he hoped would find them in the best of health and spirits. He remained their obedient son, Taylor.

The letter was taken to school and Jim showed it to Miss Virginia who read it aloud to the children. Jim struggled for several days to write an answer. Finally he asked the teacher to help him and they wrote a newsy letter telling of Lyde's approaching marriage, the happenings in the community during his absence and finished with a postscript by Miss Virginia, telling Taylor that she was going to be the bridesmaid in the coming wedding, and how much she enjoyed teaching in the Valley. She ended by wishing him luck and an early end to the war.

And then Christmas came!

Mrs. Stone kept a clean house. She always had, but this Christmas the house fairly shone. Even the Christmas spirit had to take a back seat for this wedding, and Jim was young enough to wish that Lyde had chosen some other day than Christmas to be married on.

About ten o'clock in the morning the guests began to arrive, and by noon the house was full. Out in the kitchen such a babble of voices arose as to make strong men weak, but to strengthen them again was the odor of chicken and dumplings. It was an odor that had body to it, nourishing. The overworked range in the kitchen had been stoked continuously for several days now, and mince pies, apple pies and various other pies were the last to come forth steaming hot. There were puddings and sauces and cakes besides to drive anyone, especially Jim, into a lather of salivary ecstasy.

In the parlor, the men sat around and talked about the weather, their livestock and the coming of spring. There were men with whiskers cut in all manner of patterns, great rolling mustaches, or none at all with a fringe of beard following the curve of the jaw, or goatees, but some were either whole hog or none, full beard or clean shaven. The rumble of their voices was good to hear and Jim and the others his age sat quietly in the corners and listened.

When dinner was ready Lyde sat next to her father at the head of the table. Burr's father sat next to him on the other side, and then Burr. Scattered around the table at various places were the rest of the guests with Miss Virginia, lovely as could be, at the foot of the table. Next to her sat the minister who showed his pleasure at her company so obviously that his wife tried to slay them both with dark looks. Jim ate with the children at the kitchen table.

There was no silence at this meal, and if the good of the food was blown away, it was a small matter, there was so much of everything. When Burr started to send his plate away almost untouched, his father glared at him and Burr ate it clean. Lyde ate with such evident relish that Burr felt slightly peevish.

Although the day was not a dark one, candles were lighted and the smell of them was good and homey. Mr. Stone urged food on everyone and had everything been eaten that was prepared, the country doctor would have been needed at once. By two o'clock the dishes were done and the minister's wife began to play on her violin. The Stones had no piano, nor for that matter was there one in the neighborhood. Lyde did not march in because there was no place to march from, all space being filled by the people.

So Lyde and Burr stood up. Behind and to the left stood Mr. Stone. Beside Lyde stood Miss Virginia. Henry Fuller stood to the right of Burr. Both were so nervous it was hard to tell whether they could last through the ceremony. But Lyde! She was so calm and serene that one would have thought getting married was something she did every day. There were no flowers and none were needed or missed.

Then the minister began to rumble and the music stopped. In less than five minutes it was all over and the wedding guests were congratulating the bride and groom and making preparation to get home to do the chores. Babies were getting tired and whimpered or bawled. By three o'clock the place was deserted. Burr and Lyde were on their way to Newark.

Mr. and Mrs. Stone and Jim were alone in front of the living room fireplace. Then the old man spoke, "I missed my nap today. I'm tired."

Then he laid down on the couch, closed his eyes and went to sleep. Mrs. Stone covered him with a shawl.

When Jim finished his chores, he came stomping into the house carrying the evening's milk. His mother met him in the kitchen and from the tired calmness of her face, he knew something was amiss.

"Jim, your pa is dead."

"Dead," said Jim unbelieving.

"Yes," she replied, "he just slept away."

The soft wind blew from the east. Already the snow was melting and dripping from the trees and shed roofs. Its soft thud as it hit the ground made life seem to be where none existed, and the Stone homestead seemed to be peopled by elfin busybodies.

In the rutted roads and ditches yellow water told of the yellow clay base to the soil. By nightfall, the creek in the bottoms would be full to its banks with it. Overhead the gray sky seemed to be made of one piece. The smoke rose slowly from the chimneys, white and wispy, the smoke from good dry wood.

Between where Jim sat and the house ran the road, and at right angles to it, the lane leading up to the house. The slope down to the road was not steep, nor was it steep to the top of the hill above him. No water trickled here because of the thick matting of buffalo grass, now dead and white. Blackberry bushes and elder fringed the quarter acre cemetery, with an occasional elm sapling or maple.

The headstone on which Jim sat bore the inscription, "Joshua Adams Bailey, Borned July 17, 1770, Died October 22, 1812. Rest in Peace." Jim wondered about the Baileys. There were more of them scattered about the little cemetery, but aside from these markers Jim never heard of them. His father had not even bought the place from anyone by that name. And now there would be a Stone in the cemetery—the first one.

"Maybe," said Jim, leaving his seat, "I'd better spell you. That clay gets harder as it gets deeper."

"Be glad to rest," said the hired man, pulling himself up out of the grave.

Jim dropped in and began to work. By chore time the grave was dug and Jim and the hired man gathered their tools, their coats and started for the house. The soft, slushy snow rinsed the mud off their shoes, but the road and the lane put it back. As they neared the house, Ed seemed to have made a decision.

"Jim, I reckon you be the man of the house now, at least, 'til Taylor or the others show up. I got something to tell you, and I think now would be a good time."

Jim was surprised, but now that he thought about it, he was

37

the man of the house. Of course, the minister was sort of running things now, but he wouldn't as soon as the funeral was over. So feeling a bit proud, Jim said, "Get it out of your craw, Ed, I'm listening."

"I'm going to leave here soon's I can. I have been wanting a place of my own for a long time and now'd be as good a time as any to be about it."

"Ed, I don't know what Ma is going to do, but if you want to go, it is as good a time as any. I'm practically through with school and I'm grown enough to take care. Have you told Ma?"

"Not yet I ain't."

"Well, don't. I'll tell her after the funeral. I wish Taylor was here."

"He'd be a help all right," agreed the hired man.

There is something about a funeral in the country that makes one think of auctions. It is hard to tell the difference in the people who go to them. In both cases there are those who are really interested and those who go to see what they can see. Perhaps there is a similarity, because there sometimes are auctions after funerals. People come and listen to the sermon and wonder how much this table will bring, or that lamp or the bay mare with the mule colt. With an effort they bring their minds back to the sermon and then wonder what the widow will do. Perhaps she will marry again—well no, she is pretty old. And so it goes.

Jim stayed by his mother and wished again for Taylor, but he would have settled for Lyde, who couldn't even be notified in time to get here. Perhaps that was for the best, because girls sometimes cried and, God, how he hated to see them cry. He looked at his mother and noticed that she was not crying and, come to think of it, she never had cried. He felt a new admiration for her.

The minister had been talking over an hour now. Right at this moment he was quoting from the Scripture about the daisies of the field. Jim wondered how the hell that fit in with his father.

Eventually, the sermon ended and his father was carried down the lane, across the road and up into the cemetery. Some of the older women followed to the grave, but most stayed behind to talk and mourn. Jim wondered why anyone should mourn. Not many men lived as long as his father, nor had as little to regret.

Chapter IV

FAMILY TIES ARE BROKEN

It was only a little over two years before the next funeral was held in the house, and the long walk to the cemetery made again. This time it was the mother, a victim of pneumonia. Again, Jim had helped dig the grave, but this time Taylor had been the one he helped. The grave was placed beside the other, and the ground had softened none in that time.

It had not been such a bad two years. Ed Williams, the hired man, had left at the first of the year. Jim had quit school and had taken over the farm in every way. He had never known how a person could grow to love horses and cattle and chickens. Of course, he had liked them, but it was not until he practically owned them, and had the full responsibility of them that he came to really love them. Take for instance, the way Old Belle had come to mean so much to him. He was really proud of her.

Belle was a stocky bay horse, fat and long haired. She was the younger of the team, about ten years old, with Antonio at least twenty. That Antonio was also a mare, albeit with a masculine name, is another story, but the name of the seller stuck to the horse.

Belle's head must have been extremely heavy, because no sooner was she allowed to stop than down would go her head for a snack of grass. After a nibble or two she seemed to go sound asleep.

When it came to pulling, Belle could have done a good job had she done it up even with Antonio, but no, she must lag at least two feet behind. Prodding had no lasting effect. When it came time to go to town, Belle was always hitched to the buggy, because Antonio was lame and not capable of the long trip.

It was on one of these trips that Jim decided to do a little reforming. He stopped under a maple tree and cut himself a

39

switch. Belle resumed her sleepy walk, but was promptly awakened with the switch. She broke into a gallop and it was a wonder the buggy did not fall into pieces as they clattered down the road. Soon winded, Belle would have settled back into a walk, except that Jim kept her at a trot. When they reached home, Belle was sweating profusely and lathered under the breeching.

Jim unharnessed her, got a bucket of warm water and sponged her down first, and rubbed her with a brush and curry. Then with a piece of flannel, he made her shine.

In less than a month Belle lost considerable weight, becoming a fine buggy horse with plenty of wind, and a fine steady trot. She even worked better with Antonio, but the happiest hours Jim spent that summer were those when he was caring for her, braiding her hair and oiling and polishing her harness.

It is a fact that once a person starts fixing, brushing or polishing, there is no place to stop. Belle and her harness were preened and shining, so the buggy had to be fixed, too. Jim sewed the top where it was tattered. He soaked the wheels in the pond to swell the wood and make the iron tires tight. Then he found some odds and ends of green and black paint and mixed them all together, getting enough to paint the buggy twice. Henry Fuller gave him a small can of red paint, and with this, he carefully drew in a pin stripe on the body, and painted the spokes of the wheels.

When Belle, carefully groomed with her shining harness, was hitched to the buggy, she seemed to be proud of herself. She would lift her feet much higher than necessary, snort at birds, feathers, or tumble weeds, and act like a colt. And Jim loved her. He was very proud to drive his mother to town on a Saturday for the shopping, and his mother seemed very happy, too.

Of course, a young man's motives for such feedaddling are always open for questioning, and it was Henry Fuller who first came right out and asked him about it. Mrs. Stone was in the general store and likely to be a long while, seeing how she was talking to Mrs. Fuller, Mrs. Abe Adams and Mrs. George Newberry.

"Jim," said Henry, "what you turning over in your mind to be dollin' up your buggy and ol' Belle there?"

"Nothin' much," said Jim, coloring up slightly, because he knew what the next question would be.

"You ain't thinking of sparkin' some little country girl, are you?"

40

"Could be," answered Jim, feeling the old devil pushing him into a whopping big story.

"Who is the lucky girl you got your mind set on?" persisted Henry as several other men stopped to listen.

"Well," said Jim thoughtfully, "I hadn't thought to make my business public, but I kind of got my mind set on young Widow Creech. She's got a farm and no one to run it, and I figured I'm her man."

Henry howled. The others joined in and Jim knew he had started something he might be sorry for.

"Widder Creech has got three kids nearer your age than her," said one man Jim did not know.

"Yup," said another, "she'd make a boy like you who ain't quit wettin' his night shirt a good mother."

"Now, wait a minute," implored Jim, "you know how it is with widows. They need more than just an ordinary fellow to get 'em satisfied. That's why I aim to spark a widow."

There was considerable laughter and some uneasiness. Maybe this youngster meant what he said. In a town where news was scarce and a story need be but a breath to become a scandal, each was anxious to be off to spread his version. Soon Henry and Jim were alone.

"What did you want to start that kind of a yarn for?" asked Henry.

"Henry," said Jim, "I don't exactly know why I did, but those fellows were yawping so big, I figured I'd give 'em something to yawp about. Besides what's wrong with widows?"

The morning Taylor had come home was no different from the wet spring mornings that had preceded it. The morning star had been bright and gave way only when the sun was about to show itself over the hills to the east. The swallows were darting in and out of the hayloft and were busy plastering their mud nests on the rafters. The robins were talking about rain, but the dew was so heavy that little pools of water had gathered at the stems of the thistles and plantain. Rain there might be, but there was no promise of it in the morning air.

Jim came from the house, sleepy-eyed and rolling his shirt sleeves to the elbow. His hair was tousled and his cheeks were creased by some slight wrinkle in his pillow. Jim's morning rou-

41

tine was always the same. He would bring the horses and cattle up to the barn yard from the pasture, and put them in the stable, but not until he had cleaned the stable, removed the wet bedding and put in each manger its allotment of grain. So this morning when Jim let down the bars, there was the usual stampede on the part of the stock to get in the barn to breakfast.

Jim leisurely scratched himself, and then reached for the milk bucket he had hung upside down on the fence post nearest the barn. It was then that he saw Taylor.

As morning twilight replaced the starlighted night, Taylor left the main road and walked up the lane to the house. He knew it was too early for anyone to be up and about. He was glad. He wanted to look around and settle his mind on how things were. The last news he had had was nearly a year old now, a letter from Miss Virginia telling him about Lyde's wedding and the funeral of his father. He wondered if the place had changed much. Four years is a long time.

As Taylor looked around, he felt that nothing was worse than it had been when he went away. The stock looked fat and although it would not be long before haying season the barn seemed to be half full of good hay. Taylor was pleased and relieved to know the folks were getting along all right. He walked over to the old apple tree near the barn and saw its limbs would soon be heavy with fruit, although now the apples were no larger than hickory nuts. Taylor placed his rifle on the ground and leaned it against the trunk. Then he hitched himself up and sat in the crotch of the tree.

As Taylor sat there, with a lump in his throat, thinking of the past four years shot to hell, but thanking God for sparing him his life, there was a rattle at the kitchen door, which opened. In the peach ivory light of dawn, the man who came out of the house appeared to be a stranger. His height, breadth and muscular thickness were those of a grown man, but the nose, eyes and forehead were typically Stone. "My Heavens," thought Taylor, "is that my young brother? Four years—mm—fifteen. Well, it certainly could be." Taylor started to jump down, but before he could do it, Jim walked into the barn, so Taylor sat still and watched.

From the barn came forks full of manure, adding to the growing heap outside the barn. A Dominicker hen with a dozen or so chicks scratched in the heap and called her brood to examine each new morsel. Jim was happy so he sang.

Taylor watched Jim bring the stock to the barn and watched him open the gate for them. He jumped down from his roost, picked up his rifle, and Jim saw him.

"I suppose it's you, Taylor," said Jim doubtfully. The man approaching him was abnormally thin. His clothes hung on him as on a scarecrow and his face was white and peaked. The cavernous eyes and heavy brows were familiar.

"Yes, it's me."

Jim dropped the milk bucket and raced the few feet to Taylor, and put his arms around Taylor's thin shoulders. There is a lot to talk about after four years and the two lost no time. After the first burst of conversation had passed and they regarded one another in silence for a moment, Jim said, "Come in the barn while I milk. Ma's up, but I want to be there when she sees you."

"All right," said Taylor, following him. "Are you farming it alone, Jim?"

"Yes, I am and I did all right last year, but there's enough room here for you, Taylor, and plenty to do besides."

Taylor did not answer. The only sounds came from the streams of milk penetrating the thick foam in the bucket, and the rustling of hay in the manger. He sat on the spare stool with his knees drawn up under his chin. His blue uniform was faded, but clean and very large. Taylor would have filled it four years ago. Jim wondered if he needed feeding, or if that was consumption he had.

"Taylor."

"What is it, Jim?"

"Taylor, I want that you should know you are head man here now. I'll do as you say—exactly."

"You would, Jim?"

"Yes."

"If I stay, we can get along together and there will be no need for a head man."

"You are older," said Jim as if that meant everything.

By now the cows were milked, so together they turned them out in the pasture. Then they went to the house.

"Hello, Ma," said Taylor, trying to be matter of fact.

43

"Howdy, Taylor," replied the mother, being matter of fact, "I been expecting you."

"Have you, Ma?"

"Yes."

Jim was baffled completely. He had not expected Taylor and his mother had not said anything about Taylor in months. "How'd you know, Ma?" he asked.

"Miss Virginia told me the war was over and she said she had heard from Taylor." There was no tone of jealousy and no sign of rebuke for not having written his own people.

"Yes, Ma, I have written her."

"Your work clothes are in your drawer, son," said the mother breaking an egg in the skillet. "What you need is a little work, a lost of rest, plenty of eggs and milk."

"I like the sound of your prescription," said Taylor and kissed his mother.

During the year following his return, Taylor did rest and work and eat good farm food. He gained back all that he had lost and then some, but he was built along slightly different lines from his younger brother. Where Jim was heavy shouldered and thick through the chest, Taylor was thin and wiry. Taylor was slightly over six feet tall. Jim was not over five feet ten inches, but before he had finished growing, had crowded the six foot mark missing by a fraction of an inch.

When Taylor left home to join the Union Army he was like any other young man in his personal habits. He had kept himself reasonably clean, and reasonably clean shaven. His mother had seen to it that he did. His language had been strong language, the type a boy learns from hired hands, neighbors, and his own father. Under certain conditions, strong language gives way to the superior strength of profanity, and while no great material good can be credited to profanity, there is something that seems to soothe the soul of the user. Taylor had been known to leave a strong odor of sulphur behind his profanity, but now there was a difference.

Somewhere in the red clay of Dalton, Resacca, Kenesaw Mountain, Peachtree Creek or Jonesborough, all down there in Georgia, Taylor had seen something that had caused a change in him. It did not seem to be that he had taken religion. He never mentioned religion, and he never spoke of Georgia except in answer to a direct question. He seemed anxious to forget the war completely. But a change there was and in a way it amounted to a religion. He carried the doctrine of cleanliness into the barnyard, into the barns, indeed into the pastures and wood lots. He even carried it into his speech and personal hygiene. This new Taylor was puzzling, but no one ever opposed him. On Jim, it made a profound impression, and though he never carried it so far as to take the flavor from his speech, he did accept the rest.

So, shortly after his arrival, the manure pile behind the barn was hauled away, a new hog lot was made farther from the house and the privy was moved to a new location also farther from the house. Brush piles in the woods and pastures were burned and the wild blackberry bushes in the orchard were cut and burned. To this last Jim objected on the grounds that the blackberries that grew in the orchard were better than the apples.

Taylor had been home nearly a month before he mentioned Miss Virginia and then he did so obliquely.

"That's a mighty fine job you did on the buggy, Jim."

"Glad to hear you brag on it," said Jim. They both regarded it silently. It is hard to tell whether people's minds are considering further conversation or have gone entirely blank, or are thinking of the price of seed wheat, when these silences set in. After nearly five minutes had elapsed, during which time both chewed on timothy tips, Taylor spoke again.

"Belle makes a good buggy horse."

"She sure does," answered Jim, "since I got her woke up."

Silence again.

"Did you like school, Jim?"

"Yes."

Again they considered the scene before them. Then Jim stood up, threw the timothy straw away and faced Taylor squarely. He looked like he intended to speak a piece, but his resolution left him and he climbed into the buggy and put his feet on the dash. Taylor joined him.

"Jim, is she real pretty?"

"Yes."

"Do you like her a lot?"

"I guess I do."

"Tell me all about her?"

"All?" asked Jim incredulously.

45

"Yes," said Taylor.

"But I don't know all about her."

"Tell me what you know."

"Well, she was raised somewhere out of the county. I don't know really where. When she was about seventeen or eighteen she met this Creech boy. George his name is—maybe you know him?"

Taylor shook his head negatively.

"Well, they were married—"

"Married?" asked Taylor mouth agape.

"Yes," said Jim looking straight ahead. "Married. And in five years had three children. He died about a year ago—"

"Jim, who are you talking about?"

"Why, the Widow Creech."

Taylor looked into the eyes of his brother. He saw in them the laughter of the devil, and knew that he was being spoofed.

"Jim," said Taylor quietly, "you go to hell."

"That's strong language coming from you."

"I know where the devil lives. Go on home."

"To hell?" asked Jim feigning grievous injury.

"No other place."

They laughed, and Jim said that he had supposed Taylor was asking about the Widow Creech, since Jim had set his mind in her direction. Taylor grinned wryly and said, "I want to know about Miss Virginia."

"Oh her! Why didn't you say so?" Then Jim laughed and he had the peculiar feeling that Taylor was his younger brother.

Jim told all he knew about Miss Virginia, and Taylor listened. When Jim's tongue ran completely down, Taylor cast an embarrassed glance in Jim's direction and said he wanted to meet Miss Virginia tonight. Did Jim know where she lived during the summer? Good then, they had better get the chores done early.

And so it came about that as soon as supper was over, the two brothers, clean shaven and dressed in their Sunday best, climbed into the buggy behind Belle. It was a beautiful evening and Belle made short work of the miles into town. Shortly before the darkness settled down, they pulled up before the parsonage.

"I'll tie Belle. You go in," said Jim.

"No, Jim," said Taylor uneasily, "you must introduce me."

"Me?"

"Who else?" said Taylor testily.

So they went up to the door together. It was open and somewhere in the back of the house came the rattle of dishes and the conversation of women. The brothers looked at one another. Taylor summoned his courage, and it took about as much as it had taken at Kenesaw Mountain, only this was worse. He knocked. Finally, a small child came to the door and peeked out at them.

"Papa isn't home," she said.

"Is Miss Virginia home?" asked Jim stooping to see her more clearly.

"She's washing dishes," said the little one.

"Will you tell her she has company?"

"She hasn't any company," said she, making a violent denial with her head.

"Won't you tell her we are here?" whispered Jim. Gad! how perverse women could be when they took the notion and there did not seem to be an age bracket either.

"No," answered the girl, and she shut the door.

"I'll be God damned," said Jim, sweating and uncomfortable.

"Oh gosh!" said Taylor, but there was almost as much strength in his "gosh" as there was in Jim's profanity.

"Now, what do we do?" asked Jim.

"Deploy and re-form at the rear."

"The kitchen?"

"Yes."

So they walked around to the back yard, ducking under lilac bushes and getting snagged by rose bushes. When they knocked on the back door, the same little girl answered the knock.

"Thunderation," said Jim to Taylor, "that kid is a plague."

The child stared at them and would have shut this door, but Jim's foot had foreseen this possibility, and had placed itself in the way.

"Child, will you tell your mother we'd like to see her?" asked Taylor.

"I thought you wanted to see Miss Virginia?" she exclaimed in a shrill voice that ought to have been audible in Newark.

"We do, honey," said Taylor, "won't you call either to the door?"

"Who are you talking to, Abigail?" asked a voice.

47

"No one," lied the little imp.

Seeing how they were getting nowhere fast, Jim called, "Miss Virginia," in a loud voice. Immediately the child set up a terrific bawling and two dogs, hitherto unnoticed since they were sleeping under the woodshed, came tearing out barking their fool heads off. In all this racket a person could not hear himself think. When Miss Virginia appeared at the door, drying her hands on her apron, talk was out of the question. The dog disturbance was quickly settled when she picked up a piece of stove wood and accurately let it drive in their general direction. They retired under the woodshed growling to themselves, but the child had now reached her second wind and was going strong. The mother threatened to give her something to cry for if she did not stop. There was no let up, so the parson's wife kept her promise and two other children joined out of sympathy.

On the back porch the three looked at one another and grinned. Jim took Taylor's arm and Miss Virginia by the hand and led them out to the buggy in front of the house. The two dogs had reappeared and some of their friends took up the cry. The three climbed in the buggy and, with Jim driving, were soon far enough away from the parsonage to think.

"Miss Virginia, this is Taylor. Taylor—Miss Virginia."

"I am glad to know you, Taylor," said Miss Virginia simply. "You are so much like I pictured you, I feel like I had known you always."

"It's probably he is a lot like me," said Jim.

"I liked your letters, Taylor."

"I liked yours, too, Miss Virginia."

"Call me Virginia," she said, looking at him in a way that women have of showing that the proper ingredients of Heaven are now present.

"Virginia," Taylor whispered.

Jim felt slightly ill at ease. They might, he argued crossly to himself, have waited until they were acquainted before they started sparking. At least they might have waited until he was not along. Somewhere inside him a feeling of envy turned itself over, and gave way to another of wonder.

He wondered if two people could fall in love by mail. He wondered if Belle would ever get her tail down again, and why, to-night of all nights, she had to be so everlastingly windy.

The mother's death came as a surprise to everyone. She had not appeared to be very sick and the doctor was reassuring. In fact, the evening before she died, she felt well enough to want to sit up and even to get up. By morning she was extremely ill, and she died about evening chore time, with the doctor present.

The neighbors came over and did what they could to help get ready for the funeral. Taylor and Jim seemed to have two left hands and were as helpless as men usually are in such circumstances. The local undertaker and his wife stayed at the home the night before the funeral.

To Jim it seemed that more people attended his mother's funeral than had attended his father's. He was not cynical ordinarily, but the presence of three half brothers from the earlier marriages made him think that the vultures were looking the place over. Taylor wrote Lyde a letter telling of the death of her mother, but Lyde did not get it until several days after the funeral. So on November tenth, less than two years after her husband had been buried in the little cemetery, his third wife joined him.

The minister was really wound up and preached for nearly three hours, counting the nearly hour long prayer at the grave. To Jim, the sermon sounded like a political speech, and he did not feel either reverent or sad when it ended. He was glad when the grave was filled and everyone had gone home.

The two boys lived on the place until spring. When they left, they hoped they would never see it again, for the winter had been miserable. It was not that the cooking, cleaning and dishwashing were so bad, but the big house seemed so empty and silent and void of smells of good things cooking, unless you can call the odor of burned biscuits, homey. There seemed to be no point to anything. Why churn this week's cream into butter when last week's butter, and two weeks' before was not touched?

Women are often pesky nuisances. But the worst of them can turn a house into some sort of a home, and that is something no two men can do. By spring Jim would have married the Widow Creech, if she had six children. At least he said he would, and that was not just deep breathing Taylor was doing every Saturday night at the parson's house.

The mother had not been two weeks in her grave when one of the half brothers from the first family came to see them. He said

49

the court had appointed him executor of the estate and it was up to him to settle the estate as quickly as possible.

"Do you know of anything your pa had besides this place?" he asked the boys. They did not know of anything. "Did the old man or Mrs. Stone have any debts?" Only the funeral expenses were unpaid. Then he tried to sell them the farm, but mentioned a figure so high, they were troubled to keep from laughing. Then other brothers showed up to look the place over and a first class row was in the making, indeed had already started.

In January, Jim was all for taking the stock to the brother who had charge of the estate and leaving, but Taylor persuaded him to wait. In April, a delegation of half brothers, three in number, came to the place and said they wanted the place right away and offered to let them take what they wanted of the stock and equipment "within reason, of course" to get off. Taylor looked at Jim and said, "Let Jim and me talk this over a minute, and we'll tell you what we want." So the two of them went out in the barn and sat on the feed box.

"It's this way," said Taylor, "they want us off, so they can sell the place right away in time for this year's crop. To my knowledge, there are thirty-five heirs and when they get through dividing up, there won't be a hundred dollars apiece. Do you agree with me?"

"Sounds likely."

"Miss Virginia and I are going to get married and go to Iowa. The government is giving Union Soldiers the chance at some land out there and I'm going. If I could take Belle and the buggy that's all I'd want, but you got first choice on her. Maybe you could get the cows. Come with me anyway and we'll stick together."

"Taylor," said Jim slowly, because he was thinking fast and he was stalling for time, "I got no notion to leave Ohio. There is nothing on this farm that I want. Take Belle and I'll help you get the cows. I'm going to stay in Ohio, because I like it here. There is no land in Iowa for me, and three is one too many when the other two are man and wife."

"What are you going to do?"

"More than likely, I'll go to work for Henry Fuller's pa, but there is always work for a fellow like me."

So that is how it came about that one morning about breakfast time Belle, the buggy, two cows and Taylor and Jim pulled in front of the parsonage. Miss Virginia was dressed and waiting for them, her pretty face aglow with excitement. For an hour they packed her things in the trunk they had brought from home. Then they stowed it in the rear of the buggy. Under the seat and in every crack and cranny were packages, all the way from a sack of grain to a lady's hat clear from Boston. By ten o'clock the bundles were packed away.

"Now," said Miss Virginia, "it's time for the wedding." She was so happy and thrilled by the adventure that was just ahead, that she seemed like a little girl—a very, very pretty little girl.

They went into the parlor and there they were married. Taylor and Miss Virginia were solemn as they said, "I do" to the various questions they were asked. The minister's voice seemed to roll up out of his mid-section somewhere, it was so deep and majestic.

When it was over the minister's wife cried and said they reminded her of Moses and Zipporek on their way to the Promised Land.

"Not that," said Miss Virginia, "because Moses never reached the Promised Land."

"Iowa is so far away, and you children are so young," moaned the good lady. There appeared to be more to follow, so Jim helped Taylor gather his new wife and her personal gear together, and helped them into the buggy.

"I guess we are ready," finally said Taylor.

"Then let's go," said his new wife, "or we'll take root here again."

Good-byes were said and Jim reached up for a kiss from the bride. Taylor shook his hand, and Belle started off at the light flick of the rein.

Jim watched them until they were out of sight and then he picked up the neatly rolled bundle of extra clothing, all he owned in this world, except for the ten dollars Taylor had given him, and walked into the center of town. He considered for a moment and then walked down a road he had never been on before, a road that led straight out of the Valley.

Chapter V

THE WANDERER WANDERS—INTO TROUBLE

At the river Jim stopped long enough to take his shoes off. There was no need of wearing them out in the summer time when new ones might be pretty scarce in the winter time. So he tied them together with the laces and straddled them over his bundle of clothing. He had already run a stick through the bundle, so he could carry it over his shoulder easier.

Behind him lay the town with its stores, mill, bank and lumber yard. The houses were scattered along its streets without apparent plan. Some were painted and most were not. Already Jim knew he was farther from home than he had ever been in his life before, but only a mile farther. He looked up at the sun and knew he had better get moving, if he was going anywhere. But where was he going? He did not know and the knowledge that he did not care, sent a thrill up his spine. This road was the road to adventure. Any road was a road to adventure.

"I am free," said Jim to the river, or the road, or to God. "I am free. No one can make me do anything I don't want to do. I can go where I want to and work when I want to. I am free as hell." So he picked up his load and set off up the road at a leisurely pace, climbing now as the road left the river.

In the late afternoon Jim got a ride for several miles with a doctor who had just delivered twin boys to the home of a young farmer and was now on his way to deliver a baby on up the road a piece. It turned out to be a far piece and Jim was grateful.

Darkness settled quickly and Jim bedded down for the night in a haymow. The house had burned down some time ago, if one could judge by the weeds around the foundation. The barn looked fit to fall down soon, but the mow was dry and warm. With the coming of darkness a chill had settled over the land.

He was not hungry which was strange, because he had never

52

completely missed eating for a whole day before. Neither he nor Taylor could eat a bit of breakfast. He wondered where Taylor and his wife were spending the night. As he wondered, he watched the stars through the holes in the roof and thought of God.

His father had never asked God for anything except guidance. At church the minister had asked God for everything he could lay his tongue to—everything from a clear day for the church outing to a bountiful crop for the dwellers in the valley. He wondered who was right, the minister or his father. If he were God, he'd rather listen to his father.

So for the first time in his life Jim prayed, "Lord, I never prayed to you before, but Pop did and he got along all right. I don't want anything but a sign to show me what I best do. I'll make mistakes plenty, but I won't make any you tell me not to. Kind of look after Taylor, too, Lord. Amen." Sleep came soon.

At the crack of dawn, Jim awoke. For a moment or two he wondered where he was, then memory came to him and straightened the details out. He arose and found that he had managed to get a great many—too many—hayseeds next his hide. So he went around behind the barn, stripped to the skin and shook his clothes. Soon he was back in them, but the seeds were gone. Gathering up his bundle he set off down the road.

There is something good about a walk before breakfast, ordinarily, but this morning was different. "I better get me something to eat right away quick," said Jim aloud, "because my belly thinks my throat is cut." It was with relief that Jim approached the next farm house. He was still a long way off when two shepherd dogs sighted him and set up such an infernal barking as to wake the dead. Nor were they only vocal. They came leaping at him with fangs bared and made every effort to convince him that they would relish the taste of his meat, if he set foot on their property. They had no trouble convincing him. He looked forlornly at the house. At that moment an old lady came out on the back step and called the dogs to breakfast. They left him at a gallop, so he followed up the drive way into the barnyard.

The lady stared at him all the way. As he stood in front of her, Jim could feel the heavy crowbar of curiosity prying out of him his reason for being there. He also knew she was prepared to believe not a word he said.

53

"Good morning, ma'am," said Jim cheerily.

"Humph," replied the lady.

"Tough old bitch," thought Jim. Aloud he said, "I'm feeling a need for some victuals this morning and I'd like to pay for them by helping around the place some."

"You likely would eat more'n you could earn in a day."

"Likely would," said Jim not daunted, "likely would. I ain't et since day before yesterday."

"You're pretty young to be a tramp," said the old lady.

"What's a tramp?" Jim wanted to know.

"Humph," said the old lady tight in the lips and sour enough to turn vinegar. "I ain't going to feed no tramp."

At the next farm things were much better for him. A man in the yard saw him and hailed him in.

"You had your breakfast, son?"

"No."

"You will have soon. Come on in and let the women fix you some pancakes."

"Right glad to," replied Jim. "My name is Stone. James Franklin Stone."

"Mine is Turnbull. Glad to know you. Come on in."

Jim did not exactly burst, but he was about to. Pancakes, sausage, fried potatoes and maple syrup can swamp a man that hardly knows where to stop. As Jim leaned back, Turnbull spoke, "You going some place in particular, or just looking for a job?"

"I'm not going anywhere," said Jim smiling, "I'm going away from somewhere."

"So?" said Mrs. Turnbull, a pleasant plump young-toward-middle-age lady.

"Yes."

"What's the matter? Something you can tell?" asked the man.

"Oh, yes," said Jim, feeling contented and friendly. "My folks died and the family is all broken up. I'm the youngest and the only one that ain't married. So I'm leaving the Valley so's not to be a bother to anyone."

"Licking Valley?"

"Yes."

"You related to Emanuel Stone?"

"I probably am, but I don't know him."

"He lives over on the next road here—behind us."

54

"I'm not anxious to find out," said Jim uneasily. "I'd be apt to find myself working for nothing for about five years."

"I need some help myself, but I would settle for two weeks' worth."

"I'll stay for two weeks, but no longer," said Jim. "I aim to get along more than fifteen miles before I stop next time." It was characteristic of Jim that he made no mention of wages.

So for two weeks Jim plowed and harrowed and planted. On rainy days he helped fix fence. In the evenings he played with the Turnbulls' two children, both around five years old. Exactly two weeks later, he was on the road again. This time he had a big lunch and seven dollars and fifty cents to add to the ten Taylor gave him.

If there was any place in the world more beautiful than Ohio in the summer time, Jim did not care to see it. The dark green of the elms and the light green of the maples made their outlines against the summer sky, blue, with white cotton clouds. The heat shimmered on the roads and across the meadows and cornfields. Along the roads tiger lilies and brown-eyed susans grew. Daisies made the pastures and meadows white.

May and June passed and July was upon him before Jim thought seriously of finding a place for the winter. Maybe it was his seventeeth birthday that warned him of the passing days. He resolved to settle down as soon as he could find a job. At the time he was in the vicinity of Garrettsville. He could see the town in the distance and figured it to be five miles away. Jim's bare feet made little pats of noise as they slapped down on a wheel track made by a wide-tired wagon. Jim wondered how big the horses were that could pull a wagon with wheels like that.

Somewhere ahead a dinner bell sounded. He hurried a bit so as not to be too late, but the road took to winding in and out among the low hills and up and down. It was nearly an hour later that he came over a small rise and saw the farm house. Hollyhocks followed the fences around the house in thick profusion. Over the back door and all the way to the woodshed was a grape arbor, with green grapes hanging in promising clusters. Jim knocked at the door.

"Who's there?" called a voice.

"Jim Stone, ma'am, looking for a chance to work for a dinner."

"One moment," said the voice. "Ma, it's a tramp. Can I fix him some dinner?" A conversation followed in which the ingredients of his dinner were discussed by a mother and daughter. At last, he was fed under the grape arbor, a cold but satisfying meal. The cold water from the well seemed to put strength back into his muscles.

"Where you going?" asked the girl.

"I'm looking for a job."

"You'll never find one," she said with finality.

"Why not?"

"You don't look like a man who would work."

"No?" queried Jim, amazed that a person who had worked like he had could look like he had never done so. "How does a man look who won't work?"

"I said too much," said the girl edging toward the kitchen door.

"Millie, what you talking about?" asked the mother.

"Nothing," said Millie.

"You were so. You know how no one should talk to strangers. Now, git in here."

"He's looking for work, Ma."

"Why didn't you say so?"

"You started jawing me before I could."

"Where's your pa?"

"Down to the barn."

"Go fetch him."

"Yes, Ma."

"Hell," thought Jim, "these people are looking for a hired man. I got me a job right now." He wondered if he could stand the old lady's tongue for a year. He shrugged his shoulders and wiped his plate clean with a piece of bread. A heavy clumping came up the path from the barn, Pa no doubt.

"That's him," said Millie.

"You looking for work?" said the farmer.

"I had some such idee," admitted Jim.

"You ever done farm work?"

"Yup."

"How old are you?"

"Seventeen." Jim wondered if the old boy would want to see his teeth.

"Big for your age, ain't you?"

"Yup."

56

"What's your politic?"

"Politic?"

"Sartinly, how do you vote?"

"I don't aim to vote for a few years yet."

"How'd your pa vote?"

"Pa was Republican."

"Glad to hear it."

The old man was agreeably surprised. Jim expected the next question to ask if he was a red Indian, but there were no more questions. Jim thanked the Almighty One for that.

"Tell you what I'll do, and not a man can be fairer. I'll give you ten dollars a month, board and room ye, and take care of your washing and mending. You to stay a year unless I scat you."

Jim saw a chance to get away. Ten dollars a month was about half what a man could get, if he was a good worker. Times were good now and even boys were getting that wage some places.

"Nope," said Jim.

"How say?"

"No," said he, "ain't working for ten dollars when I can get twenty. Let me pay you for the dinner and I'll be gone."

"Stand up to where I can look at ye."

Jim stood. He felt foolish and wished to be gone.

"I'll pay ye twenty," said the farmer, "at the end of a year."

"No."

"I aim to be fair, but hiring a man you don't know is like buying a pig in a poke." He looked at his boots. The mother leaned in the doorway and the daughter sat on the well curb. Jim stood with the plate in his hand.

"I'll tell you what I'll do," said the farmer, "I'll pay you twenty a month. I'll pay you on New Year for this six months and on July first for the next six months. You start today."

"We don't come from the same country," said Jim. "Where I come from a hired man draws his pay every month. No need of us dickering and I'm sorry to be beholden to you for dinner. It was very good, ma'am."

"Might's well take him, Pa," said the mother, "you ain't going to find no better, and that hay won't last forever."

"Yes, Pa, he'll do," said Millie.

"You keep out of this," said the old man, "I don't want you should even notice a man in the house." He glared at poor Millie and she sort of shrank up and looked away.

"Everyone is against me, so I might as well hire you. Mind you, I expect good honest work for my money."

Millie showed him the room he would occupy and put his spare clothes in the drawers of the dresser. Besides his clothes Jim had only his father's razor. A look in the mirror showed him he should have used it more often. He made up his mind to shave tonight, but work was expected of him this afternoon so he had to hustle.

The Jared Gordon farm was a good farm. It had not been worked out like so many farms were getting to be. The fields were not large and the hillsides were not ploughed. The buildings were weathered and unpainted, but would probably outlast old Jared.

Their only child was Millie, and all her life she seemed to have had to take a boy's place. In the days that followed, it was she, dressed in overalls, who made the load as Jared pitched the hay up to her. It was she who mowed it away in the barn. Jim was kept busy cutting hay with his scythe from breakfast to chore time. His hands calloused up like leather. Of Jared, it can only be said that if he drove his family hard, so did he drive himself.

When the hay was cut and the barn filled, the oats were ready to be cradled. The one season merged into the other so quickly that Jim scarcely felt he had time to straighten up. Even Sunday was scarcely a day of rest. It is true that Jim attended church with the family, but Sunday afternoons he cranked the grindstone while Jared bore down on the scythes, getting them ready for the next day's cutting. At night Jim was ready to sleep and did, like one paralyzed.

After the harvesting was over they spent their days in the wood lot, sawing enough wood to last for years it seemed to Jim. As more and more was cut and there seemed no letup, Jim suspected that much of this wood would be sold during the winter in town. Nor was he far wrong, because Jared figured to sell enough wood to get back Jim's wages and then some. Millie was along to stack the wood in cords after it was split.

One day in the early winter the three were in the wood lot as usual. Jim's steady rise and fall of the ax was splitting the hollow beech chunks into the right size for the stove, and Millie methodically piled it between two trees. Old Jared had gone off

58

behind the hill somewhere. Jim finished his chunk and stopped for breath. Millie came and stood before him and said, "Jim, ain't you never going to look at me?"

For the first time Jim saw what she meant—that she was a woman. He had sort of taken for granted that she was a boy, because she had worked like a boy, and she had dressed like a boy. He felt sorry for her, because she should have been in dresses, sewing and cooking and acting like a woman. She was certainly acting like a woman now for there were tears in her eyes.

Millie was flat-chested and muscular. Her hips were slender and masculine. Her face was pretty enough, but wide at the eyes with sunken cheeks and narrow chin. Her hair was scanty and all hidden in the knitted stocking cap she wore.

What could he say? Jim did not know, he said nothing—not a word. Raising his ax he went back to work.

By the time Jared came back, everything was normal—at least on the surface. In Millie's eyes there was a dangerous glint and it bode no lasting good to James Franklin Stone.

In the week that followed, Jim saw that if he had not noticed Millie's femininity, he was the only one who hadn't been aware of it, because he was never alone a minute with her. Old Jared and the Missus looked after their one child in a manner that made her virtue assured.

Jim had taken a great liking for Jared's team of bay mares. On rainy days he curried them and brushed them until they were as glossy as old Belle had been. In the winter there was no work for them, so he exercised them by riding one and leading the other down to the creek. There he would chop a hole in the ice and with much snorting and pawing they would drink.

On this particular day, he had just returned from the creek and tied the horses when he heard a whispered, "Jim!" He looked around, but saw no one. Then he heard it again and looked up the hay chute into the loft. With exaggerated facial expressions Millie said, "In the pot under your bed."

"In the pot under my bed?"

"Yes."

"What?"

"Shhh!" And then she was gone.

Now in Jim's room, the articles of furniture that were meant to be used were, in order of their importance, the bed, the dresser, the chair, the water pitcher, the wash bowl and the chamber pot under the bed. In fact, the occasions on which the latter article could with reason have been used could be counted on the index finger of his right hand. So he wondered what was up now. Whatever it was, he did not like it.

After supper he retired to the privacy of his room, and placed the candle on the dresser. Falling to his knees, he pulled the pot into the open and looked into its cavernous depths. There was a note and a pencil in it. Removing both, he read the note. In a fairly legible hand, the note produced a chill and a tingle in Jim's spine.

"Darling Jim," he read. "My God! that's me."

> Darling Jim—
> I have took this means to let you know that I love you and know that you love me. I know you can't show me you do on account of the folks, but write on this paper a letter and drop it in the jar. I'll get it when I make the bed. I will go anywhere you say with you.
> Your adoring Millie

Now, indeed, did Jim know what his father had meant when he said it was no sin to run from a woman. He would leave tomorrow and he hoped he would get away with a whole skin. He knew old Jared would be hard to talk to, and he did not dare tell the old man the truth for Millie's sake.

He laboriously wrote on the back of Millie's note the following:

> Dear Millie—
> I am seventeen years old. I do not want a wife yet. I do not love you or anyone else. I am going to leave right away, so as not to cause no trouble.
> Jim F. Stone

The following morning Jim hustled through the chores. In one respect he was happy to be leaving, in another, not. In his pockets were about one hundred and fifty dollars. He wanted to buy some new clothes and get a barbershop haircut. The old lady had hacked his hair off short enough to keep it out of his eyes, but he didn't think it looked very good. In favor of staying was the dread of making a change in the winter time.

At breakfast he noticed things were quieter than usual, but was in no hurry to start anything. Once breakfast was over, he went up to his room. A quick glance in the jar under the bed, was enough to prove that at least one member of the Gordon family knew he was leaving. He gathered his clothes together and made a bundle out of them.

Descending the steps, he was thankful that all that remained was to have a few words with Jared and be gone. A little prickle of fear went through him as he walked through the kitchen and opened the door. It was strange that no one would be here.

From the back porch he saw that the family had not disappeared by a long shot. The mother, standing on the steps, her back to Jim was crying, "No, Jared, no! My God, Jared! No!"

Millie, looking mad and defiant, with her arms crossed on her chest, stood under the arbor, now a lacework skeleton. Jared was coming out of the woodshed with a pick in his hand. He bounced it on the stone flagging and removed the handle from the pick. Jim pushed past Mrs. Gordon and walked toward Jared.

"Now, by God, we'll see about this," said Jared, his eyes red with anger. "No damned hired hand will get away with this while Jared Gordon knows his duty."

"I want to talk to you," said Jim, standing before Jared.

"I'll give you two minutes, before I beat your brains out."

"I'm quitting. I'm going away."

"That's fine," said Jared sarcastically. "You sneak around behind my back and get in to my daughter and then leave her. That makes you a gentleman."

"I did not get in to your daughter," said Jim hotly and both turned to Millie standing there scared and defiant. "Did I, Millie?"

"Yes," she said.

"Millie, you know that's a story!" said Jim, aghast at the turn of affairs.

"Where and when?" asked Jared.

"In the haymow, nearly every day," said Millie.

"Oh, my poor baby," moaned the mother.

Before Jim could as much as think, Jared took a terrific swing from the side with the pick handle. Jim couldn't dodge the blow, but took it on his left shoulder below the blade on the back. As Jared pulled back for another blow, Jim hammered an overhand right to Jared's jaw. The pick handle flew from his hands and Jim hit him twice more before he dropped flat on his back in the snow. A trickle of blood ran from Jared's mouth. His wife took his head in her lap, moaning, "He's killed you, Jared. He's killed you."

Slowly, Jim looked around. Millie had his clothes in her arms walking toward him. "I'll still go with you," she said.

"You lied about the haymow. You nearly got me killed and got your pa hurt, maybe bad, but you are ready to go off with me. Millie, I wouldn't take you to hell with me." Jim looked down at Jared. The open, unseeing eyes, and the blood from the mouth convinced Jim he had killed Jared. He picked up the limp body and carried it into the house, placing it on the bed.

"I'll get the doctor from Garrettsville for you," he said. He picked up his clothes and left. The chill wind never made him as cold as he felt inside.

CHAPTER VI

MRS. ORCHARDS TAKES A HAND

"Can you tell me where the doctor lives?" Jim asked no one in particular, because no one had even looked at him as he entered the store.

"Someone hurt?" asked a man sitting on a pile of three horse collars where he could watch the checker game.

"Yes," said Jim, "Jared Gordon."

"Jared Gordon! If he sent for a doctor, he must be going to die. Jared ain't the kind to spend money foolishly. No, siree!"

"Where does the doctor live?" repeated Jim.

"That's him playing checkers right there. He be through in a minute, 'cause he's most licked now."

"Some people know a lot," said the doctor.

"I know when a feller's done in," replied the other.

"Well, I guess you're right one time anyhow," said the doctor pushing the board on his opponent's knees. As he stood, his full gray beard came down past the top button on his vest. His stomach paunched out abruptly and came back in farther down. He looked like a man hiding a dishpan to Jim's way of thinking.

"What happened to Jared?" asked the doctor.

Jim had been expecting this very question, so without hesitating a moment, he said, "Do you remember the bay mare he had with the bad hind foot? He undertook to cut the foot rot out of the frog and she kicked him square in the face. When I left he hadn't come to yet."

"Serves Jared right for cheating the veterinary out of his work. Live and let live, I always say." Jim did not see the speaker, but there was hearty laughter and general agreement.

"I'll get my horse and buggy ready and follow you right out," said the doctor, "but if you get ahead, don't worry, because I know the way."

"Thank you," said Jim and left.

He was glad the doctor had not offered him a ride, and that he knew the way. Suppose he had not known. "Lordy," thought Jim, "that was a close one. I'm getting out of sight quick."

Crossing the street and turning the corner in the direction of the depot was quickly done. Jim entered the depot as scared as he had ever been. He had seen trains and heard them. Now he planned to ride one. His heart thumped so loudly he could hear its echo. He hoped no one else could.

In the middle of the waiting room was a huge stove, a coal burner from the look of the ashes, but it was red hot and the warmth felt good. He forced himself over to a window behind which a small important looking man was busy packing a wad of tobacco in his mouth.

"When does the next train come through for Cleveland?" Jim asked him.

The man looked at the clock. Then he jutted his jaw and looked at the ceiling, meanwhile rubbing the back of his head. "Well, let's see, if she ain't late, there will be one in thirty-five minutes to do some switching and get some water from the tank up here. You want to go to Cleveland, do you?"

"Yes."

"Your ticket'll be two dollars and fifteen cents." Jim shelled out the money. It was good to be rich enough to ride on trains, but, Lordy, he hoped Jared wasn't dead. Seeing how he was running away and all, it would probably go pretty hard with him. There was nothing he could do about it now, but get out and he was getting out as fast as he could.

He wondered what Cleveland would be like. He had never been in a big city, except Newark, and he knew Cleveland would make ten or twenty that size. He looked out the window and wondered if he would have time to get his hair cut and guessed not. He figured he'd wait until he got to Cleveland, because haircuts might be different there. He had never had a barber haircut. He felt his face. Just as he figured, he needed a shave again, but Lord A'Mighty, he seemed to need a shave every time he turned around.

Jim's heart had quieted down while he waited, but began to thump rapidly again at the first sound of the whistle as the train came into town. This whistle, Jim had been told, was always given in order for farmers to get to their horses' heads, and keep them quiet while the train went through. He saw men running now either to get going, or to get hold of bridles. The train chugged to a stop with the last car right at the station.

All the cars in this train were coal cars loaded with coal for Cleveland. Jim counted them—twenty-six. Twenty-six cars of coal and one car of mail and people being pulled by one engine. He marvelled. Six cars of coal for Garrettsville? That didn't seem possible.

"Is all that coal for Garrettsville?" he spoke to a man whose blue cap bore the word, "Conductor."

"No," said the man genially, "it's upgrade all the way from here to Solon. We can make it with twenty-one or two cars, but no more. We'll leave those six here and so will the trains behind us. When we get eighteen or twenty down here, they'll send an engine down from Cleveland for them."

"I see," said Jim thoughtfully. Railroading must be like playing. It must be wonderful to ride all over the country.

"All aboard," said the conductor. The cry was taken up by the station man and a boy who was emptying the ashes from the stove. Jim noticed that every passenger who was going to get on, was now standing, and had been standing for at least twenty minutes, less than ten feet from the steps into the passenger car. They had been waiting for the conductor to come and stand by the steps to take their tickets. Jim soon found himself in a seat right by the window, a good padded seat, he noticed, like in a buggy. There was a wild waving of arms and a couple of quick toots on the whistle. The train began to move.

Jim was thrilled as he had never been before. The smooth pull of the engine and the sense of riding on air was enough to send his mind on a wild dream of James Franklin Stone leaning from the cab of an engine, pulling a colossal string of cars. Almost before he could get well started on his pipe dream, the train began to slow down. It stopped less than five miles from Garrettsville and one passenger got on. The train struggled painfully to get started again. It was almost more than it could do.

"Where to?" asked the conductor of the new passenger.

"Cleveland."

"That will be two dollars and ten cents." Jim marvelled—only five cents to ride this far.

"I don't have to pay." What kind of talk was this? Jim turned and stared at the man. He was young—maybe twenty-three or four, but no more. He wore a black coat and a derby hat. He had a white shiny collar and a black bow tie. He had a thin, scrawny mustache. His face was long and lean, and over his blue, watery eyes he wore large glasses from which dangled a black shoe lace. The other end was pinned to his coat lapel.

"I am a minister of the Gospel. I am Reverend Knight K. Willard and here is my pass."

"Sorry to have asked, Reverend. Have a seat."

"I have a few tracts I'd like to pass out first. Here—have one." The conductor took a printed sheet and peered at it. The minister gave each passenger a copy and then sat down in the seat ahead of Jim.

The engine had now reached its speed again only to stop in a few minutes at Mantua Station. More people got on and Jim was glad to see that he wasn't the only person riding for the first time. An old couple, farm people, had gotten on and the old lady had quivered like a nervous colt. Her husband's arm about her shoulders assured her that if they were struck down, they would be together. They relaxed long before they reached Aurora.

Ahead of Jim the Reverend Knight K. Willard read from his Bible. Jim looked at the tract. "Know Ye The Day of Wrath Is Coming, by Reverend Knight K. Willard," he read. As near as Jim could tell, things were in a hell of a shape in this part of the country. People were not taking much heed of the Ten Commandments and what they were doing to some of them was a scandal. Nobody seemed to pay any attention to the Golden Rule and they were going to pay for this monkey business right through the nose whenever the Lord got tired of all this hurrah. According to the Reverend, it wouldn't be long in coming.

Jim was glad he wasn't like the people in this tract. Unless, of course, you counted this Jared fight of his, but then Jared started it. He flexed his arm and the pain from his bruised shoulder, forgotten in the excitement of the day, shot through him. He decided not to try that again, and sat back to look out the window.

The train by now was rolling free and fast. They must be near Solon he figured and, sure enough, they were. The train slowed to a stop and began taking on a large number of cans of milk. This seemed to be a prosperous town. The houses were painted and clean. The roads were muddy and the sky gray and bleak, but could not hide the town's prosperity. A large number of passengers came aboard and one sat next to Jim. The man had a gold watch chain across his belly as big as Jim's little finger. The man told him there was only one more stop between here and Cleveland. Corlett, was the name of the place.

"I like the looks of that town Solon," said Jim to his neighbor.

"Great little town, son," said the man obviously pleased. "My father and mother brought seven of us young ones from Connecticut here with a neighbor and his family, and here we have been ever since. They gave the town my middle name, and I'm the postmaster here now, Lorenzo Solon Bull."

Jim wondered what it would be like to have a town named after you. He had never heard of a town named Stone. He knew of a town of Franklin and one of Jamestown. Maybe that wasn't the same. His mind wandered off to other pastures. He wondered what Cleveland would be like.

He had not long to wait for soon the train was running through the outskirts. In less than a quarter of an hour the train jolted to a stop and Jim got off. A brown stone station stood before him. Close around it, the streets were cobbled, but mud was knee-deep everywhere else. Heavy draft horses pulled heavy wagons loaded with boxes and trunks. Whips cracked and harness creaked, wrinkles coming on horses' rumps as they pulled.

Black coal smoke arose from the chimneys a few feet, but was heavy and lowered itself to the ground. Its stench bothered Jim. Ahead of him he could see the town. To the left was the lake. It looked black, and a cold wind blew across it. Jim looked behind him. There was only a valley with a river of muddy water. Only to the right as he faced the town was there any hope. There were houses—boarding houses, probably. Jim carefully picked his way along the plank sidewalk. Mud was everywhere. This was Cleveland on December 20, 1867.

On a street corner a wooden sign had once been painted, "Broadway."

It was loose and hung by a piece of chain and might have meant either street, or none at all. In the first few houses, faces peered out from behind curtains and heavy rings knocked on windows. Jim knew this neighborhood was no place for him. He hurried on. His shoulder pained him so he did not swing his arm.

Four or five blocks farther Jim saw a modest sign before a

brown drab house, "Mrs. Orchards' Boarding House." He went up to the door and knocked. A young woman with coal-black hair and eyes opened the door. She was nearly six feet tall and looked like a woman who had better not be crossed.

"Good afternoon, ma'am," said Jim, "I'm looking for a place to stay."

"Have you a job?" asked the lady, not unkindly.

"Not yet, ma'am, I just got in."

"No money then—I'll give you two weeks' credit and no more. Come in." He entered being careful to scrape his shoes and to wipe them on the rag mat. "My rates are two dollars for the room a week, five dollars for room and board. I put up a lunch for noons and will do your laundry and mending for fifty cents a week. You get all the regular food you want, but only one helping of dessert."

"Yes, ma'am," said Jim intimidated.

"Another thing. I won't stand for drinking in this house and don't ever bring a woman here."

She showed Jim his room. It was small and on the third floor. Up here it was colder than Billy-be-damned, but there was plenty of bed clothing and Jim was used to a cold room. Here again were the pitcher, bowl and thunder mug. Jim hoped to God he never found a note under his bed. He unpacked by opening a drawer and shoving the whole bundle out of sight. Then he gingerly took his shirt off and nearly broke his neck trying to see the bruise on his back. He shaved with goose pimples standing as high as his whiskers.

When he finished he put his shirt back on and went downstairs. He might be foolish, but he had to do what he had made up his mind to do, and the sooner, the better. Entering the living room, he found it empty. There was noise in the back, so he went through the dining room to the kitchen. Mrs. Orchards was bending over the stove stirring something.

"Mrs. Orchards."

"Oh, it's you again."

"Yes, it's me. Can I ask a favor of you?"

"I don't lend money."

"Oh!"

"Never did make a practice of it."

"Would you take care of some for me?"

"What?" she sounded like her ears had not heard right.

"I never handled money and I never spent any until today. I worked though, and I've got one hundred and fifty-two dollars and twenty-one cents. I can't take it with me and I don't like to leave it around loose. Will you take care of it for me? I need me some clothes but I have no idee how to buy them for me."

"In all my days! I never heard of such a thing. What is your name?"

"James Franklin Stone, but I'd like to be called Frank. Jim, I was always called, but I'd rather be called Frank."

"All right, Frank. You want me to take care of your money. Shall I pay your board bill and buy your clothes out of it?"

"Yes, ma'am, please."

"Give me one hundred and fifty, and you keep the rest. I'll keep it for you and you can have it any time you change your mind." Jim gave her the money and felt a load ease itself off his mind. He was about to leave when she said, "Frank, take off your shirt. I'm going to cut your hair."

"Are you a barber?"

"I cut everybody's hair here and shave them when they are sick. Step out here on the back steps."

"Thank you, ma'am."

Jim felt that for once in his life he had landed on his feet. He began to feel at home and he liked this tall woman. She seemed to like him, too; at least she was friendly. He took off his shirt and followed her out on the porch.

"Where in the world is your underwear?" she asked.

"I ain't got none."

"In the dead of winter you leave home without your underwear. Have you got a mother?"

"No, ma'am."

"How old are you?"

"Going on eighteen."

"What's your birthday?"

"July 5th."

"Where'd you get this welt on you?"

"Slipped and fell," said Frank. He'd been waiting for that. The scissors began to snip, not little picky snips, but real honest to God snips. When she finished with him, he felt his head almost naked, she had cut so much. Around him there was a circle of hair and he wondered how all that had come off him.

The boy huddled under the load of quilts above him. At first he had even covered up his head, but as the bed began to get warm he shifted slightly to get his head out and was instantly sorry, because the move brought an entirely new area of cold blankets against his body. Soon this, too, warmed, and peace began to creep through his veins. He relaxed and felt soothed by the cold air he breathed.

What a day this had been! In the short space of twenty-four hours, he had not only upset one world, but had found another. He liked this world so far. Mrs. Orchards had been nice to him and motherly. He trusted her and felt pleased that she was his banker. Her husband, too, had been friendly, although not talkative. Maybe that was his way. He had liked their advice given him before dinner with reference to his age. Mrs. Orchards had said, "Frank, don't tell anybody you are only seventeen years old. Tell a story if you have to—say you are twenty or older. You look old enough to get away with it. When you ask for work you will get paid better, too."

He smiled as he thought how this age business had worked out at the supper table. There they were—Mr. Orchards at the head of the table with eight boarders not counting him. Mrs. Orchards brought the food in and put it on the table. "Eat," she said, "and if your arms are broken, you'll have to starve to death." Mr. Orchards had mumbled a blessing and everybody pitched in. It was while they were waiting for desert that someone asked him his age. He had blown his saucer of coffee just like the rest and remembered and said what his father used to say when people had asked him the same question. "I reckon I'm old enough to know better, but young enough not to give a damn."

The boarders were for the most part rough, and tough. Several worked in a warehouse on Huron Road, several more were teamsters and one little man was a Jewish tailor. Mr. Orchards worked in the ticket office of the Cleveland and Buffalo Steamship Company. Frank wondered what he would do. From the talk at the table anyone who wanted to hold a job as a teamster had to be able to fight—at least there had been several today and it had taken considerable waving of arms and dodging of heads to illustrate how the blows had fallen or been countered. He had kept his mouth shut and had listened.

70

Before he fell asleep he thought about Millie saying he had been in to her every day in the haymow. He wasn't so sure now that it was a bad idea. Maybe a little loving was what Millie needed. He moved and his bruised back reminded him that he had paid the fiddler, even if he hadn't danced. Fatigue and sleep soon won over, and he slept soundly.

He was up early, but ate alone as some of the boarders had eaten and gone to work, while others didn't have to leave until later. He knew that finding work might be hard, and that he had better get moving early. In his mind was a half formed plan to try to get work on the railroad. He didn't exactly know how you went about it, but somebody around the yards could tell him who did the hiring.

Day broke late these cloudy December mornings, so a full hour before daylight, he entered the depot and walked up to the ticket office.

"Good morning," he said to the man framed in the window. He saw the room was lighted by two coal oil lanterns.

"Where to?" asked the man brusquely.

"Nowhere. I want to find out who the boss man is—the one who does the hiring."

"Oh, him. You looking for a job?"

"Yes."

"Go down the road toward the lake and you'll see a wood station about the size of a small house. Go in there and knock on the door that says, 'President.' He's your man."

"Thank you kindly. I'll be running along. Thank you."

He had no difficulty in finding the place and with considerable nervousness knocked on the door. A voice from within said, "Come in." He entered.

"Good morning, sir, I'm looking for a job and I was told you were the man to see." The man he was talking to was about forty years old and had the largest black mustache Frank had ever seen. He sat before a desk with a roll top. A lamp hung in a bracket above him.

"Where did you work before?" asked the man.

"On a farm."

"Why do you want to work on the railroad?"

"I want to—that's all."

"Do you have any particular reason?"

"I want to see the country." Frank could think of no better rea-

71

son, except of course to earn money to keep body and soul together. Everyone had that reason.

"Building track wouldn't suit you then. We are hiring everyone
we can to build line in the west. Not this road, but railroads in
general. We only run to Erie ourselves. We are not a big line,
but big enough."

"I'd like to stay in Ohio. Cleveland suits me fine."

"Uh huh. Wait a minute." He left the room and was gone for
a long time. Eventually, he returned with a tremendous man in
overalls whose red face seemed about to burst the thousands of
little veins running under the surface of the skin. The man wore
overalls with a sweater under the jacket to keep him warm.

"Ed," said the president, "here is the young man I was talking
about."

"I might use another brakeman, if we can afford it."

"Money is no trouble right now. There's more freight than we
can haul, so if you want to break him in, I'll hire him." The big
fellow, Ed, looked at him and Frank wondered if he would be
hired. Quietly Ed said, "I'd like to have him."

"What is your name?" asked the president.

"Frank Stone."

"Age?"

"Twenty-two."

"Where are you staying?"

"At Mrs. Orchard's Boarding House near Brownell and Broadway."

"We'll start you out as a sort of brakeman, wherever Ed wants
you. We'll pay you ten dollars a week, holding back a week's
pay. I see you have your lunch so you can start today."

Frank's surprise at getting a job so easily was only matched by
his surprise when he saw the engine to which he had been as-
signed. On it in fancy lettering were the words, "Lake Shore
Railway Co." He had expected to be working for the Cleveland
and Pittsburgh Line, but had not followed directions at all. One
railroad was as good as another, he thought. Maybe Frank Stone
was luckier than Jim Stone used to be.

CHAPTER VII

LOVE APPEARS

Is three years a long time? To a man in prison it probably is, but to James Franklin Stone, happy—because his work was play —playing with engines and cars and getting paid to do it, the three years that followed his arrival in Cleveland seemed to have disappeared with amazing speed. Nor were the years all that had disappeared in that time. Frank Stone had ceased to be a boy and had become a man. His shyness and uncertain nervous reactions to things new disappeared, too. His new confidence in himself was not the cockiness of a person trying to be a man, but yet uncertain of it himself, nor was it the chestiness of a bully. It had come from the knowledge that he could do a man's work and if necessary, fight a man's fight.

He had spent every day of those three years in Cleveland. If, as he told the man who hired him, he had wanted to see the country from the railroad right of way, he should have been sorely disappointed. He wasn't. During that time, the city had seen fit to pave some of the downtown streets. Broadway was cobbled to Erie Street, but beyond, the mud and dust still was master.

In the Orchards family there had been changes, too. A son, Raymond, had made his appearance. Now indeed Mrs. Orchards worked. She seemed to thrive under it and was happy.

Boarders came and went, until little Mr. Ray, the tailor, and Frank were the oldest customers. Mr. Orchards continued to work in the steamship office, although his health appeared to be not too good. The doctor thought it might be consumption, but was not sure.

About a week before Christmas, 1870, Frank was riding the cowcatcher of a switch engine. They were going down to the roundhouse to leave their engine for the night. It was only six o'clock but already it was dark. The kerosene lamp headlight cast its feeble glow a scant ten yards ahead of the engine. Why the engineer was ringing the bell, he didn't know, but that bell and quitting time usually went together. Maybe he was just glad to be through for the day. The engine slowed to a snail's pace. This was Frank's cue to run ahead and throw the switch. He did, and climbed on the rear platform of the coal car after he had closed the switch again. Soon the engine was stopped.

"Through for the day," said Ben Judson, the engineer, "and not a moment too soon. I'm about done in."

"That's what you married men get for being married," jibed Haskell Taylor, the fireman.

"Wait! Wait 'til you get married and see what happens to you. Probably have a kid a year for twenty years and turn up on your toes and die," said Ben.

"With that ugly face of his," said Frank, "he ain't likely to get a woman."

"I get my sleep and that suits me. By the way, tonight's the night we take our turkeys home, if we want. I think I'll catch mine and have it over with."

"That's a good idee," said Frank.

The company had bought a turkey for each man in its employ. They were brought to the yard and housed in a tool shed, until wanted. There was not much to choose between, since they were nearly of a size. The employee could leave his turkey in the shed until Christmas Eve and the company would feed it, or he could take it earlier. The last turkey in the pen was certain to be the poorest turkey, so most everyone did as Haskell suggested, take while the taking was good. So that's how it happened that he walked into the house, with a gunny sack over his shoulder on this particular evening.

From the looks of the dining room table, he would eat alone tonight. The job of catching the turkey had taken some time and so had the mug of beer that he had stopped for. Catching sight of Mrs. Orchards in the living room, he said, "I've got you a surprise here in my bag."

"That's fine, Frank," she answered, "turkeys always surprise me."

"That's a hell of a way to be surprised," he said in mock dejection.

74

"I've got a surprise for you tonight. Put the turk out in the hen coop and wash up." Frank did as he was told. As he combed his hair, he looked at himself in the mirror and saw that as usual he needed a shave. Oh well, time enough for that tomorrow. He hung the wash basin on its rusty nail and dried his hands. It was cold here on the back porch so he hurried. He entered the dining room, and sat at the table. Evidently, Mrs. Orchards hadn't heard him, so he pounded on it. "Coming," cried Mrs. Orchards.

The door opened and in came his supper, but Mrs. Orchards wasn't carrying it. The girl who was bringing his supper was the most beautiful Frank had ever seen. He stared at her.

Moving gracefully, she removed the food from the tray and set it before him. His jaw dropped slightly open. The girl paid not the slightest attention to him, but was swift and businesslike. Then she returned to the kitchen. Automatically, he began to eat. The food might have been sawdust for he never tasted it. In his mind, questions rattled around like corn in a popper.

"Well, Frank, were you surprised?"

"Heavens to Betsy—yes. Who is she?"

"Why are you so interested?" asked Mrs. Orchards coyly. She sat down and took Raymond on her lap. He looked as coy as his mother.

"She's pretty."

"She's beautiful."

"I guess so," smiled Frank. He knew she was the most beautiful girl he had ever seen. He also knew that Mrs. Orchards was enjoying his curiosity.

"Are you going to introduce her tonight or next week?" he asked wryly.

"Now, if you like."

"What's stopping you?"

"Mary," she called. The girl came to the door. "Come in." She motioned with her arms so violently that Frank wondered if the girl was "deaf."

"Mary, this is Frank Stone. Frank, this is Mary Parker. I'll leave you two for a moment, while I put Raymond to bed. Sit down, Mary." She pointed to the chair and practically sat Mary in it. "I'll be back in a moment."

"It's nice weather for this time of the year," said Frank breaking the silence that followed the landlady's departure.

The girl looked at Frank and said nothing.

"It might snow. Do you like snow?"

The girl giggled and looked toward the door by which Mrs. Orchards had left. Frank was puzzled and embarrassed. Why didn't she say something if no more than "Go to hell." The girl fidgeted. "My name is Marie Parker," she said.

"Sounds like Eye-talian," said Frank. "Say it again." He cupped his hand behind his ear and the girl knew he wanted her to repeat. She did very slowly. Frank watched her lips, full, red enunciating as clearly as they could.

"Your name is Marie Parkay? I thought it was Mary Parker. Mrs. Orchards said so."

The girl nodded, but said nothing.

"My name is Frank Stone."

"Frank Stone," she repeated, "Frank—Frank."

"C'est un beau nom, Frank Stone." She smiled and her teeth were as even as rows of corn on a cob.

"The hell you say," said Frank. They laughed uproariously, but the girl suddenly became quiet, as though suddenly remembering she must not laugh. Frank got up to find Mrs. Orchards and Mary arose.

"No," said Frank, shaking his head violently and pointing to her chair. She sat down again, but on the very edge.

"Mrs. Orchards!" he called. The lady stuck her head through the door and he knew she had heard every word. "Come here and speak Eyetalian to this girl for me." She entered the room.

"She's as English as you are, Frank."

"She don't talk like it."

"She's from upper New York State."

"New York people don't talk like foreigners."

"Mary," she said, "your card—where is it?" She measured something about four inches square.

"Ma carte, ma carte," smiled Mary and hustled into the kitchen. Mary's eyes were blue and her hair very light blonde. Frank classified her as a tow head. Her shapeliness could not be hidden by her clothes.

"Ma carte," she held a white card before Frank. He took it and read, "This girl is Mary Parker. Her home is in Hopkinton, New York, but she must go to Cleveland to work. Her mind on this is firm. Please to help her and God's mercy for her mother's sake." It was signed by Father Xavier.

76

"I'll tell you all I know, Frank," said Mrs. Orchards. They all sat down again. Speaking slowly, arms spread on the red checked tablecloth, she began, "Mary here seems to have taken a notion to come to Cleveland. She had the priest write this card for her. She went to Potsdam and then to Buffalo. In Buffalo she bought her ticket for Cleveland and came over on the boat.

"Arriving here she didn't know where the residential districts were, so she picked someone she thought wouldn't harm her, and followed him home. So tonight here came Mr. Orchards in the house. The door hardly closed before this little chick knocked on it, and handed me her card. We have decided to keep her here to help with the mending, housecleaning and what not. Frank, that's all. She can't speak a word of English."

"Can I teach her?"

"Why not? She'll pick it up fast enough, but she'll like to have you teach her." Mary had watched these two talking about her and hoped they liked her. She had to admit, they seemed to.

"She's cuter than a speckled pup," said Frank, "but she must have spunk to come here all the way from New York and not know a word of English."

"From the card, you can see the priest tried to persuade her not to come. Cleveland is so big and evil, he was afraid for her. We won't let anything happen to her, will we, Frank?"

She looked at him with a smile on her lips, but her eyes were serious and troubled. A single girl like this with eight single men in the house could cause trouble, especially such a beautiful girl. For Frank, she felt a motherly feeling, but he was still a man and men often hurt the young and innocent. This girl was not going to be hurt, if she could help it.

"Nobody is going to hurt her, Mrs. Orchards," Frank said softly.

Mary knew that they had agreed on something. She knew it concerned her and she knew now that Cleveland was not so cruel and wicked as Father Xavier had said. This woman had been kind to her, and this big, good looking man seemed so capable and friendly. Maybe he would teach her to speak English like he spoke. That would be fun to learn from someone who was not a schoolteacher. As for work—what was that? Hadn't she had to hoe and dig potatoes, and pick hops? She was getting her room and board and three dollars a week—wasn't that better than picking hops for twenty-five cents a day? Mary knew the world was good to her.

"Engleesh?" she said in a hopeful voice. She looked questioningly at Frank. They all laughed. Mrs. Orchards put a finger on Mary's nose and said, "There will be no Engleesh until the dishes are done and the kitchen cleaned up." Without understanding a word, Mary knew something else came first, and she had an idea what it was. She arose and began gathering up the dirty dishes.

"Is it all right, if I help her?"

"Frank, you never offered to help me wash the dishes."

"N—no—you had a husband and husbands don't always like young men helping their wives."

"Maybe you are right. Anyway, I can speak Engleesh."

So Frank helped Mary. He stumbled around the kitchen and got in the way, but he did dry the dishes and that was a help. Mary was bashful and avoided looking at him, so he could watch her. They were nearly finished before Frank had an idea. He reached into a basket and picked up a potato.

"Po-tay-toe," he said enunciating clearly.

"*Potak*," she said.

"No—po-tay-toe."

"Po-tay-toe?"

"Good."

"Good?"

"*Un Canuk dit potak.*"

"You are learning English—I ain't learning to be a furriner. Say, 'potaytoe.'"

She did. So he held up a dish. Before he could say anything, she laughed and said, "Deesh." It was nearly bedtime before they came out of the kitchen, and Mrs. Orchards listened to their chatter and knew that Frank was one gone gosling.

During this last week before Christmas, Mary's popularity soared to new heights. Everyone was anxious to teach her to talk English, or anything else her heart desired. There was a good deal of banter at the table and Mary did not need a dictionary to know some of the remarks that were made. Frank did not like this competition, but there wasn't much he could do about it. The corner saloon saw less of Mrs. Orchards' boarders than usual. They hung around the house worse than flies before a thunderstorm.

Frank had already bought Mrs. Orchards a Christmas present and some toys for Raymond. The young one had to have something under the tree from him. Now he had to have something for Mary—what? For the life of him he didn't know. He spent several days thinking about it.

A fellow does not have to moon around for long before his fellow workers notice it. Ben and Haskell were merciless to him and made up stories about fellows they knew who had fallen in love all at once and the dire things that had resulted. Frank scarcely heard them. The night before Christmas, Frank came home radiantly happy. He had solved Mary's Christmas present in the little jewelry store on the Public Square. He had gone in timidly, but the jeweler, long trained in recognizing a smitten man, put him at ease with all the finesse the years had taught him. When Frank left he was not only lighter in the heart, but lighter in the pocketbook. The ring he bought her was a beautiful gold one, in which three tiny diamonds were delicately set. He admitted that for a girl he knew less than a week, he was cutting quite a caper. That night he slept scarcely at all.

Frank was dressed long before he could properly go downstairs. He sat on his bed and looked out the window at the morning darkness. There was no snow on the ground this Christmas and it was warm and probably would rain before the day was over. Hell, he didn't care if it rained or not—he hoped this little sweetheart—this Mary Parker who couldn't speak "Engleesh" would like his present. Finally, unable to stay in his room another minute he descended the stairs and took a long time, making a great clatter, washing. In the kitchen he heard the rattle of dishes, so he knew he wasn't the only one up this morning.

At the breakfast table he gave Mrs. Orchards her present and the ones for little Raymond, but he could not force himself to give Mary hers before all these people. Others were not so bashful and Mary thanked each one as she opened his present. Lace handkerchiefs and perfume seemed to be the predominant gifts. Frank guessed some men were born cowards and he was one of them.

After breakfast, the men cleared out. Some went for a walk, others for a walk into the saloon, and Frank sat in the parlor and talked to Mr. Orchards. He did not know whether they were talking of the price of grass skirts in the Fiji Isles or of bull fiddles on Broadway. He cared less.

Abruptly standing, he said, "I've got to see Mary."

"Oh?" said Mr. Orchards, but Frank was gone.

"Mary," he called, opening the door into the kitchen. The girl looked up from washing dishes. Mrs. Orchards watched with flour to her elbows.

"I have a Christmas present for you."

Mary wiped her hands on her apron and came over to him. He handed her the box and deftly she opened it, manipulating the little metal catch as though she had been opening such boxes all her life. She removed the ring and looked at it. With eyes wide and mouth that looked like she was about to whistle, she took it over and showed it to Mrs. Orchards, who took one look and then looked back at Frank.

Mary tried it on and the only finger it would stay on at all was her middle one. She held it to the light to catch the glint of the light.

"Frenk," she said soberly, "you ma bes' boy." With her ringed hand she reached up and patted his cheek. To Frank, every touch was a caress.

Of the next three months there is little to record. Frank worked hard, and Mary did too. Mr. Orchards was sick and his illness placed an extra burden of mending, washing and cooking on Mary. She was used to hard work and it was well that she was strong. Frank helped with the work when he could.

After Mr. Orchards returned to work, the load was lightened on Mary to such an extent that one evening Frank found her actually doing nothing.

"Mary," he said, "shall I get the book I bought a month ago and try to teach you English?"

"Engleesh?"

"Yes."

"But yes. It is long time no Engleesh." So Frank went to his room for the book. Returning, he went into the parlor. Mary indicated that he should sit on the settee. She pulled up a footstool and sat down at his knee. Behind them Mr. Orchards dozed peacefully, mouth agape. Rocking away quietly by the window, Mrs. Orchards sewed a patch on some pants.

"This book," said Frank, "says that words make up sentences."

"So?"

"And a sentence is a single thought—"

"Like what?"

"Like—'Mary is beautiful.' That is a single thought."

"So?"

"Each sentence has a subject," Frank said, "a predicate and an object."

"What is that 'predicate'?"

"Maybe I can read here what it is. Right now damned if I know. I been speaking English since I was a boy but don't know much about this predicate."

The lesson went on with the predicate getting mixed up with an infinitive, and the going got really tough. Finding himself unable to explain since he could not make head nor tail out of the book, Frank said, "Let's leave this book for awhile. Maybe I can get somebody to tell us what it is about. We can work on speaking words right." So Frank would say a word, or several words, and Mary would repeat them.

"Blue eyes."

"Blue eyes," Mary repeated. A smokiness began to appear in Mary's eyes that bespoke hidden anger. Frank did not see it.

"Pretty hair."

"Pretty hair."

Holding up his hand he counted.

"One."

"One."

"Two."

"Dew."

"Three."

"Tree."

"Four."

"Four."

"Five."

"Five."

"Six."

"Seex."

"No—six."

"Seex."

"Like this—'sicks'—six."

Mary rose from her stool and kicked it out of the way. Frank saw the storm coming this time, but it was too late to run for shelter.

"Frenk Stone," said Mary angrily, her cheeks flushed and her

eyes shooting sparks, "you teach me Engleesh! I teach you Engleesh more. Predicate from a book, eenfeenateefe from a book—
the first night I no work and you teach me Engleesh. All is to
Engleesh don't say 'ain't.' Zat ees all.

"In Cleveland are fine men. At Chreesmas say 'Mary, you nose
ees dirt. Have handkerchief.' 'Mary, you steenk. Have good
smell.' You say, 'Mary, you preety eyes. Mary, you preety hair.
Mary, you preety face.' "

She paused, her breasts heaving, her lips parted. Frank knew
he was about to get the second verse. Shaking a finger over his
nose, she continued, "Een da glass, I can see preety eyes, blue
eyes, preety face and preety hair. You need to tell me? You no
say, 'Mary, you got beeg brains. Mary, you good to mend. You
good to cook.'

"I come to Cleveland. I be dressmaker. I have beesness. I get
reech. I send for Mama. Fine Mary—so smart. First man she see—
to hell with dressmakers. Fine man—he teach Mary to count, one,
dew, t'ree, four. Four what? Four feengers! Eef you must count,
count keeses like thees!"

She threw herself on his lap and wrapped her arms around his
neck. He was smiling at her. She kissed him. "One." Again,
"Dew." And again, "T'ree." Then she buried her face on his
shoulder and began to sob.

Frank hitched her up on his lap into a more comfortable position. "Now, Mary," he soothed her. "Tut. Tut. Big girls don't
cry."

He kissed the smooth round cheek, and brushed the hair back
of her ear and hoped by twisting it in with the rest it would stay.

Within himself, Frank felt a contentment he had never known.
This girl was his. He loved her and knew it. Damn—love was
beautiful!

Mr. Orchards still slept. When Frank looked over his shoulder,
Mrs. Orchards smiled at him. "Frank," she said softly so as not
to break the spell, "you have just become engaged."

Chapter VIII

MOSTLY ABOUT MILLIE GORDON

No sooner had Frank become engaged than doubts began to come into his head about whether he was free to marry her. "Suppose," said his conscience, "that you really killed old Jared. You didn't mean to, if you did. Sure it was all that Millie's fault, but suppose you take this girl for a wife and the sheriff finds you. He'll lock you up and then what?"

"What," said Frank's mind to his conscience, "am I to do? If Jared is gone, I can't bring him back. If I go to Garrettsville they will be looking for me and I'll swing on the end of a rope."

"Isn't that better than hurting this girl?"

"Now, ain't that a hell of an idee? Once I'm on the end of a rope, I can't do anyone any good."

"But no harm, either," said the conscience smoothly.

In the end the conscience won out. Frank got a day off and went to Garrettsville. To be sure, he was scared, but in his new Sunday clothes there was a fair chance no one would recognize him. For a fact, he didn't think he knew anyone in Garrettsville he would recognize, unless it was the doctor with his dishpan paunch.

The train chugged into the station and Frank got off. So far as he could discern, not one thing in Garrettsville had changed. Even the station agent was the same. Frank walked across the street and started for the feed mill. If anyone knew of Jared, these people would, because he used to come in at least once a month. He entered the mill and his conscience complimented him, but his mind called him a fool.

"Good morning," said Frank to a portly man working over a desk.

"Drummer, eh? We got all the horse tonic and animal ailment remedies we need. What's your line?"

"I want a little information, please."

"Detective are you?"

"I'm no detective, either. Is Jared Gordon alive?"

"Jared?"

"Yes."

"Jared's over in the next building over there. He's watching them weigh some oats he's selling."

"See," said the conscience, "what did I tell you?" Frank walked over to the building indicated. On his way he stopped to look at Jared's team, certainly no better with advancing age. Then he saw Jared, who failed to recognize him at first.

"Jared," said Frank, "do you remember me?"

"Can't say's I do—Jim—it's Jim Stone."

Jared seemed not the least disturbed to see him, for which Frank was thankful. The years had not been kind to Jared. His face was pinched tighter, his shoulders more rounded. "You want to come back to work for me," he asked hopefully, then answered himself, "No—no—I suppose not. You're looking well, Jim."

"I am doing well, thank you kindly," said Frank. "I'm railroading."

"Railroading? Which line? The Atlantic and Great Western?"

"No, the Lake Shore Line."

"How do you like it?"

"Just fine."

"Better'n farming?"

"It's kinda like playing—shoving those cars around, but I liked to farm, too. I think farming is harder work."

The two men talked amiably for a few minutes about Cleveland and Frank's life there. Finally, Jared got around to the question that was in his mind, "What are you doing down here?"

"Well, Jared, I came down to see you, or at least to see about you." Frank found it hard going to tell him what had been bothering him. "When I left these parts, you and me weren't exactly like Damon and Pythias."

Jared looked at Frank blankly. "Damon?"

"I joined me a lodge since I left here. That Damon and Pythias were close friends. When I left, you and me weren't."

"No, I guess not." Jared squinted at Frank, then said suspiciously, "Don't tell me you come all the way back here after all this time just to make friends?"

"Well, not exactly," admitted Frank, "you see it's like this—

I'm going to marry me a fine girl in a few weeks, and I didn't want to do it, not knowin' whether I'd killed you or not. I was pretty scared when I left here, but when no policeman came around looking for me, I figured you was probably all right. But I didn't know for sure, and that's why I'm here."

"You always was a good boy, Jim, and I'm sorry for what happened. Come around in back and I'll tell you my side of it." Once in a spot private enough to suit Jared, he pushed his hat to the back of his head, and told his story.

"When Millie told that big yarn of hern, I believed her. Fact was I was sort of expecting you to try anytime, and I wasn't surprised when the girl said you done it. That's where I made my first mistake. Well, after you hit me with a bootjack, I—"

"I never hit you with a bootjack," denied Frank.

"Millie said you did, and her ma, but I don't remember much. Anyway, I was up and around when the doctor came to see where I'd been kicked by a horse. Don't seem like that was quite the right story, either. Kind of a good liar yourself if you're of a mind to be, ain't you?"

"Not bad," admitted Frank.

"Well, the doctor said a call was a call and he was going to dun me for it, so I told him what the fuss was about, and could he tell for sure if a woman was still a virgin. He said he could, so I told him to go ahead.

"Then Millie got uppity and said she wasn't going to show what she had to no doctor. I'd had about enough by that time, so I slammed her on the kitchen table and pulled her dress up. Her ma kept crying and begging me to let her go, and Millie tried to kick the doctor. Finally Millie admitted that she hadn't been touched and had made the whole story up."

"Gosh, then you knew that very day that I was innocenter than a lamb?"

"Sure did, and what has burned me up about it, I ain't had a hired man since." A plan edged its way into Jared's mind, and he said, "Seeing how you came all the way down here on my account, how about coming out to the house for supper?"

A suspicion edged its way into Frank's mind, and that was that he had better get out of town as quickly as possible now that he had found out what he needed to know. Of one thing he was absolutely certain—he didn't want to see Millie again. "Jared, I

85

thank you kindly for the invitation, but if I get right over to the depot, I can get back to Cleveland today. Meeting you, and getting things straight from you is one of the best things I ever did, and I'm sure glad I didn't hurt you no worse than I did."

"Can't see as how much of it was your fault, and I ain't holding no grudge."

"I'm real glad to hear you say so, Jared. Tell Millie and her Ma I asked about them."

Frank was a happy man. Mary could be his. Old Jared was alive and his account of Millie's troubles tickled his funny bone. Some people have a way with them. They see something funny, and their minds take a picture of it. They don't laugh then—no, they wait until later when they are alone, and they bring out the picture and laugh their sides out. Frank wouldn't have shared his picture of Millie with anyone, but his face got used to laughing about it, and the grin stayed on long after the picture had been put away.

He had been back from Garrettsville three days. This evening as he went home, he thought of Mary and the love he felt for her. Dear little tow-headed sweetheart, so loving—Frank Stone was so happy, he sang a song softly to himself.

Opening the door, he felt a chill that warned him something was amiss. The faces of his fellow boarders looked at him darkly, accusing. No one spoke.

"Hello, there," Frank said cheerily, and the words clattered on the floor like breaking dishes. "What the hell's the matter?" wondered Frank.

"Frank," said Mrs. Orchards coldly, "your wife is here."

Of all the things she might have said, this, Frank considered, was the craziest.

"Of course, Mary is here. Why shouldn't she be?"

"I mean, your wife. There is a girl up in your room. She says she's your wife." Mary came in bearing some silver for the table. She looked at Frank like she had never seen him in this world before. Mrs. Orchards' voice jabbed into his brain again, "Think hard. She says you married her in Garrettsville three days ago."

"My God—Millie Gordon."

Mary uttered a little cry and fled. People looked at him like he was a bigamist and rapist combined. Frank started for the stairs. Things had to be done, and there was no use waiting, but as he reached the first step, he saw Millie coming down. He stopped with his hand on the banister.

"Good evening, Jim dear," said Millie, her voice all sweetness. Frank heard a whispered, "Jim dear," followed by a long "Oh," and he knew Mary was in the room again.

"What are you doing here, Millie?" he asked her.

"A wife's place is with her husband, Jim."

"Millie, for God's sake, tell these people you are not my wife."

"Why, dear, don't you want them to know you are married? Come, kiss me." She moved toward him and Frank retreated. stumbling over a loose rug and sitting down abruptly.

"Jim, is that any way to act?" cried Millie, holding out her hand to assist him. About them the boarders stood like ghosts. There was a quiet that could only be equalled in the other world. Frank scrambled to his feet and as he did, Millie threw her arms around his neck, and Frank knew this stranglehold she had was going to be a tough one to break, because Millie was strong.

There are in life certain moments when strong medicine is the only cure for one's troubles. This was one. Reaching down, Frank picked Millie up and walked straight out the door.

"What are you doing, Jim?" Millie cried, alarm written all over her face.

"Millie, you lied to these people about being my wife. You are trying to break Mary and me up, and by God you ain't doing it, if I can help it."

At the sidewalk he turned to the right, walked about fifty feet and deposited Millie in the horse watering trough that had been put there this last year. Millie tried to fight away from it. She bit, scratched, kicked and screamed, but she went in the water nevertheless.

Frank stood back to survey the scene. As he did so, he saw Mary for the first time. Mary, looking radiant, was carrying Millie's traveling bag, her hat and coat. These she handed to Frank.

In the few seconds that this had been taking place, a score of people had gathered, including all the boarders and Mr. and Mrs. Orchards. Millie started to get out of the watering trough, but Frank pushed her back down.

"Millie," he said pityingly for Millie was a sorry sight, "tell this girl you are not my wife. Tell her you saw me last, over three years ago when I worked for your father."

Millie started to cry and tried to climb out of the water, but again Frank sat her down. For the first time Millie looked calmly at Frank and there was no shame in her eyes. "Jim, I could kill you for this. I wanted you. I have always wanted you, but you wouldn't have me. Why won't you have me, Jim? You used to love me."

"Never for one moment, Millie," cried Frank.

"All right then," said Millie, "if I lose, I lose, but it was worth a chance. Now let me out of this water." He helped her out. Her long, gray woolen skirt hung heavy with water. She put on her coat and hat, picked up her bag and left, holding her skirt as high as possible with her free hand.

"I'll be damned," said one of the crowd, "now I've seen it all."

Frank put his arm about Mary and led her to the house. He looked down at her and said, "Mary, are we having us a wedding at our house like we planned?"

"*Mais oui*," said Mary, "I 'fraid you t'row me in water I say no!"

88

CHAPTER IX

BLESSED BE THE TIE THAT BINDS

Of one thing Frank and Mary were certain—they had better get married soon. Kissing and lalligagging may be fine for a short time, but a lover's kiss, worthy of the name, is only a promise of something more.

So it came about that Frank and Mary attended church for the first time since either of them came to Cleveland. Frank's people had been religiously inclined, but had not attended the church regularly. Mary's people were devout Catholics, but not Mary. In fact, she had refused to accept the church when only twelve years old, for what reason only she knew. So here they sat quietly, holding hands, their minds wandering, wishing for the end of the service, so they could see the minister for a few minutes.

As the sermon crept into its third half hour, Frank's mind began to work. What a lot of folderol people made of marriage! Two people agree to a union, but before it is legal they must pay fifty cents for a piece of paper, like a railroad ticket. They must go to a minister, or a justice of the peace, and hear him say a few words, and he must listen to them promise to be true to one another against all the ways of being untrue the Book could think of. It wouldn't be so bad, if the ceremony were in itself proof against defection. However, since a union without the words being spoken was an invitation to hell's perils, it was best to take no chances. Anyone could see that with so small a fence as these few words between the couple and hell, marriage itself was a dangerous undertaking for a soul.

The minister was now on tiptoe, roaring at the rafters. His fist pounded the pulpit as he drove the last nails into his argument! His glasses fell from his nose, and Frank wondered what he'd say if they were broken. Then he saw the glasses swinging from a string in front of the parson's sparrow-thin stomach. "Whoa—

Nelly," thought Frank, "I've seen that fellow before. Where, I ain't got an idee, but I'll think of it." He looked on the blackboard in front and then he knew. The man was Knight K. Willard, the reverend who rode the train for nothing and wrote about the day of wrath. His name had been painted on the board in letters far bolder than the ones for the name of the church itself.

By now, the parson had smelled the oat bin, and was finishing his sermon at a gallop. Frank rode along with him easily and when the last song had been sung, Frank felt none of the strain a hardened non-churchgoer should rightfully have felt. Where Mary's mind had been, he didn't know.

The Reverend Willard was shaking hands with the congregation, beaming a smile upon one and all. Frank and Mary were the last to leave, purposely.

"Ah! Good morning, young people," cried the Reverend, "and how are you this Sabbath?"

"All right," said Frank shaking hands. "This is Mary Parker. I am Frank Stone."

"How do you do, Mary?"

"Fine, thank you," smiled Mary, looking shyly at Frank.

"Don't say it! Don't say it!" said the parson playfully. "You want to get married!"

"Yes," admitted Frank. He did not know then that a parson with experience would have been able to have picked them out of a congregation twice this size, at a Vesper service to boot, as accurately as this young minister had done in broad daylight, and them at the end of the line. To Frank the Reverend Willard had done an amazing piece of work.

"When do you want to be married?" asked Mr. Willard, the business man.

"Next Saturday afternoon, if it's convenient," said Frank.

"Next Saturday? I am always available to do God's work. Where shall it be? Here or at Mary's home?"

Frank gave him the address.

The days that followed were days of fever and excitement on Broadway, anywhere near where Mary happened to be. She found an apartment and rented it, farther out Broadway. She scrubbed it until the floors became almost white, and the windows glistened in the early summer sun. She flitted to Mrs. Orchards for advice, help and stray pieces of furniture. With all she had Mrs. Orchards was generous. In these two she felt an interest far greater than ordinary, for under her roof they had come together.

Mrs. Orchards compared this courtship with those she had read from books, and those she knew about where there were mother and father and other children. There had been no dances, no parties, no theatres for these two. The young people they knew were like themselves, working ten to twelve hours a day, six days a week. If there was any love lost, because of the lack of gaiety, Mrs. Orchards could not see it.

There was no work for Frank's engine crew on Saturday. Haskell Taylor was to be Frank's best man and Ben Judson and his wife planned to attend. Frank arose and shaved leisurely. Mary kept out of sight and Frank could not imagine where she had gotten to. When he asked, he was told to mind his own business, which sounded like a good idea. Frank's clothes had been pressed and waiting for this day since last Monday. He climbed into them. Looking at himself in the mirror, he wondered how he would look with a mustache.

Dinner was a farce. The only one who wanted to eat was Frank, and he was told to forage for himself. He did, but either he did not know where to look, or there was nothing to find. About this time, a neighbor's piano was brought in to the house for the occasion.

The first guests to arrive were Ben and his wife. Frank sat with them in the parlor and Mrs. Judson spoke so seriously of "this holy occasion" that Ben and Frank exchanged glances and uneasily talked of other things. The afternoon sun streamed through the windows and Frank felt hot and uncomfortable.

Haskell drove up in a fine looking buggy to which a beautiful sorrel gelding was hitched. Frank could hardly take his eyes off the rig, as he went to greet Haskell.

"That's a beautiful outfit you have there," he said.

"Do you like it?"

"You sure got something there. How many hands tall is he?"

"Is Ben in there?" asked Haskell, not knowing anything about measuring horses' heights.

"Yes."

"Let's call him out." Ben had been standing in the doorway. Now, he joined them. The horse pawed the ground and looked at them, his neck arched and tail up.

"We might as well tell him, Ben," said Haskell.

"Suits me," said Ben.

"Frank, this rig is the best we could find in town, and there ain't no better horse. Ben and me and some of the other boys chipped in and rented him for today and tomorrow, and every Sunday for a month. We are making that our wedding present to you."

Frank's eyes became misty and he could scarcely talk. Finally he said, "Gosh knows I thank you, but with such a fine horse, you'll drive me from railroading."

"Not much chance of that now you got a missus," laughed Ben. Both he and Haskell knew that their gift was really appreciated.

Frank and Haskell returned to the parlor where the Reverend Knight K. Willard held up his hand for silence. Behind him stood a churn full of roses. A red checked tablecloth disguised the churn, but nothing could disguise the smell of roses. The place surely did not look like a boarding house to Frank today.

Then the piano began to play and the stairs above them began to squeak. The Reverend beckoned and Frank and Haskell stepped forward. Frank saw Mary, nearly at the foot of the stairs now. His heart bounced within him. He could not have described her wedding dress to save him. It looked like something you would expect the angels to wear.

Mary's hair, lighter and shinier than ever, was swept up off her neck and coiled someway or other so that there was no knot. In a few seconds the piano stopped and the preacher began. The recording angel wrote his entry in the book. When Gabriel saw it, he shook the heavens, but the entry was there to stay. "June 1, 1871—James Franklin Stone damn well married Mary Parker."

The horse shook his head, impatient of the check of the reins upon him. He wanted to go, but Frank did not think it looked exactly right for a fellow to carry his bride off to her new home at breakneck speed. So the gait was a stately trot, not more than a jog. Mary had been overjoyed at the richness of their departure. She had expected to walk. Like children they hardly knew whether to laugh or cry.

"Meesis Mary Stone," sighed Mary, "I am so happy, Frank." Her eyes looked up to him and he knew that she meant it. It does not take long to drive four blocks. Frank pulled up in front of their new home, cramped the front wheels by hawing and backing a few feet. Then he jumped out. Mary would have stepped down, but he took her under the arms and lifted her down easily. While she waited for him, he tied the horse to the hitching post.

They walked the few steps to the door, stopped, and looked at one another. He had been warned by Ben not to forget to carry his bride over the step. It seems Ben had forgotten and the missus was still giving him Hail Columbia for it. So Frank picked Mary up and did not set her down again until they were in their own apartment on the second floor.

"Frank, please to unhook my dress. I weel change before eet get dirty." He fumbled with the hooks and eyes and eventually stood back to watch her emerge like a moth from its cocoon. She carefully folded the dress and put it in a dresser drawer. Frank watched her flit about in her lace petticoat. Coming over to him, she took him by the ears and pulled his head down to her level.

"Now," she said. "Now I put on my other new dress and we go for ride in our beeg city!"

CHAPTER X

CAPITALISM BECKONS

Frank was up before the sun. In the soft morning twilight, he rubbed the horse's skin until it was smooth and shiny. Bill munched on his morning oats. Above him through the back windows, Frank could see Mary darting back and forth. He knew she was packing a lunch. This was something like he hoped heaven would be. A good buggy, a good horse, and a wonderful wife—life was good. He backed Bill into the shafts, after harnessing him.

"Come along there, Bill old man," said Frank. Bill started off down the alley at a walk. Around on the main street, Bill was watered from a public watering trough, and was ready for the day. Frank drove up in front of the house and hitched him.

Upstairs Mary was singing. Perhaps music critics might have found a flaw in it, but to her it sounded good. "Can she bake a cherry pie, Beelly O Beelly Boy? Can she bake a cherry pie, Charming Beelly." It seems she was a good pie maker and some kind of record holder for speed, but slightly on the antique side, being twice six, twice seven, twice twenty and eleven. Not only that, the sweet young thing couldn't leave her mother. Eggs were frying on the range. On the table a basket was being filled with provisions. Those footsteps on the stairs danced lightly on Mary's heart. That boy in those shoes—that boy in a man's body—was hers. She loved him, and knew he would never be anything else.

"Bacon! Eggs! Food woman!"

"Be steel," chirped Mary in between bars of her song about Beelly.

"Danged if I won't be as old as that chippie, before I get some victuals in me, the way you skip around here," said Frank in mock ill humor. He sat at the table with knife and fork in each hand. Mary kissed him, pushed the table away from him and sat on his lap, arms about his neck. She looked into his eyes.

"They tell me, eef a man love his wife, he can't eet for first week they married. Don't you love Mary?"

"Who told you that?" asked Frank, "A fellow's got to eat more than ever to keep body and soul together."

"You are a gross peeg. A keess for breakfast. That ees all for you." Then she put his breakfast on the table.

The bacon and eggs were soon demolished and the dirty dishes stacked in the pan. With the basket on one arm, Mary on the other and Mary's twittering in both ears, Frank descended the stairs. Bill pawed the ground in welcome.

"Where we go now, Frank?" said Mary.

"Out Euclid. So far's I know, it's the only important street in town."

"Eucleed?"

"That's the one. Giddap there, Bill."

Bill giddapped and they were soon rolling across town. The morning sun was well up now, and no one in church ever thanked God more fervently for their well-being than did Frank and Mary this sunny June day.

Soon they were on Euclid. Here horses of Bill's general worth were everywhere. Frank had never seen such wealth in horse-flesh. Bill knew he was among his equals, too, and fretted to show off. He tugged at the lines impatiently. Frank saw a stretch of road which had been recently scraped, and when Bill next tugged there was no restraint. He stepped out into a fast trot. Still there was no check on him, so he sped along like a race horse. The light buggy was a scant load and Bill covered the next mile and a half in a hurry. Then Frank slowed him to a jog to let him get his wind back.

"Frank, why you go so fast? You afraid I get good look at houses on Euclid and want to move in here?"

"I was not worried about that, Mary," he told her, "if you don't have a million dollars they won't let you turn into a drive-way, unless you work at one of those places."

"You theenk we can live in house like thees in ten year?" she teased.

"In ten years, I wouldn't earn enough at railroading to pay for the iron fence in front of one of them."

From Willson Avenue to Doan's Corners they were pretty much in the country. Orchards bloomed and cattle were everywhere.

95

A few large homes were being built along the way. Doan's Corners itself was a separate little community with its own stores, hotels and post office.

Frank and Mary drove East beyond Doan Brook Valley until they came to a country road that led off to the right. Narrow and deeply rutted, it forced them to slow to a walk.

"Eet ees preety out here in the country," said Mary.

"I reckon it is them new leaves and dark green grass that makes the whole world look shiny and new. Old Bill would like to get his nose into that young timothy and clover."

"We weel let him when we stop for dinner, no?"

"Yup. We sure will."

This country road took them through a wooded countryside and onto higher ground, but eventually brought them out on a wider, more traveled road. They turned right towards town and immediately started down a long hill. Part way down they came to a stone watering trough which was full and overflowing with water from a spring a few feet above it in the hill. An iron pipe carried the water to the trough.

"Here'd be a good place to eat our lunch," said Frank, "but it's kind of early."

"Beel will drink."

"Probably will, but he's warm and we won't give him too much."

A signpost carved in wood bore the legend, "Cedar Road." As they rode on they found themselves passing prosperous looking farms, with new houses being built in woodlots and orchards which adjoined the road. They were amazed at the amount of this building and agreed that one day, Cleveland would stretch clear out here, and would be a tremendous city. Shortly after they recrossed Doan Street, they saw a little house with a store building in the front yard. In the back was a barn, a well and a privy. The place appeared deserted.

"Mary, let's you and me eat in that back yard. There is water there."

"Eet does look empty," said Mary dubiously.

"If you don't like it, we can go on."

"Thees weel do."

So they pulled Bill into the yard, unharnessed him and tethered him in the lush grass, now nearly knee high. In the shade of a catalpa tree, Mary spread the lunch, while Frank pumped water into their cups.

"Frank," said Mary later as she leaned against the tree, "you think it all right to look in house?"

"I don't know why not. On the store is a sign that says 'To Let' and another saying it's for sale. We can always say we are looking to buy property."

"We look, no?"

So they looked the place over, hand in hand. The house was of three rooms, all on one floor with a stone walled basement. While it was obviously not a new house, it had never been painted or papered inside. An old straw mattress and a broken chair were scattered around.

"There is nothing wrong with it for two people," said Frank.

"I have seen seex or more people leeve in smaller house," replied Mary.

They emerged from the house which had not been locked and stood on the front porch. The main view was of the back end of the store, squarely placed in front of them, and two stories high. A catalpa tree grew in the yard between the two buildings.

The store doors were locked, but Frank crawled through a partly opened window and unlatched the back one. Mary entered.

"Eet was a grocery store," diagnosed Mary. There were shelves on three sides and a plank counter across the middle. A huge plate glass window on each side of the front door let in light. There was an alcove of three feet or so in depth between the door and the outside of the building. On the sills were hundreds of dead flies. A bag of sprouted onions dried on the floor. A stairway led to the second floor on the back of the building. They could not enter here, but by peering in at various angles they could see it was an empty room, probably a store room, the same size as the store.

Behind the house stood the privy, slightly tilted, and the small neat barn. There was nothing in the barn, nor had there ever been.

"I suppose who owns the store fail," said Mary thoughtfully. "I wonder why."

"With the city growing out here, nobody ought to fail."

"Some people can fail een a gold mine," said Mary.

Eventually, they hitched Bill up and rode off again, but they kept thinking of the place, and an hour later drove in the yard again. They left saying, "Somebody ought to buy it," and returned saying, "Maybe we ought to buy it."

"Let's find out who owns it and see how much they want for it. Can't hurt to ask," said Frank. "Of course, we haven't any great lot of money, but there's some. I'll have to get it from Mrs. Orchards."

"Frank, she gave eet to me yesterday."

"How much was there?"

"More than you theenk, but I am not going to tell you. You would buy Beell and eet would be gone." Frank laughed. This wife of his certainly had taken charge of the financial end of the family affairs.

They drove up to the nearest house and drove in the yard. When a man in overalls came out to greet them, Frank jumped down from the buggy.

"Good afternoon," said Frank.

"Howdy, folks, won't you get down, ma'am, and come in?"

Mary smiled, "We only came to ask you sometheeng."

"Don't knows I can help you, but fire away."

"Who owns that little house and store over there?" asked Frank.

"A feller that wished he didn't," said the man. "This feller built that place and started a store, but he didn't last long. He still owns it, but his wife left him. He quarrelled some with the customers and most of them left him. He warn't agreeable at all."

"Do you know how much he aims to get?"

"No, I don't. He comes around every few days to see after it. If you say, I'll have him look you up."

"Tell heem, we weell be back next Sunday at about ten o'clock. We weell make heem an offer."

"I'll do that, ma'am. Glad to. Won't you come in? No? Well, come again next Sunday when you got more time. Henderson is my name. John Henderson. Don't know's you said yourn?"

"Stone. Mr. and Mrs. Frank Stone."

"Don't know's there's anybody by that name around here."

"No," said Frank, smiling, "me and Mary got no kin here."

All the way home they talked of how this might be done here, that there, and the other, some place else. About the store, they were a little frightened. One man had failed—could they do better? They thought so.

Chapter XI

A PLOT THAT FAILED

The sun bore down as though trying to melt the wax out of him, but Frank kept grimly at his cutting. The grass had blossomed and was ready to cut. Sun heat, or no, he was going to cut it. Behind him in even swathes, the hay was curing and this afternoon he would rake it up. He didn't want it to get wet—not this hay.

Mary was not home. She was down buying groceries to stock the little store, now all clean and polished. They had scrubbed and scraped, and scrubbed some more and at last they knew it was clean. Mary said that it was no wonder the first store had failed. People would not stand such filth.

The house had been cleaned and they had moved in the last Sunday they had Bill and the buggy. They had dickered for the place the second Sunday, bought it the third and signed the mortgage. He had figured to keep on railroading at least until the store was going, but Mary had said nothing doing. "Frank, you will either keep a store or run a railroad, no one can do both. Together we weell make out." So inspired by Mary's confidence, he had quit. This was his first day of his first week as a business man—a hell of a businessman he was, Frank thought, but he smiled and enjoyed the sensation of ownership.

Already the place was looking more respectable. He had cut the grass around the buildings first. They seemed taller with it gone. The sweat poured out of him. It was funny how a person used different muscles for different work. He knew his shoulders and arms would be stiff and sore tomorrow.

He thought of Mary down stocking the store. He knew so little about what they should carry and how much. He trusted Mary to know and was proud of her. He would do the work and let her handle the figures. She seemed to have come to that conclusion by herself and there wasn't much he could do about it. Take this scythe here—she had been going to give him the money out of their funds to buy a new one. Then she found this old one hanging from a branch in the apple tree, so she bought a whetstone and he had spent hours honing it to where it would cut.

Then he had been the one to get tight. Mary said he ought to cut this hay and burn it, but he refused to burn anything so good. He would put it in the barn against the day he could afford a horse.

When Mary returned in the afternoon, she saw him hard at work, carrying the hay into the barn in his arms. His face was turned away to avoid the prickliness of it. Mary went to the house and got the water bucket. When he heard her pumping it full, Frank came over to hear her news. Together they sought the shade of the catalpa tree. Frank examined the fine beads of sweat on Mary's flushed face.

"Well, Frank, I did eet."

"The heck you did!"

"Yes. It was so-o easy. I go to see Mr. Beel Gordon who own W. H. Gordon Wholesale Grocery Company an' I tell heem I am Mary Stone. My man ees Frank Stone. We open new store on Cedar Avenue near Doan. He say, 'Do I know heem?' I say not now you don't, but soon. He say, 'You need credit?' "

"What did you say then, Mary?"

"I say we have some money—hope eet ees enough. Then I give heem list we make, an' he say very leetle list for good store. I tell him I know, but we no want to go bust like man before, so we take it easy until we get start. He say he send man out to see how we do, an' help us start good. I say, 'I weel talk to my Frank about thees.' Then I spend all money I have an' eet weel be out tomorrow in beeg wagon."

"Sounds to me," said Frank, "that the man was very neighborly."

"You theenk I do all right?" Mary searched his face for approval.

"Mary, no one could have done any better. We are feeling our way along, and hoping we don't make us no more mistakes than a few. I think you done fine!"

In the shade, the slight breeze was cooling. So was the cold well water, as they drank from the dipper that was always in the bucket. The heat shimmered off the curing grass.

100

"Frank, why you cut the grass on that land over there?" She pointed to where he had been working.

"First off," he replied, "it needs to be cut so's not to be inviting a fire. Then next year I aim to have a garden there, and maybe we can sell some of the stuff in the store, and another thing it is too good hay to be let go to waste." Frank paused. "Any more questions?"

"No more questions from thees girl," said Mary.

On the following day, the groceries arrived on schedule. In the wagon they made an impressive pile, but once they had been sorted and put on the shelves, they seemed to have disappeared.

Mary groaned, "Frank, where have they gone, these groceries? A pile to here een the middle of the floor, but on the shelves, they are none."

"Some day the shelves will be full," he told her. She said it looked like a play store, so empty.

Love is a handy medicine. It soothes and one forgets his troubles until another day when they appear in their true size—much smaller and less formidable. Frank took her in his arms and kissed her. In the morning they would open for business —no need to worry now.

Mary wrote with her nose so close to the pencil, one might have thought her blind. Her tongue was between her teeth and a cuter storekeeper, it would be hard to imagine. Her first customer came in. He was possibly seven years old.

"Is this a store?" he asked, his voice shrill.

"Yes," said Mary walking over to him.

"I want to see your penny candy." Candy! She had never even thought of it.

Frank left the house when Mary entered the store. He visited a half dozen homes before he was saying exactly what he wanted. From then on it was easier and his self-assurance resumed control. A typical encounter went like this:

"Good morning, ma'am."

"Good morning."

"I am Frank Stone. My wife, Mary, and me have bought the little place at the corner. We are trying to set up a grocery store, and have precious little besides the ordinary things like flour, coffee, sugar and suchlike. We want to help you to trade with us and while Mary tends the store, I'll deliver what you need, if it's too much for you to carry. Or send a note down with a youngster, and I'll fetch the groceries. Mary says we can't extend credit beyond the middle of the next month."

Ordinarily, the lady would say she would try to buy something there, or ask him if he had any vanilla extract as she needed some. Frank would thank her and say he didn't know vanilla extract from bullhorn reukus juice, but Mary would.

One lady asked him if he had any fresh vegetables.

"We don't have any now, but we will have, as soon as I can find some," he said hopefully.

"We planted a garden, but my husband has been so busy at the hardware store, he didn't take care of it and the weeds have about taken it."

"Can I see your garden, ma'am?"

"Yes, indeedy, right through here."

Frank looked the garden over. There were weeds a-plenty, but if it were weeded now, he might get some string beans and cucumbers out of it.

"It's about gone, lady," he admitted, "but if I weed it, will you go halvers with me on anything we get?"

"Heavens, yes," said the lady.

"Have you got a hoe?"

"Yes, in the shed."

"I'll be weedin' it."

Much later at another place a man listened while Frank talked to the wife. When Frank was ready to leave, the man stopped him.

"Didn't I see you cutting and mowing that hay around your place?"

"Yes," said Frank.

"I got some property down here that's got a good stand of hay on it. I'll give it to you if you cut it and get it off before the builders are ready to start work."

"I'm much obliged to you," said Frank, "but I got no way of getting it home."

"No horse?"

"No."

"What you making hay for?"

"I aim to get one some day."

"Well, cut it and I'll lend you old Kate back here," he jerked a thumb toward the barn, "to haul it off."

"I can get it day after tomorrow, if nothing stops me," said Frank.

He returned that night to find Mary's spirits lower than he had ever seen them. She had sold less than five dollar's worth of groceries her first day. The profit was sixty cents. He laughed at her and told her about the garden, the hay, the people he had met and how nobody knew there was even a store here yet. Mary had to admit that her husband was a comfort.

The passing days soon became weeks, the weeks months and precious few months it takes to make a year. The shelves were fuller and there were a few bags of sugar and flour on the second floor. These were piled on a platform Frank had built from some old scaffolding the carpenters had given him when they built the house next door. The legs were sheathed with old stovepipe metal to keep the mice from getting to the stores.

Where last year there had been grass and weeds, west of the house, this year was a beautiful garden. The rows were closely planted and not a weed was in plain sight more than a day before it lost its roothold, to die in the sun. In one respect Frank had made a slight error in judgment. He had planted far too many cucumbers and when they started getting ready to sell, there were so many of them that Mary complained he was trying to cover the store up with them.

Frank solved the cucumber flood in admirable fashion. He took two empty vinegar barrels and knocked out an end of each. Standing them on end in the cool basement of the house, they became pickle vats. Then he hurried into the garden and headed off the bumper crop by picking the young cukes. The larger ones were put in the dill barrel, the smaller ones into the sour pickle barrel. Enough still got past him to grow to full size to bother Mary. She hated to see them spoil when there were too many to sell.

This year there were more groceries to deliver and Frank kept busy. A few souls were anticipating the canning season and ordering sugar in hundred pound quantities. Generally when they did so, they would come for it with their own horse and buggy, but occasionally Frank would toss a sack on his shoulder, and walk off to deliver it. He was always delivering fifty pound sacks of flour to some home or another.

Frank liked to deliver groceries. He was a sociable person and if he ever made a delivery without a few minutes conversation thrown in, it was because something pressed him to hurry. As he grew to know the neighbors, the more they talked and some of the talk was gossip. Sometimes one customer would try to pump him for information about another. Frank recognized the danger of saying anything malicious so he kept his mouth shut, just as he had done for as long as he could remember.

One day while returning from the Schaeffers' where he had made a delivery, he saw in a blackberry bramble two sets of wheels still on their axles. They were for a fair-sized spring wagon, but their rims were askew and some spokes had been broken, patched with wire, and broken again. The weather had opened cracks in the wood and they appeared to be junk.

Frank rolled them out and looked at them. He knew they were bad, but he might be able to play with them and make something—no harm to try—so he rolled them home and put them in the barn.

For weeks afterward Frank spent every spare moment in the barn. From oak pieces he made new spokes and sanded them smooth. Eventually he forced the rims back on the wheels and painted them. All that remained was to sand away the rust from the axles and grease them. In high good humor he made a neat little wagon and seat. He had an acceptable rig now, except for shafts, a harness and a horse to pull it.

Mr. Henderson had bought a mowing machine. A day or so ago he had become so interested in his new toy that he had cut far more hay in a day, than he could rake and put up in a week by himself. Frank knew he was now desperate to get it in before a rain spoiled it. He walked past the Henderson house in the early morning with groceries for Mrs. Morrison out beyond. On his way back he intended to stop in to see Mr. Henderson.

As Frank came down the road, arms swinging, he noticed the farmer working close to the road.

"Good morning, John," said Frank slowing his walk, and angling over toward the fence.

"Howdy, son," said the man, "how's things at the store?"

"Not bad. It keeps a fellow humping hisself to keep up."

"Yes, I suppose it do. Think it's going to rain?"

Frank looked at the sky. Only in the south was there the sign of a cloud. If ever a day promised clear weather this was it.

"Mr. Henderson, I never saw a day look brighter and less like rain, but the robins was singing fit to kill and Mrs. Morrison's feet was plaguing her bad this morning. I say it's likely we'll have rain before tomorrow night."

"What you doing these days, Frank? Especially today and to-morrow?"

"I'm looking for me a piece of hay to put up, close to home. I'd like to have me a mow full before winter."

"You ain't got nothing to feed, Frank."

"I ain't like most men, John. They go get them some stock and then wonder what they gonna feed it. Not me! I get the feed, and a barn full of it—then I get the stock. I'm going to have enough feed, two to one, to feed my stock, too. I don't figure to feed out, and hear a hungry animal a-pawing in my barn."

"Sounds reasonable," muttered John, "sounds damn sensible." The old fellow scratched a match on the seat of his pants and lit his corncob pipe. Through the haze of white smoke he said, "Frank, I got more hay here than I need, and more down than I can reasonable get up. How'd you like to hay it with me on shares next couple of days?"

"Sounds like a good idee," admitted Frank. "What's your plan?"

"How about four loads for me and one for you? It's cut and raked, ready to doodle and take in. Fact is, the dew is most off. We can start now."

"I'm your man, Mr. John," said Frank climbing the fence.

The fifth load was the last load for the day. It looked good there in the mow on top of the hay he had put up last year. With luck he might get two or possibly three more loads in there. He had luck and did. By the week's end hay bulged out the mow windows and he could scarcely close the doors. His wagon had lost its home and now stood in the lee of the barn. Inside the barn the only space that remained were the two horse stalls he had optimistically built, when Mrs. Gibbs had given him the lumber from her woodshed for the wrecking and cleaning up of it.

With the barn bulging with hay, Frank felt that the time had come to discuss the matter of a horse with Mary. He had wanted a horse for a long time now, but good horses cost a lot of money, and he knew Mary would never consent unless he could present a pretty strong case. With more and more deliveries, the biggest part of a wagon on the premises, and a barn full of hay she would have to agree with him that the only sensible thing to do would be to get that horse right now. So that evening he spoke to her.

"Mary, I got me an idee."

"So?"

"Canning season is coming on and I'll have to be lugging sugar to hell and back. There's always flour and other stuff. Well, I got me a wagon and I got me a barn full of hay. How about us getting us a horse!" He took her on his lap and patted her. With a most serious face, he said, "Mary, we really need us a horse."

"A horse eats more than hay," Mary objected.

"Not much. Give 'em all the hay they can eat and it's precious little grain they need."

"But how much?"

"A good horse, let's see—" said Frank looking up at the ceiling as though this was the first time that the matter had ever entered his mind. "A good horse would cost us a hundred dollars."

"A hundred dollars!" Mary gasped.

"But we don't need a good one—fifty or sixty dollars and a harness thrown in would be good enough for now. Later we might get us another one—a sort of buggy horse for Sunday and such."

"We cannot afford it, so much money. A horse to work one day and stand three—"

"Besides, I need me the manure for the garden." Frank was enraptured by the inspiration. Certainly, the garden had been a money maker and a garden needs manure. He could see Mary was weakening.

"Let me think it over," she said. "Are you sure we have enough hay for one animal this winter?"

"Enough for two," he assured her.

Several days later Frank was picking wax beans in his garden when he looked up at the sound of a horse and wagon entering the yard. Driving it was the youngest Schaeffer boy. Plodding along behind, her udder so large as to make her walk with legs wide apart, was the biggest yellow cow he had seen in ages. In the wagon lay her calf, trussed with rope.

"Whoa!" said the boy.

Mary came from the store. Frank stared. An idea that something had gone wrong filtered into his mind.

"Oh, Frank!" said Mary watching him from the corner of her eye. "Aren't they beeautiful?"

"Pretty as a spotted pup," agreed Frank without cheer.

"They are ours, Frank, I got them from Mr. Schaeffer for only forty dollars."

"Not too bad," he grudgingly admitted.

"Oh, yes! So much better than a horse! We got two for less than one horse would cost. In the store we sell the milk, and you get twice as much manure in the garden."

Frank carried the calf into the barn and put it down in the stall. Young Schaeffer led in the cow, and tied it in the other stable. Frank ran his hand down her flank, "So bossy—so bossy—take it easy now—take it easy." He felt her udder, now so swollen with milk.

"Bag is caked a little," he said to young Schaeffer, "have you milked her dry this morning?"

"Didn't have time this morning." Frank scowled. There was no use ruining a good cow because of time. He got a box from the store to sit on, and a bucket from the house and began to milk.

Mary ran back to the store. She knew how disappointed he must be and yet he hadn't seemed to be.

Late in the afternoon she closed the store for the day. As she came through the house to the kitchen she heard Frank hammering and sawing out by the barn. She decided to investigate.

"Tum diddee dum diddee tum," sang Frank not seeing her. She watched him for a moment, and then stooped down and put her arm around his shoulders. He was on his knees on the ground, hammer in hand.

"What are you doing, Frank?"

With a twinkle in his eye, he said, "I'm making me a God damned wheelbarrow."

CHAPTER XII

THE FAMILY GROWS

As time passed, Mary spoke with so slight an accent that it could be scarcely noticed. In fact, she spoke better from a grammatical standpoint than Frank did. Perhaps, it was because she had learned the language, while he had just grown up with it, speaking as his father and neighbors had spoken.

In the community now were other accents, some German, but mostly Bohemian. These people for the most part did not live in the community as families, they worked there as hired help. The foreign settlements were closer to town.

Not far from the store a church was being built. There was not much more than a foundation now, but it appeared to be going to be a fairly large one. Down on Bolton Avenue a fine brick school had been built with plenty of room for additions if they were ever needed.

Henderson's farm was cut by streets, and the land laid out in lots. It hadn't been done all at once, but in a few years there were so many houses on it, that it seemed hard to remember it as orchards and cow pastures and wood lots. Mrs. Morrison had her place cut into lots and gave her children enough to build their homes. The hammers and saws were busy and a worker's tools had little chance to rest.

In her third year of marriage Mary roused herself. Why was it that she had not been pregnant? Was she to have no children? The thought chilled her. She had to see a doctor—perhaps there was something wrong. So that is how it came about that she went to see young Dr. Kotay in his office on Euclid near Doan Street. The doctor did find something wrong and repaired it. Within six weeks Mary was pregnant. Frank promptly started that mustache he had been considering off and on for the past several years.

108

In the several months before the baby's birth, Frank kept the store going by himself. Putting up the orders that had to be delivered, he loaded them in his wheelbarrow and set out right after supper. Mary still actively handled the financial end of the business, even to totalling the day's receipts. Buying was no strain anymore, for now drummers made regular calls on them. The shelves that had been so bare, now overflowed into the storeroom above.

In early May the baby was born. The doctor had delivered the baby easily and Mary was rightfully proud of the healthy little lady. She named the baby after her sister, Calista Delilah. Frank's mustache had become a local landmark. It had grown in red and bountiful. When he thought to trim it, he looked dashing, romantic and worldly, but generally he looked like a man with a red mustache.

Several days before Mary was able to be up and around, Frank was in the store looking at the new scales they had bought. They certainly beat the dry measures they had used when they started. Frank wondered if he could put them back together if he took them apart and took a peek at the works. He decided against fooling with them. He swatted a fly and mentally cursed all fly netting. It was so flimsy that it was practically useless to put it on the screen door. The door opened and a man came in.

"Nice day, Mr. Buck," said Frank, glad of the company.

"Good morning, Frank," Mr. Buck looked like the world had settled on his shoulders. He shuffled his feet and looked down at the floor.

"What will you have yourself this morning?"

"Frank, I got something on my mind this morning."

"I see you have."

"I'd rather be whipped than be here."

"Tut! Tut!"

"It's a fact."

"Maybe it ain't so bad."

"Frank, I'm here to tell you I just lost everything I own."

"No!"

"I'm locked out—lock, stock and barrel."

"That beats hell, don't it? What happened?"

"I bought this place of mine some years back. I give a mortgage on the balance, but I never could swing it. They took the place back from me and I got to get off. I owe you and the missus a little bill of about twenty-two dollars and blessed if I can pay it 'fore I go."

"Where do you aim to go?" asked Frank sympathetically.

"I got a boy doing real well out in Berea. He offered me a home."

"It's good you got a place to go," said Frank trying to be cheerful.

"Yes, but it's hard to live with children and earn money, too."

"Maybe you got a little something I can use," suggested Frank.

"I don't reckon I have. All I got is old Methusaley who is twenty-five years old if he is a day, and just needing to be shot."

"Methusaley is a horse?"

"Yes. He used to be good, but he got lame and has been to pasture for about six years now and ain't had a strap on him."

"Have you got any harness?"

"None that is any good."

"I'll tell you what you do. You catch up old Methusaley and throw on him all the old leather you can find and bring him to me. I'll wipe your book clean as a hound's tooth."

"You will, Frank?"

"Yes, siree!"

The man brightened. "I won't be owing anybody, if I don't have you to pay."

"That's right for a fact," said Frank.

That is how Methusaley, sway-backed, smooth-mouthed beyond belief and lame in his off hind foot, joined the Stone family. He still had last winter's long hair stuck to him in patches and you could hang a hat on his hip bones. Frank knew he was a sorry creature, but with little Calista to be paid for, it would be a long time before Mary would see her way clear to let him get a good horse. At least he was still alive and that was more than Frank could promise for him tomorrow.

Josey and her heifer, Young Josey, would be crowded into one stall to make room for Methusaley at night. During the day he turned the cattle into a five acre pasture he had rented, which ran all the way from Halsey to Logan Street. There, too, he put Methusaley. The horse grazed on the tender grasses now growing lush with the spring rains and summer's sun to coax them. He knew this horse was a long way from being able to work, and figured that by the time he remade a harness from all the scraps he had gathered, and found a pair of shafts, the horse would be in better condition and strong enough to pull.

Mary was scarcely up and around before she was back in the store. Little Calista peacefully slept in a basket Mary had lined with an old blanket. For Frank, it was like a release from a prison. For Mary, it was a return to the friendly neighborliness of the community.

As soon as Frank could reasonably do so, he brought Methusaley into the yard and tied him to the apple tree. Methusaley's head sank to the ground in utter exhaustion. Although his only occupation in over six years had been to eat, Methusaley had little to show for it in the way of flesh when he came. In two weeks' time the diet of ground oats and cornmeal Frank had given him began to take effect. Frank hoped to make him look like a horse, if nothing more, and prescribed the diet when he examined Methusaley's mouth and couldn't find enough molar surface to crack a kernel of corn. He suspected the horse was starving himself as a result.

Today he fitted the harness. It was patched, riveted and wired together, but it didn't look bad. The bridle had only one blinder on it, and after a moment's hesitation, Frank cut it off. The reins were made from a new clothesline from the store. It was an elated person who finally hitched old Methusaley to the wagon. The shafts Frank had made and even paint could not conceal that fact. However, they worked and that was all that mattered. Frank climbed on the seat.

"Giddap," he said.

Methusaley thought he heard some one say, "Giddap," but he wasn't sure. He did, however, lift his head a foot off the ground.

"Giddap," repeated Frank.

Now, did Methusaley know he had heard correctly. They couldn't do this to him. He had been pensioned long ago, and "Giddap" did not apply to him any more. He looked around in time to see the bitter end of the reins swinging in the direction of his hind end. He leaned forward and the wagon began to roll.

CHAPTER XIII

VINI PROHASKA HAS TROUBLE

Mrs. Butler lay on her back and looked at the fringed canopy above her bed. Her head ached this morning, and she suspected the cocktails her husband had served last night. He always made them too strong. She felt her forehead. There didn't seem to be a fever, but there must be. Maybe she ought to call Dr. Kotay.

Looking at the clock, ticking away in its wooden case, she saw it was now nine-thirty. That meant her husband had gone off to work again without saying good-bye. He was doing that oftener now. Perhaps she should get his breakfast herself.

Jeff and Grace would be gone, too. Jeff was attending Case and hoped some day to be an engineer. Such dirty work that was —building railroads and bridges. It wasn't clean like banking or lawyering. Still, it was up to Jeff and he had made his choice.

As for Grace, she was going to school down on Euclid. If she was learning to be a lady, it certainly didn't show in her manner, for only yesterday she had found Grace in the top of the cherry tree, eating cherries and spitting the stones out where they might hit anyone below. It was immodest, too.

Mrs. Butler sat up and swung her feet to the floor. The flesh on her belly rolled into folds, and the bottom one lay in her lap. She must get a new corset, she thought. She looked at herself through the neck of her nightgown and knew she looked horrible. She consoled herself that her sagging belly was the price of having children. Still she wondered if she ought not work harder, or reduce, or quit drinking cocktails.

She thought about breakfast. Perhaps eggs and toast would be good, with a few pieces of bacon. Then she thought of her headache. Perhaps it would be better if she stayed in bed. A smile spread across her round face. That was it—breakfast in bed. Her jowls imitated her tummy and sat on her ample breasts.

"Vini," she called.

There was no answer.

"Vini!"

A door slammed below, but Vini did not come. That was the way with these foreigners, they would come when they got good and ready.

"Vini!" she screamed. Her voice carried through the open window and was heard halfway down the block. Two dogs quit sniffing one another and, with tails between their legs, hurried off in opposite directions. A sparrow in the coaming under the eave regretted the location of her nest. But if Vini heard, she paid no attention.

"God damn her soul to hell!" swore Mrs. Butler, climbing from bed and paddling barefooted down the hall. At the stairs she listened, but could hear nothing. Taking her nightgown in hand, lest she trip on it, she descended the stairs.

"Vini!"

"Errooo," came a voice from somewhere.

Mrs. Butler entered the kitchen. On the stove a dishpan full of water boiled. The breakfast dishes were piled on the table. She walked over to the door and listened. From the privy in the back someone was retching, Vini probably.

That was just her luck! Of all the bohunks in Cleveland, she had to get one that got sick. This wasn't the first time either. Mrs. Butler had forgotten her own illness, but her ill humor persisted. She heard footsteps on the gravel and in a few seconds Vini came in the door.

"It's about time you got here," said Mrs. Butler.

"Yes, ma'am," said Vini, weakly. Her Slavic beauty was lost in the pallor of her face, which was almost greenish in color, except around the mouth where it was white. Her lips were dark and perspiration stood in droplets on her upper lip.

Mrs. Butler looked the girl over. Across her face was a smear.

"Vini, are you pregnant?"

"No, ma'am."

"What is wrong with you?" she asked crossly.

"I'm going to have a bay-bay," answered Vini in her thick Bohemian accent.

"I thought so, you sinning wop," hissed Mrs. Butler. Now she'd have to break another girl in and their skulls were so thick. She shook her finger at the poor girl, "You should be arrested. What would Reverend Willard think, if he knew that I hired a fallen woman. Get out of here! Go this minute."

Vini left the kitchen to get her things. Mrs. Butler thought, "My God! What have I done? Now I'll have to do the dishes." From the room over the kitchen came the sounds of Vini packing. Soon she was coming down the stairs. When she entered the kitchen with her old suitcase in one hand and her huge flowered hat in the other, Mrs. Butler arose from the chair she had flopped on. Pointing through the open frame of the door she said in a loud voice, "Go!"

Before Vini could go, a shadow cast itself across the threshold and a man walked into the kitchen carrying a big flat grocery basket piled full.

"Good morning, Vini. Good morning, Mrs. Butler. Nice day to-day." He walked over to the cupboard and began emptying his basket. One glance at Mrs. Butler, barefooted and in her night-gown, told him the good lady was steamed up about something. As he emptied his basket Vini departed. So did Mrs. Butler.

"Giddap, Claude," said Frank, climbing on his wagon. Half a block up the street Vini Prohaska lugged her heavy bag. From the shake of her shoulders, he could see she was crying.

"Whoa, there boy! Vini, let me give you a lift to where you are going." She smeared the tears over her face. Frank jumped from the wagon and took her bag, throwing it into the wagon easily.

"Give me your hind leg and I'll heist you up," he said, but Vini climbed into the wagon and up on the seat like a boy.

For several blocks they rode in silence, but Frank couldn't stand the strain. "Where you heading for, Vini?"

"Oh, Mr. Stone," she said, "I don't know." She dragged the last word out to the length of the rest she had said.

"Why don't you let me take you to your pa and ma?" he asked her tenderly.

"They are old country people and wouldn't understand."

"Most folks understand pretty well, Vini."

"Not mine," she said grimly, "I am going to have a bay-bay." She regarded him closely. The eyes smiled at her and the mustache twitched.

"Ain't that fine, Vini?" She opened her eyes wide and her mouth

114

opened twice before she said anything.

"I have not a husband."

"Let's tell the boy and you will have."

"Oh—noo!"

"No? Well, I may be wrong."

They rode in silence for a block or two and he made another delivery. When he returned he was grinning delightedly.

"Vini, I just had me a brain storm. How would you like to live with us 'til your baby comes?"

"With you?"

"Yes. Get along, Claude, you pokey devil. You see, it's like this. Mary and me have these two children, Calisty and Howard. They are a heap of bother in the house and Mary loves to take care of the store. If you come with us I'll fix you a room over the store and you take care of the kids for us and we'll take care of you, and Dr. Kotay, when the little rascal comes. That way Mary gets her some help, and so do you." He grinned at her. It was all so simple.

"Mr. Stone," said Vini, "please ask Mary if I can come by your house."

Eventually, Vini settled into the routine life of the Stone household. One day a neighbor who was talking to Frank saw Vini about the yard and asked him who his girl was.

"That girl," said Frank thinking fast, "is as sorry a sight as I ever see. Her husband has been off to the west fighting red Indians out there, and the other day word came from the gov'ment that he got hisself killed."

"No!"

" 'Sa fact."

"Bless my soul! What do you say her name is?"

"Rogers. Mrs. Vini Rogers."

One thing was certain. Vini was pregnant. She blossomed out into the fullest woman Frank had ever seen, and in his mind were visions of twins or triplets. However, there is an end to all things, including pregnancies. Vini had her baby, a five-pound boy. Frank pondered the ways of nature, and found them confusing.

Chapter XIV

THE CLERGY OBJECTS

The church had been finished now several years and the minister was the right Reverend Knight K. Willard. The years had filled Mr. Willard out in the middle, but his face had the lean aggrieved look it had ten years ago. In the pulpit he had become a master of oratory. When the occasion demanded, "Cake" Willard, as he was known in the barber shop, could rise on tiptoe and shake the timbers with the fury of his voice. The stained glass shepherdess on the south window had been seen to reach down and comfort the lamb, as it quivered in fright. But when Cake felt the need of a soft voice he could produce a voice so low, so throbbing, that strong men had been known to wipe away a tear. If he felt so sad about the iniquitous ways of mankind that he must render a sob, he could produce one that would break his voice, as it would that of a child. Then with tears streaming down his face, he would lift his voice to the hilltops, and let it fall to the valleys below. But up from the depths, with spiritual hope and Christian clarity, would the honorable Cake Willard lead his flock in the search for—in the hope for—a new and better world.

On the rolls of the Beginners' Class was the name Calista Stone, and on the Tiny Tots, Howard Stone. Nowhere was there a Frank Stone or a Mary Stone. This grieved Mr. Willard and he said so, not once but several times. He exhorted Frank to be a leader in the community, to put his shoulder to the wheel and to give unto God what which was due him.

"Reverend," said Frank one day when Cake was particularly insistent, "I don't aim to be ungodly, and I try to live my life behaving myself. God Almighty knows I ain't going out of my way to cause Him any trouble, and with that I don't reckon He'll slam the door in my face when I hear the last trump."

"Life is more than behaving oneself," said the minister.

"How's that?" asked Frank. He had always heard that a man had done himself proud, if he got along unmarred by sin.

"A man has his duties to others. By example he must show others the true way of life. The true way of life lies within the church of God."

"And anyone outside is a going-to-hell-sinner?"

"In a way, yes. He has not given to God all that was demanded of him. You must give all your time to God and the study of His ways."

"Reverend, that sounds like a big order."

"There are many sins," said the man of the cloth darkly.

"Seems to be."

"Have you ever heard of the sin of taking the name of the Lord in vain?"

"Do you mean swearing?"

"Yes."

"It appears to me I have."

"Mr. Stone, do you swear?"

"Considerable," admitted Frank.

"That is sin."

"Parson, the man that invented them swear words might have been swearing at God, but nowadays they got to be a part of the language. As a matter of fact, I ain't so certain that swearing ain't a form of praying."

"Praying?" The Reverend didn't think he had heard right.

"That's right. Let's suppose you and me are mad at each other and you say, 'God damn you, Frank Stone!' What are you really saying?"

The parson declined to comment, so Frank told him.

"You are asking God to keep me out of heaven for vexing you. Ain't that right?"

"No. I would be sinning for asking God to intervene in our petty quarrel on my behalf."

"Do you mean you don't ever ask God to kick in with you, against your troubles or those agin you?"

"Well, no, but that is different."

"Whenever a mean swears and says God anything, he's praying and don't believe otherwise. Now take the other kinds of swearing like—"

117

"Let's not talk about other kinds of swearing. Taking the Lord's name in vain is sin. It always has been and always will be."

"If a two-by-four scantling falls off a house and hits me, I'm going to say, 'God damn it!' Maybe I could help matters by saying, 'God damn it, Amen!'"

"Mr. Stone, I am grieved at your attitude. You need the healing influence of the church, and I'm expecting you next Sunday."

"Thank you, Reverend, possible Mary and me will be there."

The minister left haughtily and Frank resumed his game of solitaire.

The sermon for the following Sunday was "Taking the Lord's Name in Vain." There was considerable comment in the barber shop on Monday by those who heard it. Frank hadn't needed a haircut but he dropped in to pass the time of the day as Monday was pretty quiet.

"Old Cake had something under his breechin' yesterday," commented George Smith, the barber. He pulled the leather strop out tight and reflectively swiped the razor back and forth several times.

"Was he gunning for somebody?" There was a twinkle in Frank's eye as he cut himself a bit of plug tobacco.

"Seems he had a talk with somebody last week about religion, and this fellow, whoever he was, was a slick one to hear Cake tell it. For every question that come up this fellow took the devil's side. Cake got hot right there in the pulpit and I expected to hear him do a little cussing himself."

"How did he make out?"

"All right. He said he and Jesus were alike. The devil couldn't tempt either of them."

"Glad to hear that," said Frank picking up the morning paper.

"I liked the part where he lit into card playing," said George Adams. "My old lady has been trying to get up a Pedro Club among the women folks in the block. His remarks was bad enough to her, but when I give her the elbow, she like to have murdered me right in the pew."

"How," said Frank, "did he ever figure that playing cards was taking the Lord's name in vain?"

"I don't exactly remember," said Adams.

"Something about wasting the Lord's time, wasn't it, George?"

"That's it. It seems all the time in the world belongs to the Lord."

118

"All of it?" asked Frank.

"That's what he said."

"Don't appear natural," said Frank, taking off his vest. Maybe he did need him a haircut, after all.

"Any off the top, Frank?"

He looked in the mirror, and turned his head from side to side. "I better say yes while I can. A few more years and there ain't going to be no top."

"It is getting a little thin for a young man," said the barber. "Can I give you a hair treatment with Clive's Hair Restorer?"

"That ain't no good to me," said Frank. "My pa was bald and all my relations was bald, and I'm going to be bald. The will of God ain't always a mystery."

There was a general laugh, while the barber snipped away for a fare thee well. Frank looked at the clock and saw in fifteen minutes Morrissey's saloon would be open, and he knew the barber had had a long dry week end.

John Henderson came in. After greeting everyone and reading the captions in the morning paper, he said, "What did you think of Cake's dadburned sermon yesterday?"

"We were just talking about it," said George Smith.

"I'm in bad with my woman over it," he volunteered grinning.

"Because of swearing?" asked the barber.

"No, because this devil of his was wasting the Lord's time with cards. Wasting the Lord's time and taking His name in vain was all one and the same according to Cake. My woman learned how to play cards and has been to a couple of afternoon parties, but they play cards instead of plan church socials. She liked them fine, and thinks I put Cake up to raising the devil about them to keep her home."

"I wonder who did stir him up," said the barber, looking at Frank.

"I ain't got the least idee," said Frank.

CHAPTER XV

RAW EGGS AND RARE LIVER

The morning was bright and cloudless, but it was cold enough to put a crust on hell. Frank worked the bay mare carefully on the icy streets, because she was not winter shod. The fact was he had just traded Robert for her. He had traded Jenny for Robert. This one was still unnamed.

In his wagon this morning he had quite a load. He would not get back until after two at the very earliest, which meant he would have a late dinner. He had three orders from the Morrison families this morning. He guessed he'd stop at Grace's first.

He stopped, loaded the basket on his arm and tramped through the snow. It crunched under his feet. The snow had been swept off the back stoop, so he noisily stomped his feet to shake off the snow. Grace heard him, opened the door and bade him enter.

"Good morning, Frank," said Grace. She was a fairly large woman as women go, blonde, pretty and witty. Besides that she was right neighborly.

"Colder than Billy-be-damned out there today," he said.

"I have only stuck my nose out long enough to sweep the back porch, but I like to have froze."

"I see your tracks."

"Will you have a cup of coffee before you leave?"

"Damned if I won't," he replied, "I need me something to warm my gizzard."

Grace poured the coffee and got him the sugar and cream. Doughnuts were already on the table, freshly made this morning for the aroma was heavy on the air. Frank sipped the scalding liquid, and then filled his saucer and blew on it. Finally, he noticed Grace and what she was doing.

"What in thunder have you in that glass?"

Grace made a face.

"Raw eggs."

"Raw eggs?"

"Yes."

"Do you like raw eggs that way?"

"I despise them."

"You don't look crazy, Grace, but I guess you are."

"I am crazy."

Tears started at the corners of her eyes and trickled down beside her nose. She swallowed several times and forced a smile.

"Clarence makes me do it."

Frank had heard of a lot of things that eggs were supposedly good for, but for Grace—he shook his head and kept his peace.

"Frank, do you know how long I've been married?"

"Let me see now, about five or six years."

"Eight."

"So long as that? Time ain't awaiting none."

"It certainly isn't. Look at me, old, wrinkled and drying up—a married old maid."

"Pshaw! Gracey—tut tut, girl."

"I am, Frank. Eight years and not one child to show for it. I thought there was something wrong with me, so I went to Dr. Kotay. He examined me and could find absolutely nothing wrong."

"There's time, Grace."

"Time!" she said scornfully. "Time to grow old and die! That isn't the worst of it!" A new tear chased the first one from each eye. Frank risked a raised eyebrow.

"Clarence makes me eat raw eggs to make me fertile."

"Good God A'mighty!"

She nodded. "Last month it was liver, cooked rare."

"Gracey, that's the saddest story ever I hear. Doesn't he think he might be lacking?"

"No."

"Has he ever been to a doctor?"

"No." Grace looked at the tablecloth and traced a design with her fingers. "Frank, is there anyway a man can tell he is all right, without being a father?"

Frank thought it over carefully. How in the name of sin could a fellow know for sure. Maybe a doctor could tell, but—"To my way of thinking, there ain't none."

121

"That's what I thought. I have eaten his damned eggs long enough. I'm going to have a baby by some man I know is a father, and I know I can trust. I am sure it is Clary's fault."

"What kind of an idee is that?" asked Frank, dying to laugh, but not cracking a smile. Grace searched his eyes.

"Frank Stone, you are laughing at me!"

"Honest, Gracey, I ain't."

"You had better not, Frank, because you are going to father my baby."

"Good God A'mighty," said Frank, sitting absolutely still and rather liking the "idee."

"You have two children and heaven knows how many more, if you can believe the gossip. One more won't hurt you."

That gossip had given him this reputation shocked him, but he wanted to howl with laughter. Maybe Grace knew more.

"You started this, Grace. Who do people say I fathered?"

"Is Vini's boy yours?"

"No."

"He looks like you."

"All tow-headed kids look alike. He's the spitten image of his ma."

"Why should you take care of her?"

"She's working for us and she earns her keep."

"All right. You haven't any children but your wife's. You still are going to give me a baby, and you are going to keep your mouth shut. Do you want me to live on raw eggs and liver the rest of my days?"

"No, Gracey, but I got to be going now, or folks will be talking."

"Clarence goes to New York for a week, leaving tomorrow. I'm counting on you, Frank, but it's got to be our secret." She ushered him out into the cold and it was a good thing she did for the red blood was rushing through his veins.

Now, wasn't this a fine howdy do? He was already the number one choice for young Jimmie's daddy. He wondered if Vini naming the youngster after him wasn't the reason for the suspicion. But now, Gracey was threatening to Lord A'mighty! He wondered what his father would have done. He didn't think he'd need a second guess.

The following morning Frank was eating his breakfast. Mary's flapjacks were always good, but this morning they were extra good. There was, so far as Frank knew, not the sign of an expression on his face.

"All right, Frank, out with it," said Mary. Frank gasped. Had Mary read his mind?

"What are you talking about, Mary?"

"Frank Stone, I haven't lived with you all these years not to know when there's something under that hair of yours that I ought to know."

"I ain't the least—"

"Yes, you have! You came home yesterday looking like the cat that ate the canary. You've been grinning about it this morning. I'm going to have it from you."

"Now, be careful, Mary. There may be some things you won't care to know."

Mary sat on his lap. This was going to be more difficult than she had supposed. She pushed his chin down, opening his mouth.

"Talk!"

"Oh—Mary!" He wondered what she'd say if he told her.

"Give!"

"Mary, suppose that you were me and making deliveries. You step in to make a delivery and the lady of the house is in the kitchen, and she says for you to come in and have a cup of coffee. You see her trying to eat raw eggs and gaggin' over 'em."

"Raw eggs?"

"Yup—raw damn eggs!"

"What on earth for?"

"It's her husband's idee. They been married eight years and no children. He thinks it is her fault."

"Eight years!" Mary looked out the window.

"Last month it was raw liver."

"Raw liver? Ye Gods."

"Well, rare—almost raw."

"Go on."

"It was her husband's plan to virile her up to where she'd have a baby."

Mary studied his face intently.

"She went to Dr. Kotay and he said it wasn't her fault. Her husband won't go to the doctor himself. He says he knows he's all right."

123

"Humph!" said Mary.

"Now, supposing this woman says that she wants a baby and she ain't got no use for no more raw eggs. She says to you, 'I know you are a father and I want you to get me a baby.'"

Mary said nothing. Her face portrayed nothing to Frank, and she did not look at him.

"What did you say, Frank?"

"I said, I'd think it over and tell her later. Then she says, 'Don't think too long,' or some such thing, 'my husband's going out of town for a week and I ain't foolin'.'"

"What do you aim to do?"

"Mary, you tell *me*. You drug it out of me."

"I'll tell you, Frank, what I'd do." Mary squirmed on his lap, faced Frank and looked into his eyes. Her own were solemn.

"I'd give Grace Morrison her baby!"

He was stunned. This woman—this Mary had read his mind as sure as sin. She even knew the woman's name. "Holy Hanna," he thought, and blushed a deep red. Mary noticed his confusion and couldn't help laughing at him. She kissed him.

"You will always be an open book to me, Frank. Clarence Morrison paid his bill yesterday and told me he was going to New York for a week. The rest was easy."

"There is one thing I am going to warn you about." She closed one eye and wagged a forefinger under his nose. "Don't get caught and don't like her too much!"

Mary put on her sweater, kissed her husband and went to open the store. Frank sat still, shaking his head, "I'll never undertake to understand a woman, so help me John Robinson!"

124

CHAPTER XVI

VIRGINITY—A QUESTION OF

Grace Morrison gave birth to a fine son. Although Mary did not get to see little Jack until he was about a year old, Frank had described him to her. That she was impatient to see him is understandable. During the months of Grace's childbearing, she had chided Frank, and once made him a present of a brass ring—the type worn by bulls.

Frank enjoyed her chiding, although he protested that he was only doing his duty to mankind. Mary protested the word, "mankind." Other than this, Mary never questioned Frank, or mentioned the affair. It was a little thing they shared with one another, and even Grace did not know there was a third member in on her secret.

On the day that Jackie came into the store with his father, both Frank and Mary were present. The lad was heavily dressed for such mild weather, and his cherubic face stared solemnly out of a knit helmet. Mr. Morrison carried him proudly on his arm, but set the child down on the counter and arranged his sweater.

"There we are," said Clarence. "Ain't that a fine big boy?"

"He is certainly a beautiful boy," said Mary.

"Oh, yes siree, he's a beautiful boy. He is the living image of Grace's father."

Frank said nothing. What could he say? He watched Mary closely and failed to note anything but admiration on her face.

"He has the old man's nose and eyes, but my chin and ears." He removed the bonnet to show the baby's ears. Mary nearly laughed too much. The baby's coloring and hair were almost identical with Howard's when he was that age. There was the same button-hook-shaped head.

Clarence's chin was small and round and so was the child's now, but Mary knew it would not always be.

She could see Frank Stone staring solemnly from this little cherub and no doubt about it. It pleased her that she could feel only pride in this baby, and pride in that good-looking, now slightly flushed husband of hers who had sired it.

When the talk shifted to the subject of the proposed street railway, and water and sewage systems, Frank felt relieved and entered into the conversation with enthusiasm. Clarence paid his bill and Mary gave him a receipt. Shouldering Jack, he made for the door.

"Good-bye, Mr. and Mrs. Stone," he said, "Wave bye-bye Jackie. Wave bye-bye. That's the boy. Tell them we are soon going to have a little brother or sister at our house." Then he left.

Mary gave Frank a look that practically froze him into an iceberg. He was surprised as well as frozen, because although he had seen Grace nearly twice a week, he had noticed nothing. In his misery, as he weathered Mary's frosty glare, Frank was jealous. If Grace wanted another child, after the good job he had done on this one, why had she failed to ask him?

"You can't let well enough alone, can you?" Mary was mad through and through. One child was enough. Why had she not known this would happen?

"Mary, for Pete's sake, cool off. If Grace is pregnant again, I am not the daddy."

"I should have known."

Before he could answer her, she flounced out of the store and left him. He looked around the store and saw that Mrs. George Smith, the barber's wife, was waiting. He wondered how much she had heard.

For nearly four months, he felt the chill of Mary's doubt. They never mentioned the cause. Sometimes Mary would warm up to him in such a way as to make him hope the matter had been forgotten. If she remembered, a killing frost would settle over the air and Frank was in bad again.

The baby finally came. It was shown to Frank by old Mrs. Morrison as he delivered the groceries. Grace was still in bed. With relief, Frank saw the tiny lady and noted her brown eyes and abundant black hair. He tickled the baby under the chin with his finger and the baby's tiny fingers grabbed it and held on. Old Mrs. Morrison was babbling about this baby being one hundred per cent Morrison, and giving voice to comparisons between this baby, Clarence and practically every other baby she had had. Frank felt a load easing off his shoulders.

Mary had supper ready when Frank got home. He called to her before he left the barn, again on the path and plunged into the kitchen. He grabbed her and kissed her, and waltzed her around the kitchen.

"What on earth is the matter with you?"

"I got me proof. I got me proof," he chanted.

"Proof of what?"

"Proof I'm a virgin for this year! Grace's baby is here." He pointed to the top of his head. "Black hair!" He pointed to his eyes. "Brown eyes!" His chin. "No chin!" He ended triumphantly, "And it's a girl."

Mary laughed and the strain was off. "What would you have done, Frank, if Grace had another tow-head?"

"Mary," he said grinning, "let's talk about something pleasant for a change."

As long as Vini was there to look after the children of an evening, Frank and Mary took to stepping out to dances about once every two weeks. These were held in the Knights of Pythias Lodge Hall, or the Woodmen of the World's hall. They made many new friends; and new friends were new customers. Perhaps it was made more enjoyable by the fact that for the first time since they had known one another, they were acting their ages.

Frank had a good clear voice and often called the dances while the regular caller took a whirl at a dance. In fact, Mary complained that he would rather call than dance. Her fresh beauty had not been lost. She was a little wider in the hips, a little fuller in the bosom, and a little thinner in the face.

It was well that they played while they could, for when Vini's little Jimmie was two years old, Mary became pregnant again, and Mary and Vini eventually changed jobs. As a storekeeper Vini was shy, and she was glad when the arrangement could again be reversed. Mary's new baby was a girl, whom she named Myrtle.

The house was now too small. They debated on whether it would be better to add a wing or build an upstairs to the house by raising the roof. They finally rearranged the partitions in the house, robbing space from the living room and dividing the bedrooms. This gave them two small bedrooms. The smaller of the two became the nursery. When Vini came over, Jimmie took his nap in there, too.

Frank's garden no longer could supply the amount of green stuff that could have been sold. They were a little slow to realize that it was not the fault of the garden, but the increased demand. One evening, Frank talked to Mary about it.

"Have you noticed, Mary, that people would buy more green goods, if we had them?"

"I have, Frank."

"Give me some money and I'll go down to the city market and buy us a load. If we get too much or can't sell it, I'll stop. I got an idee we can sell all I can haul."

"It sounds worth a try," said Mary, "get my pocketbook will you?"

Frank got the pocketbook and opened it.

"Good Lord of love, woman, how much money have you got there?" Frank's eyes were about to bug out of his head, and seeing how deep they were planted, that was something.

"Frank, we agreed once that money was none of your concern. People are paying their bills now and I haven't been to the bank."

"Do people owe us much?"

"Quite a lot, but times are better than they were a year ago. Then we were carrying nearly everyone."

"I didn't have no idee."

"There isn't a smarter man in town than Frank Stone," said Mary, "when it comes to working and making money." She smiled at him impishly, "And there isn't a man in town who knows less about keeping it."

"You maybe got something there," he said, rubbing his ear and thinking out loud, "You never gave me a chance to see."

"I never will, either. I know you from away back."

Mary gave him the money and a list of what she estimated would be most popular. He pocketed it and set himself to wake up early.

Jenny objected to being awakened at three o'clock in the morning, and showed her displeasure at being harnessed by laying her ears back tight against her head and trying to get up nerve to nip him. When he cinched the belly band, she nipped, and almost

128

instantly regretted it. She was almost downtown before she was fairly certain her rear end had worked back to where it had started from.

Frank was very careful in the selection of his produce, and with his wagon full drove back to the store. Mary was enthusiastic about the produce, but scolded him like a shrew for failing to note the amount he had paid for each item. All he knew was the total cost and the way it was divided was no concern of his. It may be entered on the record that he never forgot again.

CHAPTER XVII

FRANK SOLVES A MYSTERY

This spring Vini was cross as a bear. It took scarcely anything
to send her to her room in a cloud and very little more to make
it rain. Frank puzzled over her behavior and was stumped. Mary
told him only a man could upset a woman like Vini. What man,
Mary could not guess, because Vini would not talk. She knew he
was Jimmie's daddy, if that was any clue, but why she should be
so upset this spring, and not last, or the one before that was anybody's guess.

Frank put his mind to the task of unravelling this mystery and
the results he obtained were so startling as to leave him slightly
groggy. He took a tablet out of the showcase and sharpened a
pencil with his jackknife. Then he wrote: "A. Why is Vini upset?
—Man (Mary says); B. What happens in spring? 1. Snow melts.
2. Flowers bloom. 3. School is out. 4. Gardens planted. 5. —"
Under five he wrote: "Horses shed hair," but erased it as not applying to the problem. "C. What men does Vini know? 1. Me. 2.
Mr. Butler. 3. Jeff Butler. 4. Her pa. D. Why won't Vini tell who
baby's pa is? 1. Don't know. 2. Is ashamed of him. 3. Doesn't like
son of bitch. 4. Don't want to upset his plans. 5. Is afraid of him."

Then, wetting his pencil point with his tongue, Frank reread
his list. Under A, there was only one answer. Then he tried
"man" with the answers to B, "Man snow melts," "Man flowers
bloom," "Man school is out," "Man gardens planted." He studied
this. Snowmen always melted and he couldn't figure what a man
flower would be doing blooming. "Man school is out" made some
sense, but "Man gardens planted" did not help much. "Man school
is out" was the pick of the crop.

Under C, then he substituted the names for man, and excluded
everyone but Jeff Butler, since school had been out for a long
time for the rest. Now he had "Jeff Butler's school is out."

Under D, he figured Vini was not the kind of a girl who would not know who she had been with. If it was Jeff Butler she would not be ashamed of him. He decided there might be something to three, Vini didn't usually get worked up at all. Since she did get stirred up, it probably meant the opposite. Most likely reason for keeping quiet was number four. She didn't want to upset his plans and nobody was afraid of Jeff, him being so likeable and all.

At the bottom of the page he wrote his conclusion: "The father of Vini's baby is Jeff Butler. He is just finishing school, and she kept quiet so as not to upset his plans."

He reread his conclusion and added "as figured out by Frank Stone."

When he verified slyly that Jeff was through with school for keeps this June, he knew he was one of the great detectives of Cleveland. He just hadn't put his mind to it before.

For several weeks he plotted to bring Vini and Jeff together. His imagination worked at top speed and produced some masterpieces. In one he would drive up to where Jeff was walking down the street and say, "Hello Jeff, seems like I'm going your way. Have a ride."

"Don't mind if I do," Jeff would say.

"I hear you're out of school this spring."

"Glad to be shet of it."

"I suppose you'll be getting married one of these days."

"I don't know. I might find me a woman."

"I know you have a woman."

"You do?"

"Yes. She is Vini Prohaska who has you a fine son."

There would be tears, hearty handshakes and wedding bells.

In another plan he would take little Jimmy with him, all dressed up cute as a button, when he went to deliver groceries. He would set Jimmie in one end of the basket and put groceries in the other end. Then he'd knock on the door, polite as could be.

"Good morning, Mr. Stone," Mrs. Butler would answer the door, seeing as how she had never got her another maid when Vini left.

"Good morning, ma'am. I have you here a delivery."

"Won't you come in?"

"Thank you, ma'am."

"And is this your little son, Mr. Stone? Isn't he cute all decked out like a bazaar tent?"

"No, ma'am, he ain't my son."

"Oh? Whose little man is he? What's the little fellow's name?"

"His name, ma'am, is James Franklin Butler. He is your grandson by Vini Prohaska and Jeff." He bet that would throw the old girl on her ear.

He had other plans just as effective, including one in which he waited until Jeff was crossing the street and then he would run him down with Fan and the spring wagon. Before Jeff could regain consciousness, he would throw him in the wagon, and race like a charioteer to the house.

"Whoa, Fran!" he would holler. Vint would come out on the porch and ask what was the fuss "by our house." Frank would carry the inert Jeff up the steps and say, "I have brought you your man, Vini."

When Jeff would come to, not being hurt much, he would say, "Vini!" and collapse. When he would come to the next time the first fellow he'd see would be Cake Willard.

The whole trouble was that of so many corking plans, he did not know which to use. He studied the matter when he had time. One morning he was trimming cabbages in the store, before Mary came in, when a customer entered.

"Good morning to you, Mr. Stone," said Jeff politely. "I've slack. The young man in question had entered the store.

"Good morning, to you, Mr. Stone," said Jeff politely. "I've come to see Vini."

"Vini?" he didn't want to miss this, so he said, "Wait here and I'll call her."

"Thank you," said Jeff.

Frank scurried out the back and up the stairs to Vini's room. Vini was pulling a gingham dress over her head.

"Vini, he's here."

"Yah, I know. I saw him coom in."

"Come along then."

Frank re-entered the store. Jeff sat on the counter smoking a pipe which was cupped in his hand.

"She'll be right along."

"Thank you, Mr. Stone."

"No trouble at all."

Vini entered.

"Hello, Vini."

"Hello, Cheff," said Vini without a trace of emotion.

"I've come for you."

Vini walked around the end of the counter and Jeff met her. He would have taken her in his arms, but she held him away. "Cheff, is not you feel sorry for me?"

"No, Vini."

"Ven ve find ve are going have baybay, ve make a deal. Vini have the baybay and Cheff finish collech, right?"

"That's right."

"You finish now? Right?"

"Yes."

"I luff you, Cheff, but I no hold you to deal, if you change mind," said Vini. She searched his face intently as he pulled her close to him.

"For the love of Pete, Vini, do you think I'd be here now if I had changed my mind? I've come for you!" He gave her a business-like kiss.

"Yah," said Vini now smiling radiantly, "you my man, Cheff. Now coom. I show you Chames Franklin!" She led the way out the back door.

For big James Franklin, the results were as he had planned, but where were the tears, the sobs, and the avowals of everlasting love? Frank honked loudly into his big blue bandana handkerchief.

CHAPTER XVIII

CHANGES ARE MADE—PROGRESS REARS ITS HEAD— FRED JOINS THE FAMILY

Cleveland was growing in the early 1880's, as it had never grown before. The desire for property and homes seemed to have seized the city like a disease. Here there was no crowding into wealthy tenement houses like there was on Boston's Beacon Hill or Chicago's South Side. The people spread out and occupied the same land areas as cities six and seven times its population.

The problem of getting to work in the morning, and home at night, was a critical one. The horse drawn streetcar system was in operation on Euclid Avenue as far as Doan Street and on Cedar it ended at the Y at DeForest Street. From the far East Side, the horse and buggy was still the commuter's best answer.

In the downtown area and near business buildings and depots were livery stables of every kind. Some had a hot stable arrangement, dray horses in the stable at night and buggy horses during the day. Liveries made money.

Sibley Street ran parallel to Cedar, but one block north. It started at Willson Avenue and ran into a dead end at Perry Street. At a time when the main streets were being paved with stone, making them noisy and hard riding, Sibley was still a dirt street. Here a few members of the Gentlemen's Driving Club placed two white painted posts a mile apart. Anyone who felt so inclined could, by driving out of his way a block or two, drive his horse over the measured mile and time his speed. When two or more horses were timed at the same time, it became a race track.

Perhaps because many of the members of the city council were members of the Gentlemen's Driving Club the street was graded and sprinkled with loving care, and had every bit as good of a racing surface as the Glenville Race Track, which the club also owned.

134

In the years that followed, men would arrange small bets on their horses and would settle them in a swift dash on the way to work in the morning. Anyone wanting to bet and having none arranged, had only to drive alongside another and wave a bill. If the unknown adversary figured he had a chance, he could accept the challenge with the wave of a hand.

Certain unwritten rules governed all races. Since there were no judges to pick a winner in a close race, the race was judged by the position of the hubs of the front wheels at the end of the mile. Even that was not proof of a peaceful settlement to a close race, but it would do until something else came along. If a horse broke and ran, he couldn't win whether he came in first or not. He had to trot or pace the whole way.

For those who indulged in the sport, it was necessary to have light buggies. Eventually, men were riding to work in light gigs with bicycle-type wheels, or even sulkies, but most men conservatively stuck to a light four-wheel buggy.

Of all the horses Frank had owned since Methusaley, not one could better three minutes strictly trotting. Most had left their speed before the plow. Frank itched to get into a race and yearned for a horse that could come close to a two and a half minute mile. That was not fast as race horses go, but for buggy horses, it was mighty good. The fates smiled on him and he found the answer to his prayers in a horse named Fred. Before Fred entered the family fold several bits of family history had been made.

"Thunderation A'mighty! We need us more room," Frank told Mary one morning, as they crammed some new stock into the store. "It's getting so around here that we can't get more than three or four people inside."

Mary stopped working at the cash register and came over to where Frank was working.

"I've been meaning to say something about it before," she said, "but never got around to it. Let's build a new store."

"Can we do that?" He watched her face closely.

"Yes, and if we are careful we can get a new house, too."

"What's your idee?"

"We need a store two or three times the size of this one. Let's build it right up to the street where your garden is. We can run it back about even with our porch, and build a new house right onto the store. We have never had all the room we need, and with the children growing up, we have to do something about it."

Frank sat on a sack of coffee beans and thoughtfully pulled the generous lobe of his ear. Mary watched him for some sign of approval.

"Mary, wouldn't you rather have the store here and a new house somewhere else?"

"No," she said firmly, "I wouldn't."

"Why?"

"Because we are—I don't know how to explain it. Maybe it's like this—we have been happy here in this little place, but now it's too small."

"You mean, like we are gettin' too big for our breeches?"

"In a way I do. I want everything to be just like it is here, only bigger and handier. I want your barn to be in the back, and I want to live where I can run into the store in a minute if I want to. If Mrs. Henderson's boy brings her a few bushels of peaches of a Sunday when he comes to see her, and they are apt to spoil if they aren't canned right away, I want to be where I can get her the sugar, or jar rubbers." Mary picked up an armful of canned goods and began putting it on a shelf. Over her shoulder, she continued, "There's no use joshing ourselves to where we think we can get rich here, but we can do mighty well if we don't get too big notions."

"You know me, Mary. I'll do anything you set your mind on. If you got us the money, let's be about it. I don't mind telling you, I'll probably swell up with pride to where I look like a poisoned pup."

In six months the new store and house was completed. There were two full floors for both, with an attic over the house. The roof line ran parallel to the street on the house part, while the line of the store ran at right angles to it. There were seven large rooms, including space for two bathrooms which would be installed when sewage systems permitted. City water was already in use. A long porch extended from the store's side entrance to the ell formed by the main part of the house. In a way it seemed that the new turned its back on the old, for the driveway, porch and entrances were all to the west.

While Mary was in a spending mood, Frank broached the subject of getting a new delivery wagon. His old one was all right for hauling manure and gravel and trash, but he wanted one with a covered delivery body. It would be high wheeled and slightly higher in front than in back. The tail gate would close and a canvas curtain could be drawn across the back to keep out rain or dust. Over the driver's seat and out over the dash would be a continuation of the top. There would be a gentle curve to it. On the side would be the steps and a brass handle. "Frank Stone, Grocer" would be painted on the panelled sides. The body would be painted green and red, striped with yellow. The wheels would have yellow spokes and there would be black rims and hubs. The wagon would have the best type brake with a foot pedal to lock it in place. The shafts would be curved and painted red, with leather loops for hold-back straps. He saw it all, and as he described it to Mary, she looked away with an enraptured look on her face.

"Yes," she said when he had finished, "we must have that."

"And a new harness, all black with brass rings all shiny, and a red tassel on the bridle."

"Yes," said Mary.

"And," began Frank—

"No!"

"No what?"

"No new horse!"

"Mary, you are the dangdest woman I ever see."

"Weren't you going to say a new horse?"

"Yes, but how did you know?"

Frank built a new barn on the very back of the lot and moved his cows, two senior Joseys and Beulah a heifer, and Maude his current horse into the new barn. He filled his barn with hay from out Cedar Avenue. There were no farms close around any more.

What a crop this garden had raised this year! In its new light yellow paint, the building glistened in the sun and Frank's heart was full of gratitude. It had been done in sixteen years. Was that long? It hadn't seemed long. Here was Calista, going on thirteen but helping in the store and as tall as her mother. Howard was a big help, too. He watched little Myrtle picking her way carefully about the yard, picking up nails that had been scattered about. She was as cute as a speckled pup.

Speaking of pups, Howard had been given one. It had large

137

ears and was all woolly and fat when he brought it home, but now only half grown, it showed promise of being only two sizes smaller than a horse. He guessed it was a cocker spaniel crossed with a Shetland pony. Curly was here to stay and the children loved him.

Frank had planted a quince tree near the back door of the house, an apple tree by the west fence, a lilac bush and one whose name he could never remember, probably a Bullhorn Reukus, elsewhere in the yard. He planted hollyhocks along the walls of the barn.

He was greasing a front wheel of his new wagon. He had a shed for his wagons now and it was easier to keep them clean. Out of the corner of his eye he caught a glimpse of Mary, darting out to empty some garbage into the can. What a sweet girl she was! Sixteen years they had been married! He wondered what difference there was in her.

For one thing, there were little crinkles in the corners of her eyes, and lines where her smile was. Mary's eyes would always be the same, blue and happy. Was this all that sixteen years had done? No, there was more. Mary had changed from a girl to a mother. In his mind he found it hard to define, but there was a soft pleasant bossiness about her—a sort of mature sense of direction.

He thought of his love for her, and wondered if it had changed. Honestly, he thought it had. Love had been an adventure, a thrill of sensuality when he was married. It was still that, but it was respect, confidence and the pleasant companionship between them, too. The long hours and the trials they had experienced had become a bond between them—a bond forged with love.

Into this new house, more had been moved than furniture. Love of the children, love of Mary and love of life had been moved. No one had seen it come in, but it was here and this was home.

Frank spun the wheel. Contentment oozed from his pores and he felt himself purring.

The little house they had just vacated was getting a new tenant, Mrs. Orchards. Widowed now some six years or so, she had made a gallant stand with her boarding house, only to be forced to succumb to the steam roller advance of the business district. She re-established her boarding house farther from the center of town, and lost most of her clients to the hotels in the center of the city. When Raymond ran away from home, she decided it was time to alter their way of life.

Frank and Mary had kept in touch with Mrs. Orchards, although sometimes many months had elapsed between visits. Now she turned to them for help and found them moving into their new home. It fitted together perfectly. Mrs. Orchards and her two daughters, Effie and Olive, moved next door, and a neatly painted sign was placed on the store, "Sewing and Dressmaking." As a sort of postscript in small letters were the words, "In the Rear."

Living above the old store in Vini's old room was old Ben Judson. He was a widower now. He had been with the railroad long after he had been taken off the switch engine, as a sort of janitor and errand boy, but with only himself to think of, he hunted Frank up. Ben was astounded at the prosperity he saw. When Frank suggested he come into the neighborhood, and make his living as an odd job man, he readily did so.

Of a night, old Ben would sit on the top step of the stairs and play his violin. It had been put away unused for so many years, that Ben's fingers had become clumsy. As he played, their old agility came back to them and he could be heard many an evening thereafter, playing away for dear life on some old-fashioned hoe-down.

Over the little store, a tough battle raged. Frank Morrissey, who had kept a saloon in the neighborhood for years, rented it. He made the mistake of moving his gold-lettered sign, before he moved his stock. Reverend Cake Willard had thrown a fit of unusual proportions, even for him. Searching Frank out, Cake had, with eyes glittering, nostrils distended breathing fire like a dragon, delivered an ultimatum.

"Frank Stone, you—you son of Satan, you will not desecrate the Lord's property by putting a saloon so close to the church! I will not have it! Before God, I challenge you to place that evil thing there!"

"Cake," said Frank uneasily, "I think I know how you feel about it. I had me no thought about it before."

"Yes, you did, you scoundrel—you lying, cheating, adulterous son of Lucifer. You put that saloon there as an insult to God!"

"Take it easy, Cake Willard." Frank felt the hair on his head rising and anger surged into him. It was a new sensation, one he had rarely ever felt before.

"It's men like you, who steal the bread from the mouths of

your neighbors, and line your money chests with gold made by their blood. God will strike you down for your sins, and I will stand beside Jesus and point to you the road to hell."

Frank felt a new urge—an urge to laugh. The picture of himself being struck down by God, but enough of him surviving to see which way Cake Willard was pointing as the road to hell, struck Frank as being slightly ludicrous.

"If the Lord asks me, I'll tell Him you warned me," said Frank, anger abating.

"How often I have regretted the day I soiled my hands by marrying you and your wife! May Heaven forgive me!"

"To my way of thinking, Cake, that is the only really good job you ever done. I'll thank you kindly to talk about my deviltry and leave Mary out."

The Reverend Willard saw that his barb had struck deep. As much as his better judgment warned him against it, he had to strike again.

"In your house and under your roof all the evil of the worldly find sanctuary. Your wife courts the devil and his pasteboards and stays away from the fold of the church. All the other sins are yours."

Frank reached for the buggy whip, and Cake departed in something resembling a fast walk. If that was not enough, he was prepared to run, because nothing would have caused such a sensation as to have a parson horsewhipped.

Frank knew that when the minister had come in to see him about the saloon, right was on his side. It was bad enough to have saloons on the side streets and in the alleys, without having to face them from the steps of the church. He would gladly have refunded Morrisey's money, and have found a more suitable tenant. All Cake would have had to do was to mention it, and in a gentlemanly way ask him to reconsider. Now, the saloon would go in if he had to fight an injunction to the Supreme Court.

In the church Cake let go an earth-shaking blast and circulated a petition, but there were so few signatures, he subsided muttering and murmuring to himself. Frank Morrisey moved his liquors and beer, and swung his shiny walnut doors at the entrance.

Cedar Avenue was now in a state of continual confusion. The street was torn up by the street railway people and no sooner restored than it was again opened up for the sewer. The water people and the gas people each took their turn and it was time to start all over again. Frank estimated that in the last few years Cedar Avenue had been plowed and harrowed to the depth of about fifteen feet.

As a result of the mud and dirt, many housewives who had always purchased their groceries in person, began giving Frank lists of their needs for later in the week. Consequently, there was more and more delivering to do and Frank kept himself exceedingly busy.

And then at canning time! That was the real nightmare.

"Frank, watch the market for me will you? I want to put up about four bushels of peaches this year. When you see some nice ripe clingstone peaches, just buy them for me and bring them out, not on Saturday, of course, but any other time."

Just as sure as fate, if he did pick up the peaches, the lady would be in Mentor, Elyria or Chagrin Falls for the week, and Frank would be faced with the job of placing them elsewhere. Not infrequently did Mary find herself and the children confronted by an all night canning bee, after a long and tiring day. Frank was always on the job, assisting with the peeling and making remarks about what he would tell the lady when next he saw her.

It is odd that some of the pleasantest memories should have been born during these enforced sessions, memories which the children would carry to their graves. Perhaps it was because they were given a share in settling a family problem.

Mother Stone's Saucer Pies got their start in much the same way. With all her Mason jars full and fruit about to spoil from being over ripe, Mary once made about forty pies, baked in saucers. They were at once an outstanding success for they made ideal lunch box desserts, and Mary Stone knew how to make pies! Her customers clamored for more. This was good training for Calista and Myrtle and they absorbed the pie-making technique at early ages.

The first bathtub was also installed, and the water closet. It was installed in the downstairs bathroom, space for which had been included in the original plans. The tub itself was of copper sheet metal, soldered at the seams. Completely surrounding it was an oak panelled box, with a lid which closed when it was not in use.

What a luxury it was to climb into this tub with its light green metal and stretch his legs out full length. The bottom burbled and bubbled as the bather shifted his weight, but from now on the round washtub stayed in the basement.

Throughout the house was the soft light of gas mantles. They hung from chandeliers in the parlor, living room and dining room, and as many could be lighted as were needed. In the other rooms single jets swung on arms from the walls.

In the parlor was the upright piano, given to Calista after they moved. On its top was a violin, supposedly for Myrtle, but she was too busy to more than make an occasional pass at it. In a bookcase was a set of the complete works of Charles Dickens, given to Mary for a birthday present. Frank had bought them on a weekly payment plan and Mary fumed.

"When in time will I ever read them?" she asked. "Ye Gods! I haven't time to make me a dress to cover my nakedness, and you buy me the complete works of a man who appears to have never done a cursed thing but write!"

Frank grinned, but he had a hard time finding the money to pay for them, for Mary was tighter than the bark of a tree. In the beginning he had reasoned that he could pay for them out of his tobacco money, but he never really expected to do so. But that was exactly where it had come from.

In the parlor there was, besides the cherry settee and chairs they had bought to furnish the other house, an umbrella stand so ornate as to defy accurate description. An oval mirror in the panelled back was surrounded by wooden knobs on which it was expected coats would be hung. In the bottom was an iron disk to catch the drippings from wet umbrellas.

A white marble fireplace with a mirror above it, and an iron basket full of gas doughnuts in the fireplace, completed the room. Although opening on the shaded porch, the room was well-lighted for it extended the width of the house, and a bay window did the rest.

The entire house was heated in the winter time by gas stoves. In the summer they were removed and cleaned and stored away. On the windows were wooden shutters, painted brown. In hot weather these were closed; and in the semi-darkness, the heat seemed less.

It was small wonder that Ben Judson thought Frank was a rich man.

This morning was market morning and Frank had returned from downtown with his wagon loaded with fine vegetables and fruit. As he unloaded his wagon, he was not absolutely the happiest man in his end of town by a long shot. Grace Morrison was pregnant again. This was her third baby since Jack, and every time there had been a coolness in Mary. It had been nowhere near as bad as the first time, but suspicion had put a chill over the house, nevertheless. On the two previous occasions the babies had been dark-haired girls. He hoped his luck would still hold.

"Runaway!" The shout was echoing down the street. Frank ran to see. Far up the street and coming like the wind was a runaway horse, pulling a dairy wagon. People were scattering in all directions, and drivers pulled their rigs to the roadsides, so as to leave the runaway all the street possible.

Frank had seen runaway horses before, but there was something about this one that was different. The horse was a large black. The wagon was bouncing behind him, with the rear wheels slewing from side to side. There was no driver, and the lines were run through the front window and hanging from the ceiling inside. Past the store, fairly flying, went the horse.

Nearly a block down the street was a heavy tired dray, loaded with steel rails for the car tracks, going in the same direction as the runaway. The driver neither heard nor saw the black, bearing so rapidly down on him. He was in the middle of the street and stayed there. As the horse passed the dray on the right side, the rear wheels slewed to the left, locking with the right rear wheel of the dray.

There was a tremendous crash. Wheels, milk cans, and wreckage flew twenty-five feet into the air as the wagon disintegrated. As Frank watched he saw the big black, feet uppermost sail through the air and land on his back, roll over and over, finally knock down a picket fence and disappear from sight.

Frank was halfway to the scene before the horse landed the first time, which is not bad for a man as unused to running as he was. Coming up to the picket fence, now reduced to kindling wood, Frank saw the horse climb to his feet. The horse spread himself and shook violently. Stray bits of harness fell to the ground. He sniffed the grass on the lawn and began to eat.

By leading him around the lawn in a circle, Frank assured himself that the horse was in all respects whole, and only superficially damaged. Then he surveyed the wreckage.

The driver of the dray appeared to have wet himself. The huge draft horses had merely stopped and watched things fall around them. One wheel was still rolling half a block away, while another spun itself out like a top in the road. A mound of butter lay heaped by a bursted ten gallon can.

A buggy raced up to the scene and stopped. A man jumped off, surveying with dismay the scene before him. Frank eased over to him.

"This your rig?"

"Yes," said the man blistering the air with his profanity.

"Too bad you wrecked your wagon and lost your butter," commented Frank.

"Butter," snorted the man, "when that son of a bitch ran away all I had was cream."

"Tell you what I'll do," said Frank. "I'll trade you horses sight unseen."

"If you got anything that'll burn hay, you done made a swap!"

Frank was elated. It had been so easy! He took the horse by the forelock and led him, bruised and limping up the street. Behind him strode the dairy man, still breathing forth sulphurous fumes.

Mary had seen the runaway from inside the store and her heart dropped when she saw this big lack-brained man of hers leading the horse up the street. From the satisfied look on his face, she knew he made another swap. This time Mary was afraid.

"What have you done?" she asked, knowing full well.

"I made me a swap, sight unseen with this man."

"Oh, you didn't," she said walking beside him and holding his arm.

"Yes, he did, ma'am," said the horse's former owner. He had been looking at Maude, and what he saw pleased him. He felt he had made a good trade. At least she looked sleepy enough to not run away.

"You wouldn't hold him to a swap like that would you?" Mary asked him.

"Lady, he's a grown man. When he opens his mouth and words come out, he's responsible for 'em. I'm going to unhitch my horse."

On Frank's face was a grin from ear to ear. He took the harness as it came off Maude and put it on this black. He was still adjusting it when the man walked off with Maude.

Mary sat on the steps to the front porch and watched him. Calista stared from inside the store, while Myrtle draped herself over the porch railing and ate a string of licorice.

"Frank, why did you do it?" Mary could not for the life of her see why he would trade a perfectly lady-like horse for this wild son of Satan.

"Mother," he crooned to her soothingly, "did you see this horse run away?"

"Yes."

"Have you ever seen other horses run away?"

"Yes. Yes. Yes. Don't be so confounded mysterious. What about it?"

"Mary, when horses run away, they break and gallop. They run blind and wild. Did you notice Fred?"

"Fred?"

"I just named my horse."

"Oh! No, I didn't notice anything."

"He was trotting as pretty and smooth as a race horse. He wasn't running away. He was taking him a morning run for the fun of it."

"But he was going so fast, Frank," she moaned.

"Wasn't he though?"

"Pa," said Myrtle in a gratey voice she was affecting this week, "he'll run away with you, too. If you aren't careful, he'll split you clear to the neck."

Frank laughed.

"Of course, he'll run away with me, but not more than five or six times he won't. I know that for sure, Myrt."

"A horse," said a solemn voice from the store, "is made to do man's will."

"Clisty, a man only tries to make a horse do his will. Some are awful stubborn, but this big fellow I guarantee won't like running away."

"Frank, it's your life we are worried about." He walked over to Mary and whispered into her ear. She didn't get it, so he repeated it. She tried to slap him, but he grabbed her hand, put it back of her, and pulled her to him. Kissing her smack on the lips several times, he let her arm go and she put it around his neck.

"Clis," grated Myrtle, "ain't love wonderful?"

"Love," said Clis, "is made in Heaven."

Fred gradually healed his wounds and showed no inclination to run away the first week, nor the second, but that third week—!

Frank was delivering groceries on Streator Street and as usual set the brake before he climbed down from the wagon, lines in hand. The lines he tied around a spoke of the wheel, near the hub. With his basket of groceries on his arm, he started up the side walk.

Fred watched him on his way and then playfully reared on hind legs, and made several tremendous kangaroo hops, as a stylish preliminary to this runaway. As the front wheel turned, the lines wound themselves around the hub. They were new and stout. As they wound up Fred found his head being pulled back farther and farther.

The rear wheels being locked screeched on the dry cobblestone pavement, and heads popped from windows and doorways to watch. By now Fred was standing about upright, but the steady turn of the wheel forced him to sit down on his haunches, forefeet pawing the air like a puppy begging a morsel from the dinner table. On the seat sat Curly, watching.

Frank put his basket down, but otherwise made no move. Fred's tongue draped slavishly from the corner of his mouth, and slapped against his cheek. Into his mouth you could have put a watermelon, but by now Fred had quit pawing.

Frank watched tickled pink with the whole procedure. He made no move to untangle the horse—just stood there. Mrs. Kennedy Johnson came running up to him, paring knife in hand.

"Mr. Stone, aren't you going to help him?"

"Mrs. Johnson that horse got hisself in that fix and I aim to see if he can get hisself out of it."

After about five minutes Frank took hold of the wheel and slowly unwound the lines. When there was complete slack, Fred stood up. His mouth, however, wouldn't quite close and his tongue draped from it thick and purple. He was very delicate about moving his neck and stood as docile as a lamb.

The memory of horses being what it is, Fred decided to pull another shenanigan the next day. Frank was out of sight in the rear, probably passing the time of day with some good lady, or tasting her root beer.

146

This time Fred put his head down and charged ahead. The lines again wound up and the brass rings on the back pad popped from their moorings. Fred had taken a nasty jar when the slack had gone. Now he backed and the loose lines fell to the ground and got between Fred's forefeet. He charged ahead again. Again, the lines wound up but Fred was under a full head of steam. His head went down, down and back. The hold back strap on the breeching broke and Fred wound himself back against the whiffle tree. His head was now between his legs, and still being wound back. Fred kicked at the wagon now so tight against his rump, and found himself sitting, tail to the dash on the shafts. His hind feet were a good six inches clear of the ground, while his head lay flat against his belly.

How long he was in that position, Frank didn't know. He unwound him by climbing on the wagon and kicking off the brake. Fred's forefeet braced as they were, backed the wagon down, and unwound his head. It took Fred a good ten minutes to recover and it was several days before he felt inclined to twist his neck to see what was happening beside him or astern.

Several weeks passed. Frank was hitching Fred to the wagon for a late delivery. He had him in the shafts and was busy putting the finishing touches to the tugs when an apple sailed through the air from over beyond the little house next door. It fell short but Fred took fright. The lines were still on the harness. Going like a streak Fred dashed out the drive. As he passed the porch he suddenly remembered. All four feet landed in a sliding stop. The wagon slewed halfway around, but Fred had stopped cold.

"God A'mighty," thought Fred, "two more jumps and I would have been turned inside out." He would have been, too, because just then a firewagon drawn by three white horses charged past the driveway.

Frank knew that some mischievous boy had heaved the apple and would likely do so again. He hid in the bushes behind the apple tree and tried for weeks to catch the little devil, but without success. Apples, sticks and stones continued to fall. Once Frank got close enough to the kid to identify him, and if it had been anybody other than Wallace Willard, Cake's youngest boy, he'd have gone to his father.

He contrived intricate traps, but either the kid was too wary, or didn't show up. Just as Frank would settle down, there would be a thump and Fred would rear up and snort, but he never ran away. A shirt tail would flap in the breeze and young Cake would be gone.

One day Frank was telling his troubles to old Ben Judson. Ben listened and finally said, "If it was me, Frank, I'd catch the kid."

Frank was silent as he whittled a toothpick. He looked Ben squarely in the eye and said solemnly, "Ben, trying to catch that boy is like trying to catch you a fart in a skillet."

CHAPTER XIX

IN THE CLUTCHES OF THE LAW

In the years that had gone, both Frank and Mary had written to their relatives occasionally. Lyde and Taylor were doing well and they sent their love. Mary's mother wrote that times were hard, but that all was well. She was glad to know they were rich. Father Xavier had written for her as he always did.

But this summer another letter came from Grandma Parker. This time there was trouble. "Mary," wrote Father Xavier for her, "it is with sadness that I tell you of the death of your sister Marvinia, and her husband. Marvinia died of a fever and John fell dead scarcely a week later of a heart illness. The children are with me, but I have scarcely enough food or room in my poor house. Will you take your sister's children into your new home and care for them? They are so sweet and anxious to remain all together. Victor is fourteen now, Vilas twelve and little Blanche almost eleven. I am sure they would be a great help to you and they need a home." Grandma Parker added a little more about the rest of the family and hoped soon to hear from her.

Mary read and reread the letter many times. Surely, they had the room, but what would Frank say? Three children whom they had never seen, all about the same age as their own—

"Frank, I received a letter from home today."

"Everybody fine, I hope."

"No. Here, read it."

He took the letter and slowly read it aloud. When he finished, he looked at Mary's worried and anxious face. He knew what worried her. This was as much his home as hers, but these were her folks that needed help. He knew what she would have said if they had been his.

"Have you packed you a suitcase?"

"Do you mean I can have them?"

"Mary, you can have the whole kit and kaboodle, and I'm as happy to have poor Marvinia's children as you. Get you a new suitcase and go on up there to Hopkinton. When you come home, me and the kids may have things mixed up some, but not hurting too bad."

She pushed him into a chair and sat on his lap, as she had done so many times before.

"Do you know it costs a lot of money to outfit three children with new shoes and new clothes?"

"Them children will be worth more than any shoes they wear out. Get us those children and the old lady, too, if you are a mind to."

"I did find the best man in the world here in Ohio. Mind you, Frank Stone, you are a sinner, just like Reverend Cake says, and more he doesn't know about, but you have something most people don't have and never will have."

"I reckon it's my everlastin' beauty you're mentioning now."

"No, Frank, you are different."

"Of course, I'm different, Mary. I am a Bullhorn Reukus."

"What is a Bullhorn Reukus?"

"That is a something that you don't know exactly what it is, but you need you a name for it."

"Frank there is no doubt about it. You certainly are a Bullhorn Reukus."

Mary didn't bother to write any letters. Like most women she had to have a new dress before she would stir. She and Mrs. Orchards went around for the next few days with mouths full of pins, and planning on which children should go where. The whole household was in a fever of excitement over the new cousins Mother was going after.

At length, the day came when Mary was to leave. Frank took her to the train in his spring wagon and more than ever he felt a need for a buggy. Mary was so excited she wouldn't have cared if she had been riding a dump wagon. Soon she was on her way, armed with tickets and money, but before she left, she gave Frank last minute instructions on everything from feeding the dog, to seeing for sure that Myrtle washed her feet before going to bed. The train pulled out and Frank was alone for the first time since he had been married. He felt lonesome already. So as not to waste the trip to town, he went down to the market and bought a load of produce. The kids were running the store with old Ben Judson sitting in, lest they need help.

As he neared the store he saw the flit of a shirt tail beyond the saloon. It looked familiar and Frank had an inspiration. As he turned into the drive, he stepped off the wagon. Fred walked on back to the barn, unaware that the driver was gone.

Frank, too, went down the lot line the other side of the saloon, and there gathering apples was Wallace Willard, his back to Frank. The kid stayed behind the elderberry bushes, so that they would screen him from the sight of anyone in the Stone yard. Frank hid in the bushes, until the boy let fly his first apple which fell short. As he pulled back to fire again, Frank grabbed him from the rear. An agonized look of terror on the lad's face gave Frank a deal of satisfaction, but he didn't intend to stop there.

"Let me go!" squealed the boy.

"After me having so much fun catching you?" Frank laughed menacingly and turkey trotted young Willard over to where Fred had stopped.

"I'll tell my father on you!"

Frank said nothing, but took the buggy whip from its holder on the dash. He had surely never used it on a horse, but it was there, perhaps just for such an occasion as this.

"You won't like this, Mr. Willard, but if your pa had tended to you, the neighbors wouldn't have to."

"No!" screamed the boy, and he started to yell like someone was skinning him, before Frank ever laid the whip to him. Starting down near the knees, Frank laid the whip on all the way up the lad's setter. If there had been a doubt that this was Cake's boy, it was entirely dispelled when he pulled out all the stops and really yelled. Leaping and turning as he did, he made an elusive target. Frank had a good hold on his wrist and he could not get away. There had been dust in young Williard's breeches at the start, but none came out when the last lick was struck.

"Now, you go home and tell your pa," said Frank releasing the boy, who took off down the drive, still yelling like a red Indian.

"You tanned him good," said Myrtle who had been watching the show.

"Didn't I though?"

"He'll tell his pa." Myrtle somehow sensed trouble. "Can you lick his pa?"

"I can lick three like his pa at once," confidently observed Frank.

Within Frank the purring machine was working. Contentment and satisfaction were there in quantity, but mirth was there, too. In Frank's memory was the look on the little devil's face as he was caught.

Sleeping peacefully on the porch swing after dinner, his hat over his face and his hands clasped over his stomach, Frank felt someone shake him.

"Umm-m-ph," he said.

"Daddy," said Calista, "the police are here!"

"Police!" Frank lifted his hat. Calista's white face had the look of tragedy imbedded in it. He sat up, and there on the porch was Mike Corder, the policeman whose beat included the corners.

"Hello, Mike, have a chair." Frank motioned to a rocker, badly worn, but good enough for out here.

"Mr. Stone, I have a warrant for your arrest."

"Assault and battery?"

"Yes."

"Mike, I figured I'd be arrested."

"What did you do?"

"I lambasted Reverend Cake Willard's boy, Wallace."

By now Myrtle, Howard, Calista and three fourths of the neighborhood children were standing around.

"I got to take you over to the station house," said Mike, pulling his helmet off his face a little.

"No need of walking," said Fred, "wait 'til I hitch Fred to the spring wagon and we'll ride."

"I got the Black Maria," said Policeman Corder unhappily. "I hate to take you in, Mr. Stone, but orders—"

"Tut! Tut! Man—I never rode in one before."

They walked out to the front followed by the crowd of youngsters. Grown-ups were stopping now to see the excitement.

"Well, Johnny Jordan," exclaimed Frank, "I haven't seen you in ages. How's the missus?" Jordan sat on the driver's seat. He looked embarrassed.

"Fine horses you got there."

"First class," said Jordan.

"I never drove a four-in-hand. How does it go?"

"It's easy," said Mike getting an idea, "would you like to drive?"

152

Jordan effusively seconded the motion and Frank and Mike climbed up. Frank took the reins and shook them and the horses started off. Frank turned around by cramping hard to the left and they were off down the street at a trot.

"Whoa!" Frank pulled up on the lines and the horses stopped. "After I post my bond, do I get a ride home?"

The two policemen looked at one another. Hitherto, all rides in the Black Maria had been one way. They had never heard of anyone asking for a repeat performance, but they said they guessed there was nothing in the book against it.

As Frank climbed down after driving to the jail at Doan Street north of Euclid, he saw a little girl about Myrtle's size get out of the paddy wagon. It was Myrtle.

"Myrt, where did you come from?"

"In there," said she pointing to the wagon. "It was fun."

"It was," said the daddy, "wasn't it?"

They entered the building and it was like Old Home Week. He knew most of those he saw, because they were either customers, or old friends of the square dance era.

"What you in for, Frank?" they asked.

"I whaled the dust out of Cake Willard's brat," he answered.

Frank was urged for details and told his story while Myrtle flirted outrageously with the policemen.

Eventually, Frank posted bond and was told the trial would be held at ten o'clock the next morning. The return trip was made as before with all four on the wide driver's seat.

The judge brought his gavel down.

"Frank Stone, Cedar Avenue grocer, charged with assault and battery."

"Where is Frank Stone?" asked the judge.

"Right here," said Frank, walking through the gate and up to the judge.

"How do you plead?"

"Not guilty." In the room were all of Frank's barbershop friends. Ben Judson, Cake Willard and a dozen or two others from the neighborhood.

"Do you have counsel?"

"No. I don't need none."

"Very well," said the judge, "proceed with the case."

153

"Your Honor," said a clerk, "this man horsewhipped another man's son. He dragged the lad by brute force to his own yard and there brutally whipped the boy."

"Where is the boy?" asked the judge.

"Right here. Wallace Willard!" Cake and the boy came forward. Cake's face was blank and set, the boy's frightened.

"Is it necessary to swear in a minor?"

"I guess not," said the judge.

"Are you Wallace Willard?"

"Yes," trembled the boy.

"Were you horsewhipped?"

"Yes."

"By whom?"

"Mr. Stone."

"Do you know Mr. Stone?"

"Yes."

"Is he in this room?"

"Yes, over there." The lad pointed at Frank.

"Why did he whip you?"

"I don't know." Wallace looked at the floor.

"That will be all, unless Mr. Stone wishes to question the witness."

"Don't mind if I do," said Frank. He got to his feet and looked at the witness. He felt sorry for the boy. "Wallace," he said, "you had something in your right hand when I caught you. What was it?"

"An apple." His voice was so low it could scarcely be heard.

"What were you going to do with it?"

The lad looked at his father, who stared coldly back at him. He gulped once or twice and then said, "I was going to eat it."

"In your other hand, you had several more apples. Were you going to eat those, too?"

"Yes."

"Why didn't you eat the one you threw over in my yard?"

For answer the child started to cry. Frank sat down. Wallace left the stand and his father took it. After the usual preliminary questions, the judge asked him to describe the condition he found his boy in after the whipping.

"The boy's body was a welter of welts and bruises," said the pastor. "From the back of his knees to his shoulders were livid red welts." The boy, he testified, was hysterical. He pictured the distraught mother with tears in her eyes as she looked at her son, now a mass of tattered tendons and frayed muscles. He described his own feelings and those of the neighbors. He was about to deliver a sermon on capital punishment, but was headed off, and turned over to Frank to question.

"Reverend Willard, you got your idee that young Wallace came home a welter of welts, whatever that is. This happened yesterday. Let's have the boy up here and examine him. Seems like he'd have a few welts still to show on his back, if they was so bad yesterday."

The Reverend hadn't expected this, and he knew he had been making his story good—a little too good. The welts were in the boy's pants.

"I should not care to undress my boy before the public."

"The judge has got him a back room somewheres," suggested Frank.

"No," said Cake, "never!"

"That's all from me," said Frank, "as far as he's concerned."

"Have you anyone else to call?" the judge asked Cake.

"No—I'm through."

"Mr. Stone, will you take the stand and tell us your side?"

"Don't mind if I do."

Frank was sworn in. He took the stand, crossed his legs and faced the judge.

"I licked the youngster, all right, but I done it in self-defense."

The judge never batted an eye, but he was the only one that did not.

"I got me a young and skittish horse. He's a good horse but lively. One day an apple came from somewhere and the horse took fright and started to run away, but didn't really go far or damage anything. Every few days rocks and stones came flying over, and the horse would shy, or rear up, and by the time I got him quiet again, the shirt-tailed young-un that throwed the stuff was a couple of blocks down Cedar. I spent weeks trying to catch the little devil.

"Yesterday I saw this shirt tail whip around the corner and so I let the horse go into the yard by hisself. I got me over into the bushes of my place next door and there was Wallace picking him up a load of apples. He sneaked back of the bushes and

155

hove an apple over in the yard, but it didn't go far enough to scare Fred. He pulled back, and right there was where I grabbed him.

"I rustled him over into the yard and got me a buggy whip and I tanned his hide for him. I put every lick on the spot that the Lord provided for such things and, Judge, just between you and me, that's the first good licking the boy ever had."

"How do you figure the self-defense angle?" asked the judge.

"What's to keep Fred from tramping me to death if the boy keeps it up? I got no guarantee he won't do it."

"Was the boy on your property?" asked the judge.

"He was off it about ten feet, but them was my apples he was stealing." Frank paused. "Of course, if he had of eaten them instead of giving them back to me, I could of arrested him for stealing."

"Are you through, Mr. Stone?"

"Yes."

"Step over here in front of me. Mr. Willard, bring the boy and come here."

They were lined up in front of him. Every ear in the little room was straining to hear what was said.

"Frank Stone, I find you guilty of assault and battery. I am fining you five dollars and costs, totalling ten dollars and thirty cents."

The judge took off his glasses and shook them at the father. "This whipping will do more to teach Wallace the rights of others than several Sunday school lessons. If Wallace ever annoys Mr. Stone again, he should swear out a warrant for you and the boy," he looked around the room. The gavel rose and fell.

"Next case," said the judge.

CHAPTER XX

MARY RETURNS—THANK GOD

In the two weeks that Mary was gone, Frank made several important discoveries. One was that drummers were highly entertaining people and that there were a few things that needed doing so badly that it was a shame to neglect them longer. He was entertained in the saloon next door no more than forty-five minutes before he saw the wisdom of having his name put on the plate glass window at a very nominal expense, since gold leaf was now relatively cheap. It required two hours in the same establishment, plus a deal of persuasion, before he signed the contract for the establishment of a canvas awning on a pipe frame, with a crank to raise and lower it, across the entire front of the store.

After these improvements had been made, Frank admired them greatly. He decided it would be the better part of good judgment to have an awning, to match, the entire length of the porch. This, too, was done.

Frank and Howard admired the effect of all this from across the street where they could get a proper perspective. There was no doubt about it. The green-and-yellow-striped awnings did something for the place. They gave it a touch of elegance, like the highly polished doors on the saloon next door. No one could look upon the Stone Grocery now, and not know that it was prosperous.

Frank was proud of himself. It had been so easy. The lettering could be paid for in thirty days and the awnings in three months.

"Daddy," said Howard, "Mother will have a catfit."

This astounded Frank.

"How in the world can she find anything to yell about in that?" he asked the boy. "It's pretty as a speckled pup!" For a minute he considered Mary's reaction, and there was a possibility she might not care for the expense, but she would see everything in the proper light when the facts were laid before her.

Thus reassured by logic, Frank decided it was time to get a family rig of some sort. Imagine Mary's surprise when he would meet her in a shiny new carryall! He went to see the Hammond Buggy people. He dickered for, rode in, and finally selected a high-wheeled trap, and it only cost one hundred and ten dollars, payable in thirty days.

The trap was beautiful beyond description. Its four wheels were rubber tired. Its panelled body and curving well under the front seat allowed a sharp turn. It was graceful and ornate. All entrance was through the front seat, the right half of which folded neatly out of the way, permitting entrance to the rear. Here a seat extended across the vehicle at the back which could comfortably seat three persons. Two folding seats could be let down from the sides just behind the front seat.

The upholstery was of horsehair with green corduroy. On the floor were carpets, and hanging from each side of the front seat were two huge kerosene lamps with bright reflectors. The trap was suspended lightly on long curved springs and was a marvel of smoothness. It was a fair weather rig, for there was no top, but that was no drawback as far as Frank could see. The shiny black enamel paint, the yellow scrollwork and the red curving shafts, made it a joy to behold.

The morning Mary was expected back, all was in readiness. Even so, Frank was up at sunrise to wipe off the dust, to add a dab of grease here and to polish a harness buckle there. Fred, all shiny from a long grooming, was backed into the shafts and hitched. His huge head and large ungainly body looked fairly respectable, but he still looked like a delivery horse. His long legs were the only clue to the speed he had shown the day Frank got him. Fully two hours ahead of time, Frank set out for the station.

He had long wanted to run the measured mile with this horse, but no horse can pull a heavy delivery wagon in a speed trial. Frank eased over on to Sibley Street and let Fred warm up slowly. The horse was anxious to run and was held back by a stiff rein.

A block from the mile post, a huge man in a gig, driving a sleek, racy, chestnut gelding, pulled alongside. The man was conspicuously dressed in a black and white checked coat with cap to match. The trousers were a solid gray. Out of the corner of his mouth drooped a badly chewed cigar. He held up a bill.

Frank patted his hip pocket to make sure his purse was there. In it was fifteen dollars, carefully hoarded against just such a moment. With a graceful wave of acceptance, he eased Fred out a bit. As they neared the post they were even for a fair start.

"Go!" roared the man, laying the whip lightly to the chestnut. Fred felt the check fall from the lines and uncertainly stepped out. A slight flick of the bitter end of the lines across his rump was all that he needed to really get himself going. The chestnut had about a length lead in the first several hundred yards.

Once that lead was erased Fred was never headed. He crossed the finish line thirty yards to the good. Frank slowed him to a jog and then a walk, before stopping entirely.

The man in the checked coat came up alongside.

"This is the first time in six months I've had to eat dirt," he said. Climbing from his rig, he handed Frank the bill. Frank pushed it in his waistcoat pocket. He was flushed with pride and pleasure. "That skate doesn't look like he could run like that."

"First time ever I run him," said Frank.

"Would you consider an offer on him?"

"No," said Frank, "I got no idee of selling him."

"Good luck," said the man, and whipped up and turned over toward Euclid.

Fred trotted along on the smooth road. Reaching in his pocket, Frank pulled out the bill and holding it delicately in his fingertips, he kissed it. "Gold from Californy—diamonds from Africy— I wouldn't trade Fred and this here bill for all put together." Then his eyes bugged out. This was a hundred dollar bill!

"Lord God A'mighty! Lord God A'mighty!"

Frank turned around and went back to Willson Avenue and then to Lexington Avenue where he paid the Hammond Buggy Works one hundred and ten dollars, cash money. He pocketed his receipt and continued to the depot.

At the station Frank hunted up the agent and told him he was an old railroader himself. They ended up by discussing railroading as it had been in the old days, before automatic couplers, safety valves and suchlike had made it child's play. "Them were the good old days," was the verdict.

159

The train came in. There was Mary, her face dirty, and tired as she could be. Close behind her were the children, a little scared and a little awed by it all.

"Mary!"

She saw him and waved. Soon they were together.

"I thought you'd never get back. Are these our children?"

"Yes, Frank. This is Victor. This is Vilas and here is Blanche."

"How do you do, Uncle Frank," they said.

"Mary! They talk English! I expected a bunch of Frenchies."

"Everyone is talking English upstate now—except the old people."

"Bless my soul—I expected 'em to sound like furriners." To the children, he said, "Has your Aunt Mary been stringing you along about Cleveland?"

They shyly said they didn't know.

"How much luggage you got?"

"It's all here," said Mary, pointing.

Frank picked up the two largest suitcases and Victor took the third. Several bundles were assorted between the rest. Frank led the way.

"Here we are," he said, watching Mary out of the corner of his eye.

"Frank!" She looked sternly at him.

"What's the matter, Mother?"

"This rig—whose is it?"

"Why—it's ourn."

Mary said nothing, but there was misgiving in her heart. The children's eyes were as round as saucers. Uncle Frank and Aunt Mary must be really rich. Once they were loaded in, Fred started off at a brisk pace.

"Frank, is this buggy ours really?"

"Yes," he said.

"How much did it cost?"

"One hundred and ten dollars," he said.

She echoed, "One hundred and ten damn dollars."

"Take a look at this." He fished out the receipt.

"Paid for!"

"You're blamed well right."

"Have you been spending money from the store?"

"Mary, you know people don't pay up this time of the month.

160

I haven't touched a penny from the store."

"How?"

He pretended not to hear, but she insisted. They were talking low so the children wouldn't hear.

"If I told you, you would know as much as me," he finally said. "I am quite a hand at fie-nance."

Mary subsided, but she was apprehensive. From far down the street she saw the awning. The porch awning was not visible then, but when it came into view, Mary could contain herself no longer.

"What have you done?" she wailed.

"I have got us some shade."

"But how? You have spent a mint of money."

Frank smiled broadly. It was all so simple. Women were such children when it came to money matters. "Wait and see!"

Pulling up to the front porch, Frank cramped the wheels and unloaded his passengers. Myrtle saw them first and loudly announced their arrival. Calista, Howard and several neighbor children came on the run.

"Children," said Mary, "these are your cousins." She introduced them to one another, but for the most part they just stared. Finally, Myrtle broke the ice. Pointing to Vilas, she said, "I can lick you."

"Oh, Mother," said Calista, "while you were away guess what happened?"

"What?" asked Mary.

"Daddy got put in jail!" shouted Myrtle.

Chapter XXI

FRANK ADMITS HE IS WITHOUT SIN

While Frank dug an occasional nugget from his new-found gold mine, he found himself generally too busy with work that must be done, to prospect correctly. This irked him. One day he made a discovery that solved everything. The trap wheels fit the spring wagon perfectly, and a trial run over the mile at six o'clock the next market morning proved that Fred could handle this rig as easily as the trap itself. Thereafter Frank altered his plan of work and went to market between the hours of eight and ten in the morning, and the awnings and gold leaf were paid for promptly.

Fred seemed to watch his opponents out of the corner of his eye and would win, but by not too great a margin. Sometimes it appeared that had the course been a furlong longer, or even a few yards, Fred would have been licked. He ran this type of race regardless of the speed of his opposition. Frank's job seemed to consist of making the bets and collecting his winnings. They worked perfectly together and had one additional advantage—the horse did not look fast and his master did not look too canny.

Mary had been unable to solve the riddle of his purchases, or to find a deficit in the books. Nor could she get any clue from Frank. She began to get leads from various other directions.

Mary and Calista were doing the family laundry. Calista was turning down the sleeves and searching the pockets of the shirts in the wash. As she searched one of Frank's, she drew forth a bill from a pocket.

"Mother-r! Look what I found in Daddy's pocket!"

"A bill?" asked her mother.

"Five dollars!"

Mary examined it, but it was like any other crumpled five dollar note.

162

"Look in the other pocket," Mary suggested.

Calista did so and brought forth a wad of five one dollar bills. Mary and Calista stared at one another, nonplussed. They knew Frank well enough to know he was usually insolvent, or almost so. Where then, did he get this money, and leave it around so carelessly? A search of all his dirty clothes brought to light a ten dollar bill, which was found in a pants watch pocket.

"Mother!"

Mary sat on the cellar stairs, chin in hand. The trap, the awnings, the lettering and now this—could it be that her husband had held money out through the past years? As she considered, she laughed. No that couldn't be.

"Mother, he has robbed a bank!"

"Nonsense!"

"Where did this ill-gotten gain come from?"

"I don't know, but I'm going to find out."

Frank was out making his morning round of deliveries, as Mary climbed the stairs. She opened the closet door and tossed his clothes on the bed. She searched every single garment without success, until she picked up an old vest that had fallen to the floor in the closet, and had not been ejected with the original consignment. Four of its six pockets yielded loot, fifty-five dollars in all.

Mary swore Calista to secrecy and put the money in the back of the sideboard drawer. Now, if anything, Mary was more puzzled than before. If Frank ever showed concern over its loss, Mary never noticed it.

Some women she knew would search their husband's pants pockets without a morsel of regret, and the pocketbooks were always violated. It took Mary a long time to work herself over to that point of view, but curiosity being what it is, and human nature—female variety—being what it is, she did. Frank slept loudly after his usual busy day. His pants draped from the top of the closet door. She lifted them down and extracted his wallet, and retired to the bathroom, locking the door.

Even in the dark, she had felt its fat and bulging promise, although here in the light she was scarcely prepared for the glitter of wealth that hit her eyes. Money in all denominations lay before her. No attempt had been made to sort it, or, Mary surmised, to count it. She carefully plucked two hundred dollars and put the purse back in his pocket.

As Mary lay beside her sleeping husband, she felt the urge to laugh. This big, dopey man of hers had found a way of making money and was secretly doing it. She knew now that however he was doing it, he would never tell her for fear she would make him quit. As for the money, she would put it with the rest and he could have it, if he ever asked for it.

Frank never knew his pocket had been picked. Perhaps in the next several years, had he stopped enjoying himself long enough to wonder about it, he might have discovered the shortage. That was asking a great deal of the man who owned Fred.

The boys had taken over the chores and did so many odd jobs around the place that Frank found himself with considerable leisure. Mary, too, found time to relax. Calista, Myrtle and Blanche helped in the store, helped in the kitchen, and in general worked wherever they were most needed.

To add a bit of confusion, the Stone home had become a sort of meeting place for most of the youngsters in the neighborhood. Effie and Olive Orchards were generally there, as were Jack and Clara Morrison. Howard had a sweetheart, another Myrtle, and she was one of a large family. Sometimes they would join forces and the walls would seem to bulge.

The bicycle had developed into a vehicle of two wheels of the same size and the craze struck the neighborhood with a hearty impact. The younger members of the family found bicycles as necessary as blood, to guarantee the proper continuation of their existence. Not infrequently were some of both spread over the countryside.

Sunday afternoons formerly were given over to reading the funny papers, napping, or playing pedro with Mr. and Mrs. Sewell, or Mrs. Orchards and Ben Judson. Now all that was gone, for right after dinner the entire younger generation would take off over the countryside on bicycles, to be later met at a spring, or a creek or a park by Frank and Mary. This was no day of rest for Fred. While he only pulled the trap, the older folks and the dinner going out, he usually had a full consignment of people hitching to the trap on the way home.

The Sunday the entire family arose at four o'clock, had an early breakfast, and went to the beach, caused Fred to no more than raise an eyebrow. Many a lesser horse would have taken a less reasonable view of the long flapping bathing suits the boys wore, and the be-legged, be-skirted suits of the girls. Fred merely stood to his hocks in the fine sand and watched.

It was because of this Sunday's deviltry that the Reverend Knight K. Willard called on James Franklin Stone at eight o'clock on Monday morning. Frank as usual at this time of a Monday morning was cleaning the barn.

"Mr. Stone, I have something to talk to you about." The minister was losing no time getting to the point of the matter, even to the extent of overlooking the formalities of greeting—not so Frank.

"Well! Well! Good morning to you," said Frank extending his hand, "how's the missus these days?"

"Well enough," said Cake crisply. "Now, to get down to business."

"I haven't seen you around much. Have you been well?"

"About this matter—"

"This business you mentioned?"

"Yes. I—"

"Well, shoot it out where we can take us a look at it."

"Your children and niece and nephews were not in church yesterday." His face was solemn and disapproval was written plainly.

"Nope, they went to the beach yesterday. Had them a fine time, too. Mary and me had fun just watching them."

"They should have been in church."

"How's that?"

"They belong in church. They owe that much to themselves and the church. Worse than that, your children are very influential in the community, because of their worldly wealth. I can't take that from them, but I can insist that they use their leadership for God's purposes."

"Isn't this the first Sunday they have missed since they had the measles?"

"It makes no difference. A person can be good all his life, miss once, and be a sinner. So with church attendance—people must never fail."

"I'm one gone sinner then, I guess," Frank smiled as though the idea had just occurred to him for the first time. The minister looked at his hands, and plucked a fingernail.

"The worst sin in the world is not attending church," said Cake solemnly. "I say this because there is no hope for a man to find forgiveness for his other sins, if he hears not the word of God. Other sins are taking the Lord's name in vain, worshiping the Demon Rum, wagering money that could be better given to the church, and the others of the Ten Commandments."

"What do you want I should do?"

"Make your children come to church. Come yourself, and give up sin."

"You may have something there I could use," said Frank. "I'll agree to be there next Sunday and we'll see how fast the sin leaks out of me."

Reverend Willard was flabbergasted. He had long ago given up hope of converting anyone, least of all Frank Stone. He left, feeling victorious. The missionary spirit had been reborn.

The sermon that greeted Frank this first Sunday morning was "Lo, The Prodigal Returns," the second "Hark Ye The Warning," the third "The Day of Doom Approaches," and the fourth, if you could trust the bulletin board on the front lawn, was going to be "Repent Ye Sinners."

For three Sundays Frank had listened. For three Sundays Mary had been beside him and they both felt the minister tugging at the bark of sin which clothed them. They attended the fourth Sunday, but without enthusiasm. He was getting, Frank told himself, a belly full. Just as he figured, this sermon was the one which Cake believed would finish the job.

Right after the second hymn Frank's nose began to bleed. It did a pretty thorough job, but Frank sat quietly and held his handkerchief to it, and the flow abated until it practically had stopped. During the sermon Cake laid rough hands on the Devil and chivied him from here to yonder. He developed the theme that there was some good in all of us, but also an unreasonable amount of sin. "Will the man among you stand who is without sin?" His fist pounded the Bible before him and his voice rattled the door.

Holding his bloodsoaked handkerchief so that all could see his life blood, Frank stood. All eyes were upon him, as he made off up the aisle.

When Mary came home, she found him in his old clothes, puttering around the wagon shed. She hustled up to him, breathing fire.

"Frank Stone, why did you do such a thing? I was never so

166

embarrassed in my life, nor so ashamed. If you don't want to go to church that is all right, but if you do go, at least act human!"

"Now, Mary, take it easy."

"I am taking it easy."

"All I did was leave to take care of my nose."

"You could have sat right there and taken care of it, but oh no! You have to wait, until the parson wants to know if there is anyone without sin. Then you must take your nose home to fix it."

"It was all Cake's fault."

"And why was it his fault?"

"He made me do it."

"No one made you do it!"

"He did so—he practically hounded me for years to come, and listen to his brand of fire eatin'. I agree, and you and me go listen to him. We listen to the Prodigal sermon, the Day of Doom, and heavens knows what else. Today was the 'Sinner Ought to Repent' or some such. Every word that Cake has said is levelled right at us."

"Suppose it was? I'm inclined to agree with him."

"And then today he screams like a jaybird that he wants to see a man without sin stand up. If the good Lord himself had been there, he would have kept him his seat, and Cake knew it. He gave me a bad pain in the setter. If Cake had said, 'Let the man amongst you, who stayed to home last night and behaved himself, stand up,' every blessed one would have sat there and looked foolish. A speaker like Cake gets the edge on people, because they are afraid to stand on their feet where people they neighbor with can see them."

"Did that give you the right to walk out?"

"Mary, I had me a bloody nose."

"Don't you dare talk to me until you see Mr. Willard and tell him you are sorry for what you did."

"Mary!"

"You heard me, Frank Stone."

"I won't do it."

"Yes, you will."

"Mary," said Frank, not feeling much anger but anxious to stall for time, "from now on you may consider me a boarder here and nothing more." His tone said this hurt him more than it did her.

Mary looked at this man of hers. She loved him and knew his

goodness, his generosity and his inability to resist teasing people who were pompous. But ministers were not to be toyed with and she meant to cure him of the desire.

"I will not consider you as a boarder," she said, "I am far more careful in selecting my boarders than I was my husband."

Frank laughed. He looked at Mary and laughed again. This time he was being pompous and Mary had turned it on him. There was only one thing to do. He grabbed her and before she knew what he was up to, he had thrown her over his shoulder and was on his way down the drive.

"Frank! What are you going to do?"

"Me and you are going to see Cake."

"Oh! No!"

"Oh! Yes!"

"Put me down."

"Not by a jugful."

"Frank, please, I'll do anything, but not this!"

He lowered her to the ground. They looked at one another, and there was no anger between them. There probably had never been any, for they were kissing one another and laughing.

Chapter XXII

THE PEN IS MIGHTIER

Frank was on his way to market and as usual when the road was dry, he went via the measured mile, and as usual was acting as innocent as a newborn babe. Fred jogged along, ears flapping, when a sleek bay mare came alongside and would have passed. Without a word from Frank, Fred kept pace with her.

"Do you feel up to a little bet?" asked the driver.

"It's agreeable with me," said Frank, but he looked doubtful and said it hesitatingly.

"How much?" asked the other.

"Not over ten," said Frank.

"Make it twenty and it's a race," said the driver.

"If you want it that way, I got me that much," said Frank.

As usual Fred took a half length and held it. At about the three quarter mark Frank was bounced by a hole in the road and lost his balance on the seat. The loose ends of the lines smote Fred sharply on the rear. Never in his life had he been urged like this, so disregarding the mare, he lengthened out and ran for all that was in him. By the time Frank recovered his balance the race was over and Fred had won by a full city block.

"So I fell for Old Simon Pure," mused the man dourly as he handed Frank the twenty dollar bill. "I'll never live it down."

"Thank you kindly," said Frank, stuffing the bill in a vest pocket. "I never saw the old boy run like that. Must have been something he et."

The barroom at the American House, with its marble counter gleaming and its mirrors the full length of the bar, was a busy place. The white-aproned waiters and bartenders kept a steady flow of food and beer going to the large round tables at which ten to fifteen men were sitting, and to the patrons who were

169

standing at the bar. Shining spittoons were placed at convenient intervals on the sawdust-covered floor.

A door at the end of the bar opened into a large room, and when it opened occasionally to let in another customer, it could be seen to be brightly lighted, full of smoke and a very luxurious place. A dozen men sat around the table and one of them was speaking.

"I don't know what you men think about it, but Old Simon Pure has got to be trimmed!" He was a heavy man with impressive jowls. He wore a large stickpin high up on a dark tie that seemed to be choking him. "There isn't a member of the Gentlemen's Driving Club who hasn't made a contribution to the old son of a gun in the last few years."

There was a rumble of assent and a few remarks of an unkind nature.

"Are we sure, Mark, that Old Simon Pure is one man and that the horse is always the same one?" The speaker was a tall thin man who drummed the table with his fingers.

"That is one of the reasons that I have asked you all to meet with me here today. There is some reason to think that Old Simon is one of our own members who is pulling our leg. I'll sum up the reasoning along this line, and after I'm done you lawyers tell me what you think." Mark took a big drink of beer from the stein in front of him, and inelegantly wiped his mouth with the back of his hand. "The first time I raced him was several years ago. I was driving one of my best buggy horses, but certainly not a racer. Simon was driving a large black horse with a white blaze and three white stockings. His buggy was a two seater, but new and rubber tired. He was dressed in a business suit and wore a derby. He looked like a prosperous newcomer to Cleveland. He beat me badly and I ate a peck of Sibley Street dust.

"After that a bunch of you other fellows lost to him. Sometimes he was wearing overalls, and had a light spring wagon, or the same buggy I mentioned. Not one of us ever reported that we had won a race, and I did not think much about it until Bill Gordon here got beat by him when he was driving Clingstone. Clingstone had won the $3,000 feature at Glenville the week before. Bill, can you tell anything more?"

"Not much," admitted Bill Gordon. "I was going to run Clingstone against a stopwatch, when this fellow comes along with this ugly big horse. I figured my horse would make better time if he was in a race, so I challenged the fellow. He didn't look very prosperous to me so I suggested a dollar bet, and he said his horse would run better for five. We took off in a perfect start, but the black pulled out to a strong lead. I never worried about his early foot, until I gave Clingstone his head and tried to catch him. Then I discovered we had given too much away, and we could never overtake him. Cling's time was 2:14, and we lost by fifty feet."

"Has anyone ever seen this horse around the racetrack?" asked another man.

"I have never seen that horse except on Sibley," said Mark, "Have any of you seen him anywhere else?" There was a general negative shaking of heads. "There's your answer, Colonel Edwards. If he does any racing or training, it has to be at some fairgrounds or out in the country."

"Why do you think he might be one of our members?" asked another.

"I was getting around to that," replied Mark. "For one thing, where is an ordinary person going to get a horse that can run like that except from a dealer in race horses? Reason number two is that he will cover any bet regardless of size without batting an eye. Reason number three, at least twice and maybe oftener, he has won his race, and then swung on down South on Perry Street without waiting to be paid off on the bet."

"I hadn't heard about him not getting paid," said Bill Gordon. "Who lost and didn't have to pay off?"

"John D. Rockefeller!"

"My gosh," laughed Bill, "and him the one person in town who has a private railroad siding at the mint!" There was a laugh and a few wise remarks, but John D., the thin man who had spoken earlier, only smiled.

"Now let's hear from Judge Rufus Spalding. What do you make of Old Simon Pure, Judge?" Mark took another drink from the mug, and again used the back of his hand as a napkin.

"Obviously he is a man of means," said the Judge. "He is also a man who is at heart a sportsman. He is also a practical joker. This is the sort of thing Tom Johnson would like to do, but he couldn't get away with it. I don't think your man is a member of the Gentlemen's Driving Club who is wearing a disguise. He is probably one of your neighbors, who is enjoying his little joke." The Judge paused long enough to wash down a bit of pretzel with his beer. "If I were to make a guess, I'd say to watch your Euclid Avenue sleigh races. He'll show up there, too."

"We thought we had him a year or so ago at the sleigh races," said Mark. "This fellow showed up at the starting line at Case Avenue, and I got into the same heat with him, but by the time we got to Erie Street, I knew we had the wrong man. The horse wasn't a pacer, and wasn't very fast at that."

There was a hum of individual discussions, as the various members talked the matter over. Finally Mark banged the table with his beer stein. "Listen fellow, listen!" When quiet was restored, he continued. "Brother J. B. Perkins has an idea. Want to tell them about it, Perk?"

"My idea is this—let's get Maude S, hitch her to a buggy and lay for Old Simon Pure. All we want to do is beat him at his own game."

There was a general chorus of agreement.

"How are we going to work it," asked one of the members. "Old Simon is pretty cagey and only shows up every so often. What I mean is he doesn't overdo it."

"Still he does show up every week or so," replied Mark. "Has anybody ever seen him in the afternoon?"

No one had.

"How about before eight o'clock?"

It was soon decided that the best time to get to meet him was between eight and eleven o'clock. At other times or on a wet day, he had not been seen.

"I'll get Maude S lined up," said Mark Hanna, "but I can't be there every day, and that means we are going to have to take turns laying for Old Simon to show up. You fellows are going to have to help out, but it ought to be a hell of a lot of fun driving Maude S, and if we ever get old so-and-so into a match race with her, it will be one time that we'll knock him off."

"It's a beaut of a plan, but I see one problem," said Judge Spalding with a laugh.

"What problem?" asked Mark.

"Maude S belongs to William Vanderbilt, and she is his pride and joy! What makes you think he will let you take her?"

"I wish all my problems could be settled as easily as that one,"

172

Mark said confidently. "Brother Vanderbilt runs railroads. I control half the freight in and out of this town. Maude S will be ready whenever we are."

Several horses and buggies were in a cluster on Sibley Street, near Willson Avenue, and the men in the buggies were talking earnestly. Every so often they would scan the street behind them. They seemed to be in no hurry, and their horses stamped their feet impatiently.

"It sure beats all how that fellow keeps out of sight!" There was general agreement. The man who had spoken continued, "My boss at the *Plain Dealer* agreed this would make a whale of a story, and I've been here for ten days with you fellows, and we have a photographer at the finish post waiting to get a picture. And this Simon Pure never shows up! I'm afraid the old man back in the office is going to pull me off this story pretty soon."

"Simon is sure to show up soon. I'd say he was overdue right now." The speaker sounded more hopeful than convincing.

Several hours passed. The horses swished their tails at the flies. Conversation lagged. Several horses and rigs turned down Sibley Street, but were all obviously not the outfit they were looking for.

Frank stood back and took an appraising look at Fred. In his hand was a bottle of black shoe polish, liquid style. He had finished applying the polish to Fred's white legs, and now seemed undecided. "Fred, you old son of a gun, I never did black up that white face of yours before. Wonder what you'd look like as a brunette." With that he blacked the white face completely. Apparently satisfied with his artistry, Frank backed Fred into the shafts, hitched him up, drove out of the yard and down Cedar Avenue towards the center of town.

Back on Sibley Street the sun was getting higher and hotter. The reporter looked at his watch, yawned and stretched. "Hell," he said, "I'm going to give up."

"Might as well," replied Mark. Then looking around he saw a horse and spring wagon turn off Willson Avenue at a brisk walk. "Could this be our man?"

"Horse is black," said the reporter.

"Wrong horse," said Mark. "The horse we want has a white face and has white legs."

173

"Yeah, I guess so," agreed the other. As the outfit pulled up along side of them, he spoke to the driver, "I'm going your way, would you like a little fun?"

"What kind of fun?" asked the driver.

"Thought you might like to run the mile for a small bet."

"You got you a nice looking horse there, but maybe I would, if the bet was in my range."

"Five dollars?" asked the reporter.

The driver nodded hesitantly.

"Maybe ten would be better?"

"Can't say that it would," replied the other.

"Don't be a piker! Make it ten!"

"All right," said the driver, "but no more."

"It's a deal then." Looking at Mark, the reporter said, "So long, now. I don't know whether I'll be back tomorrow or not. In case I don't, good luck."

"Damn that lousy coot!" Mark Hanna was grouchy. "Damn him all to hell, anyhow!"

"Well, so long," said the young man, and picking up the buggy whip, he eased his horse away from the curb and started him trotting down Sibley Street toward the starting post.

As they moved down the street Frank gave Fred a slackening on the reins, and the horse responded by lumbering up even with the smoothly trotting bay horse. The start of the race was smooth and even, but at the halfway mark Fred began to take charge, and ended with a powerful run to the finish line. The reporter and his horse was fifty yards behind. Frank pulled Fred to the side of the road and waited.

As Frank twisted around on the seat to wait for his defeated companion, a photographer ran up, set his tripod legs in the lawn of an adjacent home, and disappeared under the black cloth which covered the camera. A few twists on the bellows knob, and he slapped a plate holder into the camera, squeezed a bulb, and took a picture.

The reporter pulled his rig up behind Frank, and jumped out. As he scooted past the spring wagon to Fred's head, he seemed to be extremely intent upon a mission. He wiped a hand across Fred's face and then held up his fingers to get a good look at them. He walked back to where Frank leaned over the side of the wagon, and in somewhat of a daze, handed Frank a ten dollar bill. Then a worse side of his nature seemed to take hold of him.

"You old bastard you," he shouted. "You old bastard! Old Simon Pure! By God I'll get even with you for this, if it's the last thing I ever do! What the hell is your name?"

To Frank, the man seemed to be a mighty poor loser. However, Frank had found that few friendships of lasting duration could be formed when a person was as upset as this man seemed to be, so he pulled Fred away from the side of the road, and started down the street.

"What is your goddamn name?" yelled the other. Over his shoulder, Frank gave answer, went on down to Perry Street, turned left and went to the farmer's market.

Frank had hardly left when Mark Hanna raced up with Maude S. He was half standing as he pulled the horse to a stop. "Was that Old Simon?" he yelled.

"You were never righter," said the writer sadly.

"How do you know?"

Instead of answering, he held his hand up for Mark to see the color of it. "Shoe blacking, or stove polish! He blacked out the white!"

"I'll be damned!"

"Me, too! Ten bucks worth of damnation! Goddamn his ugly hide! I'll get even with him somehow!"

"Ten days I've waited for him, and then let him get away!" Mark's soul was in agony, if the look on his face could be trusted.

"What's the matter with you guys?" asked the photographer. "I got a picture of the guy. Isn't that what you wanted?"

"Hell, no!" said Mark.

"Hell, yes!" said the *Plain Dealer* man. "Let's go develop it, and I'll write my story!"

"Be damn careful what you write," said Mark, "or I'll nail your ass to my barn door."

It was Sunday afternoon and raining. Calista and Effie were in the kitchen washing dishes. Mrs. Orchards and Mary were discussing the relative merits of patterns in a catalog. Myrtle was reading the funny papers. Olive picked a piece out with one finger on the piano, while Blanche tried to help her by humming the tune. Vilas read the sport pages without a great amount of interest, while Frank was upstairs taking a nap.

Suddenly, Vilas sat up straight in his chair. He looked again. "Myrtle, look here!"

"Where, Vile?"

"Here." He pointed with his finger. "Isn't that Uncle Frank and Fred?"

"Yes," said Myrtle, "what's it say?"

"It says 'HORSEMEN BEWARE!' and then it says 'Dastardly Tricks of Old Simon Pure Unmasked by *Plain Dealer* Reporter.'"

"What does it mean?"

"How should I know? I haven't read it yet."

"Read it aloud," ordered Myrt.

Vilas read, "For the past number of years, the name 'Old Simon Pure' has been a byword in Cleveland racing circles. Many of our better known downtown horse fanciers have been racing their horses for small side bets on the smooth stretch set aside for such purposes, on Sibley Street. A legend began to be told about a horse that couldn't be beaten, and the name 'Old Simon Pure' was given to the driver. The horse looked like anything but a racer, the wagon appeared rickety, and the driver looked very innocent and not quite up to city ways. Many horsemen fell for the ruse, but the truth is this horse has beaten many of the fastest horses in Ohio. His victims include such famous horses as Gentleman Jim, Clingstone, Mary's Pride and Tabernacle—all well-regarded horses at the Glenville Race Track. Just how much money in bets he has earned can only be guessed at, but it must have been considerable. In view of the little likelihood of anyone beating this horse, your *Plain Dealer* reporter set a trap for him."

"Gosh!" said Myrtle.

"Wait, there's more."

Vilas read on. "For ten days your reporter and a photographer have lurked on Sibley Street waiting for 'Old Simon Pure' to show up. When he finally did make an appearance the horse's three white legs and white face was colored with shoe blacking to conceal his identity. However, this reporter was not fooled, and coaxed him into a race. Of course your writer lost, but while he was paying the bet, our photographer took his picture.

"When Old Simon Pure realized that he had been discovered, he started to drive away hurriedly. When he was asked his name, he identified himself as Mr. Rutherford B. Hayes, but this hardly seems likely.

"In the meantime, wary horsemen should study the picture on this page, and if they fall a prey after that, they can blame themselves, and not this reporter or his paper."

"Is that all?" asked Myrtle.

"Isn't that enough?"

"Let's show it to Mother."

"Do you think we should?" asked Vilas.

"Sure," said Myrtle, "it's not everybody who gets his picture in the paper."

"But it only shows Uncle Frank from the rear."

"Mother, Daddy's picture is in the paper."

The announcement had the effect of a bomb. Everyone crowded around to see. It took several readings before the idea had finally settled into everyone's mind. To some it was a complete mystery, but to Calista and Mary it was the answer to a lot of questions.

Said Mary, "So that is where he got it! Thank heavens! I thought he had been playing poker on lodge nights."

"The shame of it all!" was Calista's reaction. "Until now, not a breath of scandal was ever connected with the name of Stone."

"I don't know where you been keeping yourself," said Mary with a smile.

"The Power of the Press," that intangible something of which editors brag and are not always so certain exists, never was so thoroughly proved as in the case of "Old Simon Pure." Fred was a marked horse and the veriest newcomer was always warned of impending doom by some well-meaning, anti-racketeering ex-competitor, before Frank could get him past the first mile post. This was discouraging to say the least. There was some pleasure to be had from the reputation and an occasional run against time showed that Fred was ready any time the unwary should come along, but this shadow racing lacked the tang of racing blood, bones and other hooves. So it came about that Fred found himself pulling the big delivery wagon to market oftener. Except for a nostalgic raise of the tail and an inquiring look around, he even learned to pass Silbey Street without heavy pressure on the opposite line.

CHAPTER XXIII

CAN THIS BE LOVE?

"Where is everybody at tonight?" Frank looked at the long white table. There were only three places set.

"There are only three of us to home, Mother and you and I," said Mary, hurtling through the swinging door into the kitchen. When she reappeared Frank spoke.

"Where are the young'uns?"

"They are down at the theatre tonight, working in the cloak room. Vilas is at a church social."

"Why in sin do they want to work nights? Ain't there enough to do here?"

"Children nowadays are different from us, Frank. When the people are all in the theatre, the girls can watch the performers."

"Mary, is that where Clis gets them airs of hers?"

"She reads a lot, but mostly from the stage, I guess."

"What's wrong with young people? They don't swear. They don't dance. They talk solemn and read poetry. The boys like Vile and Howard part their hair in the middle and slick it down with goose grease."

"It's just their way."

"If I hadn't seen them ride bikes, I wouldn't believe they were alive. They all put on airs. Look at Effie—she got her hair combed over some contraption to make it look high in front. Myrt is the nearest human and she laces her belly into where it touches her backbone. Clisty handles a fork like it was about to burst, and has her finger like this." He demonstrated.

"I don't know what's getting into them, but it isn't just our kids."

"You are right there! Little Clara Morrison did a bob of some kind the other night when Vile introduced that friend of his to her. I thought for a fact she was going to squat right on the carpet."

"No, you never!"

"Sure did." He grinned at her.

Mary went into the kitchen for some bread. When she returned, Frank had already seated himself at the table. Mary went into the living room and called her mother. Returning, she sat at his left and took his hand in hers.

"Why doesn't Grandma come to supper?" he asked.

"She has dealt out a round of Pedro and is playing all four hands."

"Oh!"

"Frank, before she comes—have you noticed Jack Morrison lately?"

"I sure have. He spent a couple of hours with me several days ago—no 'twas yesterday." Frank looked at her proudly, "Mary, ain't he a grand boy?"

"Yes, he is. What did he talk about?"

"About horses and buggies, mostly. He said something about studying at Western Reserve to be a doctor, and did I think he'd make himself one."

"What did you tell him?" Mary leaned forward eagerly.

"I told him the world needed good doctors, same as it needed good vets. I didn't see why he shouldn't be a good doctor."

"He doesn't want to be a doctor."

"How do you know?"

"He told Myrt." Mary leaned back and watched Frank closely. Grandma came in and sat down quietly. Frank knew from Mary's manner that she must have told him a secret, but he didn't see it, so he said nothing. Mary squeezed his hand.

"Frank, Jack Morrison is sweet on Myrtle."

"God, no!" Frank was so alarmed that Grandma fretted, but Mary quieted her with a quick smile. "Mary, that can't be!"

"It is true, Frank. He is twenty years old."

"My God, has it been twenty years?"

"Yes, Dad, it has been twenty years." They looked at one another and their thoughts were a long way away. Grandma Parker started to help herself to the supper. She was hungry even if these children were not. So mechanically they followed her example.

"What are you going to do?" Mary knew he didn't know.

"I am going out to the horsebarn and set me down on a bale

179

of straw and think myself out of this mess. Are you sure, Mary?"

"Absolutely."

"Have you got any idee?"

"Not the first one."

"I may have to tell the boy the truth about hisself, but I ain't aiming to do it unless I have to."

"I don't blame you."

"How do you know they are sweet on one another?"

"Frank, the way his eyes follow her around the room, the way he lifts her down from the trap, the way he says, 'Oh, you kid' —there are dozens of ways to tell when a boy is in love."

"Damn me if I'd noticed it. I'll note it now, though."

Mary felt the urge to tease Frank strong upon her, but it was without malice.

"Frank, if you had it to do over, would you play stud to Mr. Morrison's mare?"

He smiled and looked at her out of the corner of his eyes. Without haste he rubbed his ear. What kind of an answer did she want? Did she want him to be sorry for siring this big handsome lad? He didn't think so.

"Mother," he said with a slow shake of his head. "I sure would. The colt does me proud and I got me plenty of time to figure this out."

"You got some time, Frank, but not plenty, meaning more than enough."

"I expect you're right. I got me a job cut out."

CHAPTER XXIV

DRAMA COMES TO FRANK STONE

"Please, pass me the pepper." Frank surveyed the table. It was the first night in several weeks that all the children had been home for supper. Now they were all talking at once and he found it hard to make any sense out of the conversation.

"I liked the part where Helene came on the stage and said, 'For the sake of God and country, go! Go now before some new catastrophe befalls us.' That was wonderful. He fell to his knees and said, 'No, Helene, if I go, you must go, too,' and she said, 'Never! Never! Never!'" In Calista's voice was all the drama of the stage. The third "never" rose in crescendo and slid down the scales like the whistle on Twenty-eight.

"But Helene was so snobbish," objected Myrtle.

"Snobbish? Nothing of the sort," said Calista. "She was noble. She had a noble plan and carried it out, because it was her duty."

"Caringwald didn't have to fall in love with her," said Blanche taking Calista's side.

"Her gracious beauty entranced him," said Clis.

"Pass me the pepper," said Frank.

"The play I liked," said Vilas, "was Bertram and Pinkerton in *The Gruesome Twosome.*"

"A farce!" snorted Calista.

"Rubbish!" agreed the others.

"When Bertram came in balancing the fish bowl in one hand and Lord Billingsford's walking stick and cloak in the other, I thought I'd die laughing."

"There was nothing funny about it. Some people are so crude that they laugh when people trip and fall," mused Blanche.

"Pinkerton tripped him by pulling the rug out from under him, but he was only doing as he was told," explained Vilas.

"That is hick stuff. Only yokels and country bumpkins would be amused." Calista added a fair amount of disdain by inflection.

181

"Mary, pass me the pepper."

"What?"

"The pepper."

"Here you are."

"*The Gruesome Twosome* had no character portrayal like the part of Elizabeth Manning in *The Lord Only Knows*. Elizabeth was on the surface a giddy school girl, but down deep inside her she was a scheming woman."

"So beautiful, too," sighed Myrtle.

"A little large in the hips," said Blanche.

"Oh! I don't know," said Myrtle defensively. "She had a beautiful bosom, and there are lots of people like that."

Blanche retreated, "I suppose so."

"She was fat." This sordid comment came from Vilas who kept his eyes on his plate where he chased a green pea, stabbing at it with his fork.

"You didn't see *The Lord Only Knows*. How can you sit there and say she was fat?"

"Of course, he didn't."

"Such nerve!"

"Howard saw it, and he said she was fat as all get out."

"Vilas Morrow! You awful fibber—Howard did not see it!"

"He sure did. He told me all about it. This Elizabeth was secretly in love with an Earl or a Lord or somebody, and he didn't know it. She found out he was going to marry an heiress for her money. Elizabeth knew he didn't love the girl. She didn't have one penny to rub against another herself, but she made out like she did, and she got the Earl to fall in love with her. Before he gave the heiress up, she told him all."

"A lot you know about the stage!" said Myrtle contemptuously.

"I should say so," added Calista.

"So dumb," sighed Blanche.

"What's the matter?" asked Vilas bewildered.

"Matter?" cried Calista, "All you have done is get the wrong play. That was Elizabeth Jennings in *Hold Back Your Tears*."

"Oh! I'm sorry," said Vilas.

"I'll have me the cream and sugar, please," Frank didn't really expect to get it right away, but he did.

"That was very much like Vera Montague in *Silence Is Golden*," commented Myrtle.

"The situation was different, but the love motive was the same."

"Isn't the love motive always the same?" asked Frank.

"Oh, no! Daddy, you never go to the theatre. How would you know anything about the love motive?" Calista was indignant.

"Who me?"

"Yes, you!"

"I got me a good idee."

"All plays," explained Myrtle to her father, "are made up of situations. It is like a problem and the play goes on to solve the problem."

"I see," said Frank. "This here situation is always different?"

"Yes."

"But the fellow always gets the girl, after having himself one hell of a time."

"Yes, generally, but you don't understand."

"Where does the love motive come in?" he asked.

Myrtle made a gesture indicating the hopelessness of ever explaining. "The love motive, dear Father, complicates the situation."

"Damn me, if it don't," agreed Frank, with a sideways look at his wife.

"In *Some Like It Hot*, Charlene O'Sullivan gave a wonderful portrayal of the character of Evelynne," said Calista with the air of a critic who knows firm ground when he sees it.

"I cried through the entire third act," cried Blanche, paling at the memory.

"It was so sad," agreed Myrtle.

The front door opened without notice and the three Orchards came in. Mrs. Orchards in a plain gingham dress, Effie and Olive in pleats and spangles.

"My goodness," said Mrs. Orchards, "I didn't expect you would be still at supper, or we would have come later."

"Tut! Tut! Pull up a chair and have some strawberry shortcake with us," cried Frank rising. "We been gabbing when we should have been eating."

"I'd love to have a piece of strawberry shortcake," sighed Effie, "but I'm afraid it will make me fat."

"The way you are geed up, you got you no room for a piece. Let out your belly band about six notches and the devil with being fat."

"It's not fashionable to be fat, Uncle Frank," said Effie.

"Oh, I don't know. Elizabeth Manning got her a man and she was fat."

"Elizabeth Jennings—not Manning. Dad doesn't really know one actress from another," Calista explained. "We were just talking about, *Some Like It Hot* with Charlene O'Sullivan."

"Oh, yes!" squealed Olive anxious to hear more. "She was gorgeous as Constance."

"Evelynne," said Myrtle.

"Oh, I guess it was as Evelynne," said Olive subdued.

"But Elizabeth Jennings wasn't in *Some Like It Hot*," objected Effie.

"No, she was in *Hold Back Your Tears*," said Blanche, "but Uncle Frank gets mixed up."

"Who me?" asked Frank from behind his mustache cup.

"Certainly!" said his children, nodding heads vigorously.

"We were talking about Melinda Morgan as Helene in *The World Is a Wonderful Oyster* to start with, but got off the subject when Uncle Frank didn't know what the love motive was," said Blanche.

"Mary, did you hear what she said?" Mary smiled.

"I shall never forget where Caringwald asked her to be his betrothed," gushed Effie.

"Nor I," agreed her sister.

"He said, 'Helene, the world lies at your feet. It is your world but mine, too,'" cried Blanche in a passionate imitation tenor voice.

"When Helene ran her fingers through his hair, I thought I'd cry," cried Effie. "There he was on bended knee, imploring her to be his betrothed. Helene merely looked beyond him and said, 'No, Caringwald, my love is not mine to give.' Then the curtain came down."

"He loved her tremendously," said Myrtle.

"He worshiped," said Clis, tilting her head upward and closing her eyes, "the very ground she walked on."

"Didn't this Caringwald get this Helene?" asked Frank.

"Not until the next act," said Calista.

"Pretty damn slow, if you ask me."

"Uncle Frank, tell us what you said to Aunt Mary when you got engaged," said Vilas.

184

"Not me," answered Frank.

There was a chorus of delighted cries.

"That won't take long," said Mrs. Orchards smiling.

"Yes, please tell us, Daddy," said Myrtle.

"Well, all right, but remember, you asked." Frank faced Mary and held up her left hand. Pointing with his right index finger, he counted.

"One."

"One," replied Mary, taking her cue with a smile.

"Two."

"Dew."

"Three."

"T'ree."

"Four."

"Four."

"Five."

"Fi—"

"Six."

"Seex."

"No, Mary, six."

"Seex."

"Here's how—sicks—six."

Mary rose from her chair and kicked it away from her. "Frank Stone," she said in mock severity, "you teach me Engleesh! All is to know, don't say 'ain't.' I come to Cleveland. I be dressmaker. I have beesness. I get reech quick. Fine Mary—first man she see to hell with everything. Fine man—he teach Mary to count, one, dew, t'ree, four. Four what? Four fingers. Eef you must count, count keeses like thees."

She threw herself on his lap and put her arms around his neck. She kissed him and counted them. Then, burying her face on his shoulder, she pretended to sob.

He hitched her up on his legs and patted her.

"Tut! Tut! Mary, big girls don't cry." He kissed her cheek and brushed her hair back of her ears. It hadn't changed much. It was white now instead of tow, but it still wouldn't stay. Frank looked across the table at Mrs. Orchards. Her black eyes were filled with tears.

"Frank," she said softly, "you have just become engaged."

There was a long silence.

185

"Was that all?" demanded Calista.

"A God's plenty," Frank assured her.

"There must have been more," said Effie.

Frank kissed Mary as she sat up, laughing.

"Do you know what I think of Caringwald?" he asked.

"What?" said the girls.

Frank jutted his lower jaw out and emitted a Bronx cheer.

CHAPTER XXV

AND SO TO SLEEP

The cool evening breeze fluttered through the house and shook the lace curtains as it passed. Darkness was settling over the city, and there was quiet, except for the occasional rattle of a streetcar. Frank dozed peacefully in the huge leather-covered rocker in the living room. In the dining room Mrs. Orchards, Ben Judson, Grandma and Mary played cards. It was Saturday night.

From the parlor came the soft music of the piano. Calista played and her beau turned the music for her. Frank slept while Calista played, but when she stopped, he awoke. His nap was finished and his mind returned to the problem that had confronted it for several weeks and for which no answer had been forthcoming. He would have joined those in the dining room, except for this. Perhaps he could get a solution to the problem, if he put his mind to it here in the quiet darkness.

"Clis, for the love of Mike, let's go for a walk." Frank recognized her beau. George was a small lad, dark, handsome and apparently persistent.

"I've told you for the last time, no!"

"Why not?"

"Young ladies do not walk with their escorts after dark unchaperoned."

There was a silence while Frank thought what he'd have said if he had been sparking Calista. George did not say anything and the piano began to tinkle again.

"I bid seven," Mrs. Orchards must have been pretty confident.

"Pass."

"Pass."

"Twelve."

"Ben," said Mrs. Orchards, "you know you can't make twelve. I'm going to set you, see if I don't."

"After looking at this widow, I'm inclined to agree. Here's my ace. Got a pedro for it, Grandma? Good girl."

"George! Stop it!"

"Here's low you won't get," said Mary.

"There's what I want," said Ben. "Ace, jack and two pedroes makes my bid. I'll give you deuce and game."

"Very nice," said Grandma, exulting.

"Let's see if anyone is in here," whispered a new voice. Frank recognized it as belonging to Blanche. "Uncle Frank." He pretended to sleep and wondered what would happen now.

"Let's go out on the porch," said her beau.

"Myrtle and Jack are there."

"Damn quiet if they are," thought Frank, as he breathed heavily.

"Let's go out to the swing in the back yard," whispered Blanche and they departed, shoes creaking ever so slightly.

"George, can't you keep your mind on the music?"

"Clis, I've been calling on you for over a year. You know I love you. Let me ask your old man and get this foolishness over with."

"Hush! I hardly know you. I am not sure of my own heart and there is always my duty."

"Your duty?"

"Yes, my duty." The piano spoke up and Frank wondered what Clis's duty was. He strained an ear for this eavesdropping might be entertaining.

"Myrt, it's no use." Ha! This was Jack out on the porch swing.

"Four years isn't so long," said Myrtle, ever so softly.

"I'm a coward, Myrt. My father decided I should be a doctor when I was born. He has every hope in the world that I will be and I am afraid to disappoint him."

"Perhaps he knows best."

"He wanted to be a doctor, and couldn't. That's why he wants me to be."

"I suppose so."

"Myrt, I wish I was a teamster. I'd marry you tomorrow."

"I know Jack, but is four years too long?"

"It's too long when a fellow doesn't want to be a doctor."

"Suppose you didn't go on. What would you rather do?" Frank would have asked that himself.

"I don't know, Myrt, because what I really want to do, I can't possibly do."

188

"What, Jack?" There were several soft noises that to Frank sounded like kisses.

"You won't laugh?"

"No."

"Promise? Cross your heart and hope to die?"

"I promise."

"I want to own a livery stable. I want only fine horses and fine rigs—no plugs and no junk wagons!"

Myrtle laughed.

"Stop it, Myrt. You promised." There were sounds of a slight scuffle and Myrt's laughter was muffled and gave way to more of the kissing sounds.

"What was so funny?" asked Jack. His voice sounded hurt.

"You sounded just like my Dad," giggled Myrtle. "He would love that."

"No, your Dad is different. He would have the livery, but he'd never rent his horses out. Can you imagine him hiring Fred out? Howard nor Vile have never been able to use him. Your Dad would have to go along to drive."

"Maybe, you are right."

Frank wondered how he got into the discussion. The swing squeaked, but otherwise all was quiet. Frank was about to doze off again, before someone spoke.

"I think that was a dirty trick." It was Blanche and Elmer again. "We were there first. I don't see why Effie and Charles had to join us!"

"Uncle Frank is still sleeping," said Elmer.

"Uncle Frank," whispered Blanche with conviction, "is a nuisance."

"Let's slam the door," said Elmer, "maybe he'll wake up, and go to bed."

"I've got a better idea," said Blanche. "Mother Orchards is playing cards here. Effie is in the swing. Let's go sit on their porch."

"Let's," said Elmer and they tiptoed out.

"Going somewhere?" It was Myrt.

"Don't be nosey, Posey," replied Blanche. Their heels clicked on the sidewalk and faded away. A streetcar clattered past. Frank did not remember when he had had as much fun.

"Your man seems to be pretty near fagged out," said Mrs. Orchards.

189

"Frank was up at three this morning," replied Mary.

"Seven," said Ben.

"Eight."

"That's good here."

"That's a bushel."

"If I quit school, would you marry me, Myrt?"

The swing hummed its little song.

"Yes, I would marry you, Jack, but not for some time. People would think you quit just to get married. Your father would never forgive me."

"I guess that is right. Would you marry me now and go off somewhere?"

Frank for the first time felt alarmed. He listened closely and then relaxed.

"No, Jack Morrison, not on your life. There is nothing we have to be ashamed of or to run from. This is a free country and if you don't want to be a doctor, you don't have to be. Whether you are or aren't makes no difference to me. I'll wait for you."

"Bless your heart, darling, you are right as usual. If I wasn't such a coward, I'd tell Dad tomorrow."

"I'm glad you are that kind of a coward. You don't want to hurt him and that isn't being afraid."

There had been low conversational tones from the parlor, but Frank had not tried to hear them. Now they were louder and slightly angry.

"Damn it, what is this duty you keep talking about?"

"My duty is to my parents. They need me, George. They are old and must look to their children. I cannot lightly throw aside my obligations.'"

"Oh, hell," said George in exasperation, "the old man is good for seventy more years, and your mother is, too!"

"It is my duty."

"Clis, the *Maine* was sunk last week. Maybe I have a duty, too. I might join the army!" George did not sound very convincing and Frank thought he was just talking.

"A true woman never stands between a man and his country. If duty calls you, go," said Clis.

"So help me Hannah, I will," said George, "but first I am going to help myself to a kiss."

"George," mumbled Clis, "you unhand me this moment."

190

A door opened and slammed.

"Going somewhere?" asked Jack.

"I'm going to join the Rough Riders," said George as he fled down the steps.

"Did he go?"

"Yes, Clis, he's gone," answered Myrtle.

"Where did he say he was going?"

"To join the Rough Riders."

"Oh!" wailed Clis, "I have sent my lover to his death!" She charged up the stairs, and those were real tears splashing on her bodice.

"I suppose, there's no use trying anymore," complained Blanche. "Uncle Frank is here, Myrt and Jack, Effie and Charles, Olly and Bill, Clis and George everywhere else."

"There's no one in here," whispered Elmer.

"There isn't?"

"No."

"Well, thank goodness."

Frank waited for the piano to start up, but there wasn't a sound. "Well," thought Frank, "I got me a earful, and I got my problem settled as far as Mr. Jack is concerned." He felt pleased with himself as he joined the card players in the dining room.

Chapter XXVI

FRANK SOOTHES THE FEVERED BROW

The next morning being Sunday, Frank pulled the trap out of the shed shortly after breakfast and turned Fred loose to graze on the back lawn. He sang fairly loud for there was happiness in his heart. As he pulled the wheels off and dabbed a bit of axle grease on the axles, he talked to himself, and chirped a bar or two from some song. Mary knew something had happened to please him, but what it was, was a mystery. She took a pan of potato peelings out to the garbage can and dumped them, then went over to where Frank was polishing the body of the trap. She climbed into the front seat.

"Whoa there! Mary, you going somewhere?" He smiled up at her as she sat so primly above him.

"I want to talk to you, Frank Stone, and I don't want any foolishness out of you." Mary eyed him sternly, but it was all a pose.

"I'm a great hand to talk, old girl, as you ought to know. Just give me someone that'll listen and I'll tell 'em anything they want to know, including the price of Bullhorn Reukus trees in Chiny. If they happen to still listen, I'll tell 'em the love story of our Josey, and how she jumped the fence and was gone for three days. How when she came back there was a different light in her eye and how so far as we know, her heifer calf is a virgin of virgin birth. There, she stands, a brindle calf named Blizzard who at least got her a name, if not a father."

"Frank, I'm worried."

"Waste not—worry not!"

"It's supposed to be, 'Waste not—want not.' "

"Pardon me all to hell, sweetheart, darling, lover girl."

"You feel good this morning, don't you?" Mary looked down from her seat on the trap. Her eyes were crinkled at the corners

192

as they tried to read what was on his mind. Her lips were parted. Frank saw her puzzled face and he felt the love he had always had for this girl tingle in his veins.

"I always feel good," he assured her.

"Always?"

"Yup—always."

"What about Clisty?"

"What about her?"

"She's all broken up this morning. She and George had a quarrel last night, and he went off to kill himself."

"So?"

"I don't know anything about the fight they had, except that George left all huffy and Clisty says he's sure to be killed."

"They probably had them a little to-do over something, and he skedaddled," suggested Frank.

"Clisty loves him," said Mary as though that settled everything."

"Why didn't she tell him?"

"Girls don't run around telling their beaux they love them," said Mary, exasperated.

"Hm! Hm! I seem to have me a bad memory," cried Frank.

"People are different from us, dear boy," said Mary pulling his hat over his eyes. "Besides you were so stupid!"

"I hope George does stay away for a while. Serves her right!"

"I hope he comes back tonight. Clis is ready to wear the widow's weeds right now."

"Ain't that too bad?"

"Frank, you aren't even sorry!" There was deep reproach in her voice.

"Of course not, Mary. What man is going to stand for this, 'don't-touch-me-Willy' stuff? She has been reading those books where people are so polite that they apollygize to themselves when they take off their underwear to take them a bath. The girls are so good and innocent they got them no idee what them things on their chests is." Mary took a swing at Frank, but he stepped back and grabbed her hand. He kissed it with formality. "The fellows in these books are all like that fellow Caringwald. Remember, he was the fellow who fell to his knees and grabbed Charlene by the skirt—"

"Helene."

193

"All right, Helene. Now Clisty expected George to be another Caringwald, but George is a spunky little devil who ain't going to spoil the crease in his pants for no woman. They have a scrap, and he lights out. That's all, Mother." He spread his hands. It was all so simple.

"Clis is sure tore up over it."

"A bawling cow soon forgets her calf," said Frank.

"This is different." She looked at Frank and his assurance was comforting, but no mother likes to see her girls hurt. "What about Jack Morrison and Myrt?"

"Easy," said Frank.

"What do you mean?"

"Just leave it to James Franklin. He's the man to cure your troubles."

"Are you going to tell him the truth?"

"Not by a damn sight!"

"I don't see how you are going to stop them. They are thick as thieves."

"Aren't they though?"

"Frank, Myrtle kisses him."

"Probably does," said Frank, "I thought so all along. In that she sort of takes after her Maw."

"It isn't funny."

"It's awfully nice, and I bet Myrt kisses awfully sweet."

"How can you stand there, grinning like a jackass, when everything is going wrong with your children? Don't you love them? Don't you want to see them happy?"

"Of course, I love them, but I got me no intention of breaking out in a sweat over something I can't help. You sit back cozy in your rocker and tend to your knittin' and watch old Daddy Stone settle these troubles."

"Frank, you are a comfort. Sometimes I think you don't have the sense you were born with, and other times I think you are the smartest man in kingdom come."

"That's me—smartest man in kingdom come."

"I wish I could have more proof."

"By the way, Mary—" Frank paused uncertainly and felt in his pockets. From one of them he drew forth a large and completely empty coin purse. I need some 'baccy money."

"You sure?"

"Yup—absolutely busted."

"Why don't you get a race for Fred?"

"Mary, I gave that up a few years back. That newspaper story ruined me for all time. No, I'll let Fred take it easy. Have you noticed how fat he's getting? I've had to let out the harness to fit him and if he trots a couple of blocks he starts puffing."

"I'll give you five dollars when you come in for dinner," she said climbing from the buggy.

"Can you make it ten?"

"No."

"I thought I'd ask." He put his arm about her and walked a few steps toward the house with her. "Mary, I'll have me a kiss."

"Aren't you ever going to grow up?"

"I'm still on my honeymoon," he told her, "a fifty years one."

"You are an old buck."

"I love you, ain't that enough?"

"That is a lot," she admitted, as he tipped her face up to his.

From the lawn Fred watched. Trotting over he rubbed his long neck against them.

"Sure, he is jealous. Women, horses, babies and dogs all love me." He winked at her and whispered, "It's my everlastin' beauty that gets 'em."

George did not return, and nearly two months elapsed before anyone even heard from him. It was Jack Morrison who brought word that George had not joined the Rough Riders as threatened, but had joined the Sixth Ohio Calvary and was now on strike duty in Idaho. In his letter to Jack, George depicted himself as pretty much of an Indian fighter, or at least a person who would take no "sass" from anyone. He knew Jack would tell Myrtle, and she would tell her sister. He also sent a couple of photographs of himself in a wide brimmed hat. With a black curly lock of hair on his forehead, obviously planted there, his blue eyes and new black mustache, George looked scarcely menacing. Calista managed to get permanent possession of the pictures from Jack, and that, too, was planned.

Jack was busy at school and except for Saturday night and Sunday was seldom seen. He was playing football at Western Reserve and studying. From all accounts he appeared to be doing a tremendous job on the gridiron and considerably less than that in the class room. He took the girls to see several games and from Myrtle's description of the game, Frank decided George was safer fighting red Indians than Jack was playing football. These conclusions appeared to be confirmed when Jack appeared one night with a beautiful black eye.

"Looks to me, Jack, like you were talking when you should have been listening," said Frank. The whole family except Grandma was in the big two-seated swing in the back yard. Jack stood on the ground gently swaying as he rocked them.

"That is a result of this afternoon's football game," said Jack, feeling the puffy bruise.

"If it was me I'd lick the fellow who done it," opined Frank.

"I might have given it to myself for all I know. I started into the flying wedge all right, but when the whistle blew and we unpiled, I had this shiner. I probably got walloped with a knee."

"Did you win, is what I want to know?"

"We did this time," laughed Jack, "but we don't often."

"Would you want it poulticed?" asked Mary.

"I should say not," said Myrt giving him her hand, and stepping from the swing. "I wish I had one to match. Then we'd go sit in the front at church tomorrow and Reverend Willard wouldn't be able to preach, because of his curiosity."

"People would think we were married," said Jack.

"Damn me if it ain't about time you were," said Frank.

"Daddy!" said Calista.

"Frank! What are you saying?" asked Mary.

Only the young folks were not flustered or embarrassed. Jack smiled broadly as he took Myrtle's arm and led her down the drive.

"That's the first good idea you have had in twenty years," Myrtle called over her shoulder.

One woman by herself can chill an atmosphere if she is of a mind to do so, but give two women what they consider good cause, and see what happens. Frank was in for it and knew it.

"I was never so humiliated in my life," hissed Calista. "Don't you know that the boy should come to you to ask for your daughter's hand? Fathers don't go throwing their daughters at men's heads."

Frank looked surprised. This rule of paternal eitiquette had been overlooked, but innocently, if you could believe his expression.

"It is about time, Clis, that they got married. He's been galivanting around here more than a year now, serious-like," Frank tried to sound reasonable.

"A year!" snorted his daughter. "One year! Father, how can a girl know a man in one year?"

"It only took your Maw three months." Frank was careful not to look at Mary.

"She won't know *you* any better in fifty years," said Calista.

"Calista, run along now. I want to be alone with your father. There are a few things I have to tell him." Mary sounded ominous.

"I guess I'll be going, too," said Frank rising. The swing swayed dangerously.

"Sit down, Frank Stone," said Mary pointing to the seat opposite her.

"Woman, don't you know I'll catch me my death of cold in this night air?"

"Sit down!"

"Yes, ma'am."

"Clisty, get going."

"Yes, Mother."

After they were alone, they sat and looked at one another, Frank smiling, Mary grim, her arms crossed before her.

"I suppose that is what you meant by telling me to sit back and tend to my knitting and just leave everything to James Franklin. If you meant this as a joke, it is not funny." Her voice was low, but scolding.

"Now, Mother, listen to me. There are few women in the world I can't figure out, if I set my mind to it. I got this figured out and it would be a fine how-de-do if somebody spoiled it for me."

"Go on."

"We don't want them to get married, do we?"

Mary did not answer.

"No, of course, we don't," Frank went on. "Now suppose we tried to break them up like most people would. We tell Myrt she's got to never see Jack again. I chase Jack away every time he comes over. What happens?" He waited for her to answer, but none was forthcoming, so he answered her. "They get themselves married right now.

"But suppose, I just tell Jack he can't marry Myrt 'cause I'm his daddy. He's apt to say something at home that'll give it away and we'll have the start of a hell of a how-de-do. Besides, I can only tell him as a last chance.

"Since we don't want to hurt the youngster and we don't want to start any deviltry, there's only one thing to do—urge them to get married."

"You are crazy! Frank, you are raving mad!"

"No, I'm not, Mary. You don't know women. In Africy, the men put rings in their women folks' noses, but by Judas, they can't lead them around by them rings. No—a woman won't lead and she won't be pushed. The only way to get your way with them is to let them have their head and kind of point them where you don't want them to go. I got me a lot of idees on women."

He leaned forward and took both of Mary's hand. She was thoughtful and solemn.

"Frank, why do you talk about women? Isn't Jack the one who is choosing a wife?"

Frank snorted.

"Good land of love, girl, don't you know that men do the courtin' and women do the marryin'? Women set their mind on a fellow and they let him court them, until they decide whether they want him or not. Myrt is the one I'm after, not Jack. She'll do his thinking for him."

"I know you are wrong, but don't know what is right."

"Suppose you leave everything to J. F. Stone."

"There isn't much I can do, but Frank, please don't hurt the children."

"Lordy, Mother, I don't want to and God willing, I won't. There's only one thing to do—wait and see what happens."

CHAPTER XXVII

SHOULD AULD ACQUAINTANCE BE FORGOT?

As he drove along, Frank found his mind wandering. The maples with their brilliant reds, the browns of elms and the light green of birch all spoke of an autumn almost gone. He had tried to make his mind think of his troubles, but it had mutinied and thought instead about the odor of burning leaves, their joyous sounds, and their beauty.

Fred hurried. He was homeward bound and he thought of the delicious odors of the oat bin and the haymow, his clean stable and a quick rubdown, a gentle massage for his fat muscles. The wagon rattled noisily over the cobbled streets, but neither consciously heard it.

When the store came into view, framed by the trees at the end of the street, Frank sensed that something was different. It was not until he approached closer that he saw the reason. A large crowd of people were milling before it. He urged Fred into a trot and soon reached Cedar, crossed the street and entered the drive. Climbing off, he let Fred go to the back.

The trouble, he was glad to note, was not in the store, but seemed to center around Morrisey's Saloon. He entered the crowd, and pushed as far through as he could.

"What's going on here?" he asked.

"I guess there's a bunch of drunks in there wrecking the place from the sound," said one man.

"They are women drunks," said another. "Listen to them."

"No, them are anti-salooners, sure as hell," said a third man.

Frank listened and sure enough, between the hoarse cries of Morrisey and the cracking of tables and glass, were sinister squeaks of women. Just then, a big plate glass window crashed to the street, smashed from within. The crowd moved back into the street, blocking the progress of a streetcar whose occupants were craning their necks to view the situation.

"It looks to me like Morrisey needs him some help," said Frank to no one in particular. He walked through the rest of the crowd and started to enter, when one of the walnut swing doors splintered and flew from its hinges. Before he could move out of the way a woman almost exploded from the place, colliding with him. At the impact, he put his arms out to keep her from falling. Looking over her shoulder he saw six or eight more women, all bearing hammers or hatchets. The saloon was a wreck and Morrisey's shirt was torn, scratches showing red on his bare shoulder.

"Jim—Jim Stone," said the woman in his arms.

Frank stepped back and looked at the hard faced woman before him. Dressed in black, her hat awry, dirt on her face, and a hatchet in her hand was Millie Gordon.

"Millie!" said Frank almost unable to believe his eyes.

"Yes," said she, "I'm Millie Gordon. I don't suppose—"

"No!" said Frank.

"No, what?" she screamed.

"No, ma'am," said he.

"Is this your saloon?"

"The building is."

"And this is your store!" She glared from him to the store. Behind her, her legions stood with hatchets at half mast, ready to do her bidding. In their eyes were the half quenched fires of hysteria.

"Yes." The crowd pressed close to hear every word.

"Girls," said Millie, "we will smack the store to the ground."

"Wait!" said Frank. "What the hell is wrong with grocery stores?"

"Nothing," asid Millie. "The trouble is with property owners who permit saloons and get rich renting to them. You are as bad as the saloonkeeper! Forward!"

Raising her hatchet aloft, she whirled and led her women toward the store. The crowd fell back as Millie dangerously swung her hatchet. Frank followed, dazed and unable to think of anything that would head her off.

"Just keep coming, Millie Gordon!" The voice belonged to Mary, but it was a few seconds before Frank was able to see what was happening. Millie had stopped and her army with her. Standing before the door, pulling her sleeves above her elbows, was Mary. Beside her stood Calista.

"Come on," said Mary, "and here is where I get my two hands full of your scrawny neck." She paused for breath. "Come on!"

"You shall not put a foot on our property," said Calista, right foot advanced and right arm held at shoulder height, with palm outward, her fingers stiffly pointing skyward.

Behind the two women and leaning against the door was Myrtle. She said nothing, but on her face was a delighted grin and swinging idly about in her right hand was a cooper's mallet her father had used to start a bung in a new barrel of vinegar this morning.

Millie considered. Fighting men was one thing, but this was apt to be difficult. Turning on her heel, she led her army through the crowd and boarded the streetcar. The prospects of a battle gone, the crowd broke up and scattered in small groups. The streetcar clanged and rolled off toward town. Frank mopped his face and head with his red bandana handkerchief.

"Spunky family you got there, Frank," commented Mr. Smith, the barber. "Whatever set the old witch agin you?"

"I ain't got me the least idee," said Frank. Anxious to head off further conversation of a personal vein, he pointed to poor Morrisey who was even now sweeping the glass from the sidewalk. "There's the fellow she's really after."

"Frank, come here!"

"Yes, Mary, coming right along. So long, George—I'll see you later."

"Bye, Frank. I better hurry home. The old lady'll want to hear about the ruckus."

When he entered the store, he saw his family ranged before the counter, Myrtle grinning, Calista solemn, and Mary with a grim look of satisfaction on her face. As they looked at him in silence, he felt embarrassed, although he assured himself he had no reason to.

"All right," said Mary, "talk!"

"About what?"

"Millie Gordon! Why were you hugging her?"

He could have been no more stunned had Myrtle belted him with the mallet which she still had in her hand.

"Ye Gods, woman, I wasn't hugging Millie Gordon!"

"I saw you," said Mary. "Don't lie to me! I didn't get to see all of it, because I was working in the store. I heard the commotion

201

and looked out the window and there was my husband, hugging a woman in front of all those people. Of all people, she had to be Millie Gordon!" This last was said in the jerky manner of a woman who is about to cry.

"Who is Millie Gordon, Mother?" asked Myrtle.

"The Other Woman," cried Calista ominously.

"And when—?" Frank started to ask.

"Be still!" A customer entered the store. Frank was never so glad to see anyone. He started forward eagerly, but Mary thrust him back, while Calista with a lugubrious mien waited on the lady. There was silence until they were alone again.

"Who is Millie Gordon?" insisted Myrtle.

Frank was silent—not so, Mary.

"Millie Gordon once claimed to be your father's wife."

"Did you divorce her?" asked Calista of Frank.

"Hell, no!" he shouted.

"Oh, Myrtle!" cried Calista. "Just think of the shame of it all! Our father and mother living in sin, and we children born out of wedlock!" She started to cry.

Frank had enough of this and was getting mad. Taking his hat from his head he threw it violently toward the side door. He picked the weeping Calista up and sat her soundly on the counter. He took Mary next, but Myrtle beat him to it and sat facing him. Waving a finger at the three, he spoke.

"I've heard enough about Millie Gordon for one day. I got me no intentions of hearing any more." He looked sternly at Mary and tapped her crossed arms with his finger. "I wasn't hugging the damned wench—she run into me. She has caused me more trouble than most people get in several lifetimes. I never was married to her! I ain't married to her and I never will be married to her!"

"Just the same, Frank Stone," said Mary, "don't you ever bring that chippie around here again."

"Oh oh! Oh oh!" Frank said it so quietly, and his voice was so sympathetic that all looked at the side door, the direction he was gazing.

"What's the matter, Dad?" asked Myrtle.

Frank moved off rapidly, picked up his hat and disappeared through the screen door. His head reappeared momentarily.

"I forgot me my horse. He ain't unhitched or fed yet."

202

Chapter XXVIII

EAT, DRINK AND BE MERRY

It was Halloween, and all through the Stone house were signs of the revelry that the night promised. Calista scurried up the stairs as Myrtle dashed down. In the kitchen Vilas was very much in the way as he pressed his pants. Supper was over. Mary washed the dishes, Frank dried them and Grandma put them away. Blanche rushed into the kitchen to have someone hook her dress in the back, and disappeared. Vilas burned himself getting another iron off the burner, and dropped an iron holder in the blaze, making a minor fire with a major smell. Myrtle and Calista raced in to say the house was burning down, and both fell over poor Curly who could only find a place to sleep squarely in the middle of the floor.

"Somebody's going to get run over and killed here in the kitchen," opined Frank. "Maybe we better wait until the kids are gone."

"Rinse that platter before you dry it," ordered Mary.

"Get a dry towel," asid Grandma.

"All right, ladies, I was wrong. We ain't in no danger."

"I'm through now," said Vilas. "I only scorched one leg a little near the cuff. Do you think it'll show, Uncle Frank?"

He regarded the pants critically, as Frank wiped the platter.

"Vilas, there is one thing I can tell you about your scorched pants. If you run according to form, nobody's going to see your pants leg, because it'll be under some table while you eat peaches and cream and cake."

"That's right," agreed Vilas, departing on the run.

A minor riot seemed to have broken out in the living room. They listened, but no one made a move to discover the cause. Frank held a plate up to the light to see if it was dry. It wasn't, so he made another wipe and handed it to Grandma.

203

"Hello, Mom, am I too late for supper?" It was Howard.

"You can raid the ice box if you like. Is Myrt with you?"

"Yes, she's here and about five sisters and cousins, too. I got home too late to eat with them."

"Well, hop to it, before Curly gets hungry and beats you to it," said Frank.

"Myrt's ma and pa are going to drop in to see you later," said Howard, dropping a slab of roast beef into his mouth.

"Yoo hoo! Anyone home?" The call came from the front porch.

"Who's that?" asked Mary of her husband.

"I'll go see. The dishes are most done anyhow," volunteered Frank.

He walked around the dog and went through to the living room. Elmer was there for Blanche and his folks had come along for the walk, they said.

"You got no idee how glad I am to see you," said Frank hospitably. "Let me take your things."

"We are only going to stay for a minute," said Mrs. Sewell. "Elmer was coming down and we hadn't seen you folks for such a long time. It seems as if people get real busy, and sort of forget one another."

"It does seem that way, for a fact," agreed Frank. "Mother is in the kitchen. Make yourself to home—in fact, I just laid me down a dishcloth out there." He smiled at her, and she was immediately put at ease. Frank knew that if you can give people something to do for a few minutes, they invariably make better company. Mrs. Sewell hurried off to the kitchen, and soon a terrific clatter of tongues told him that the older girls were happy.

"What do you think of the war?" asked Mr. Sewell.

"The war? Teddy Roosevelt has already won it!" Frank's political views were barber shop formed. He knew it and preferred to talk about something else. With the racket arising from the girls, their giggling and squealing, there was little chance to be heard if a person did talk.

"Hurry up, Blanche! We'll be late!" shouted some little lady up the stairs. An unintelligible reply echoed down the stairs. About that time someone started playing the piano, and Frank led his guest out on the porch. Here he found Jack Morrison, Elmer, and a half dozen other young men. They rose and greeted him and the introductions were made somewhat formally. Frank ruined the formality of it by his genial gift of gab and the fact that he knew their folks, even if the "younguns" had got past him.

Mrs. Orchards, the two girls and Ben Judson came up the walk. A few words were exchanged before Effie and Ollie entered the house to cause a din. Mrs. Orchards joined the other women in the back while Ben sat on the porch railing with the rest. The porch swing was now empty, since everyone was too polite to sit in it.

"For a fact," said Frank to Jack Morrison, "I'll be glad when you take that parcel of females wherever you are going. Mind you, I ain't agin women, bless their hearts, but women in flocks is pretty strong medicine. Git you a couple of dozen, all skittery and needing breaking, and you got you a mess."

The older men nodded. The younger ones looked embarrassed and fiddled with their wash ties and shiny collars. Jack was an old campaigner in the Stone house and it took a lot to embarrass him.

"We'll get them out of here, just as soon as we can," said Jack, "but honestly, did you ever try to hurry a girl?"

"It don't do no good," said Ben.

"Nope," said Frank, "it is almost impossible to hurry 'em, but I can get them women ready in two minutes. S'pose you tell me which one of them females raises the most hell?"

"That's easy," said Elmer, "Myrtle!"

"All right," said Frank, "those girls are ready and have been for fifteen minutes or more. They are just waiting for someone to make her a move—then they'll come pourin' out like the house was afire. Jack, you go in there and tell Myrt if she ain't ready you'll meet her at the party. Don't tell her why or anything."

"She'll wring my neck," said Jack.

"Tut, tut, boy, you're over six feet and all man. Spat her setter if she gets rough."

"That's all right for you to say," said Jack, "you're her dad."

"Do as I say—just this once."

"Well, all right," said Jack dubiously. He entered the house and emerged in less than a minute with Myrtle on his arm. Closely following were the rest of the girls. There was a noisy sorting out process and then the entire crowd of young people went down the steps and disappeared around the corner of the store.

"Frank sure knows how to handle women," said Mr. Sewell.

"Seems like it," agreed Ben. "How'd you get to know so much?"

"That is easy," said Frank settling in the swing. "Lots of room here—set." They did and gently swung back and forth. Ben lighted his corncob pipe. "You see, it's like this. My pa was a great hand with the women and I sort of take after him, but I'll tell you fellows one thing—don't ever get you an idee you know *all* about woman, 'cause sure as hell you have made you one mistake right there."

"They tell me all of 'em aren't alike," said Ben.

"No, once in a while you'll get you one that is hard to figure out. Then the only thing to do is to leave her alone and see what the hell she does."

"The aloner you leave her, the better, I guess," said Ben.

"Correct you be."

"You ought to know about that, Frank Stone," said Mary. She and the other women had been listening through the screen door. Now, they came out laughing.

"What a wonderful evening!" exclaimed Mrs. Orchards.

"I expect we'll have a frost in the morning," said Mrs. Sewell. Frank looked around. It was a wonderful evening and there might be a frost. People were funny—six people could not get together and sit still and enjoy the evening without making something up to talk about. In a few minutes someone would suggest a card game, and that was the last thing he wanted to do. Of course, he'd have to play. He waited.

"When Howard's Myrtle's folks come that will make two tables. We can have a game of Pedro," said Mrs. Orchards.

"What a fine idea," said Mary.

"I knew it!" thought Frank. "I've got to scotch this business now." His mind turned over several plans and discarded them. Finally, he had the glimmering of an "idee."

"Ben, until they come how'd you like to play us some old timey music?" He knew Ben liked the suggestion, but did not want to appear too eager.

"You don't want to hear me," said Ben.

"What the hell's the reason we don't? Git your fiddle like a good fellow. If you don't care, you can use Myrt's."

"I'll go git my own," said Ben, pleased.

Ben evidently tuned his fiddle at home, because he was ready to go when he returned. Sitting on the railing he started to play. The folks kept time with their feet and clapped their hands very sedately in rhythm. When Ben swung into "Turkey In The Straw" and "The Irish Washer Woman," Frank began to call square dances.

"Frank used to do that good," said Mary, "but we don't get out much anymore."

"Join hands and around to the right."

"We haven't been to a dance in ages," said Mrs. Sewell.

"Grab your gal and hold her tight," sang Frank.

"It used to be so much fun," agreed Mrs. Orchards.

"Whoa!" yelled Frank. The music stopped and they looked at him. "You girls just gave me an idee. Let's have us a barn dance tonight. Mary, have you got any doughnuts?"

"Yes, but not very many."

"Us men'll hang lanterns in the barn and clean it out while you girls make some more doughnuts. Ben'll play, I'll call and we'll invite the neighbors to come exactly as they are when we call on 'em. Shall we?"

"What'll we do with the cows?"

"We'll put 'em in with Fred until we're through."

"I'm game," said Mary enthusiastically. "How about the rest of you?"

They were soon all busy. Frank only had two lanterns, but passed it off by saying they would probably need the dim light in case there was any lalligagging. Ben said that everyone who came would bring a lantern, if they were told about it. Soon the barn was ready. The cattle had been moved and the trap pulled outdoors.

The men entered the house where the smell of new doughnuts laid heavy siege. They breathed deeply and sampled the brown delicacies.

"Them things are hotter than Dutch love," said Frank, and added with a twinkle in his eye, "and just as good."

"A lot you know," said Mary.

"We are ready out back."

"We will be there in a few minutes. There's five gallons of sweet cider down in the fruit cellar, how's to bring it up?" Frank brought it.

"We are going to invite the neighborhood now."

"This is going to be fun," said Mrs. Sewell.

"We'll be back in about half an hour." The men left by way of the front door. "Bring your fiddle, Ben. When we knock on a door, you play and we'll walk in when they open the door."

"You are the bossman," said Ben.

They knocked at the first door. Ben played as arranged, and when it opened, Frank called out, "First couple come out tonight, bring your gal and bring your light."

"What in tarnation goes on here?" asked the bewildered neighbor. His wife peered around his broad shoulders.

"We're havin' us a barn dance tonight. Come as you are. We need your lantern, and want you to come with us now."

"I have only a gingham dress on," wailed the lady.

"And I done took my shirt off," said the man.

"Got you a shirt, but ain't nobody can have fun dressed to kill," said Frank. In a few seconds they were knocking at another door. In less than the half hour, they returned with a dozen couples and as many lanterns, which were hung about the barn.

Ben climbed on the oat box and sat on a bale of straw that the men tossed up for him to sit on.

"You get you your partner for the first dance," said Frank. "We'll start off easy with a plain quadrille. Form up here and here and over yonder!" He pointed to the spots. "All ready here? Fine! We need us another couple here—over here, Henry. Gad! Maude looks younger every day. All ready, let her go, Ben!"

The party was off with a rush, even if it did get a late start. Mary brought plates of doughnuts and pitchers of cider. She put them in a manger where everyone could help themselves. As the evening progressed more people came, including Howard's in-laws, and everyone danced except Frank and Ben. During one of the dances Jack Morrison and Myrtle came in, took one look around and departed. Within fifteen minutes at least a dozen couples of young folks came in. Apparently their party was over. The leg-weary oldsters were glad to see the youngsters, for this was more exertion than some had bargained for. Frank welcomed them and got them dancing. Mary showed them the refreshments and the party was already a huge success.

"Frank," whispered Mary during an intermission, "we are running out of cider."

"I haven't any more sweet cider," said Frank thoughtfully.

"Mary, I put several barrels in the basement under the store to make vinegar about a week or so ago. Do you think it has worked too much?"

"Get a pitcher full and let's see."

"All right," he said hurrying off.

Soon he was back. He poured Mary a glass of it, and she tasted it. Smacking her lips, she proclaimed it sweet. Frank tried it, and was a little doubtful, but Grandma and Mrs. Orchards agreed with Mary, so the cider question was settled.

Ben played some waltzes and a schottische and Frank lounged back on his bale-of-hay seat. Mary had been busy flitting about serving late arrivals. Now she came over to where he was.

"You have been hiding from me," she charged.

"I been right here," he answered.

"Why didn't you ask me to dance?"

"And get me a pitcher of cider on my alabaster bosom? Not me."

"Come on, let's finish this one out."

"All right, Mary, but I'm warning you—I'm a wicked man with a schottische." He stood up and clasped her lightly to him. They swayed to the music and took off across the floor in perfect rhythm. Mary looked up at him and laughed.

"I'm having a wonderful time."

"I think everyone is for a fact."

"Aren't the children sweet?"

"They are having them a big time."

The dance ended and Ben climbed down from his perch. Mary went to get him some food and Frank was alone, but not for long.

"Mr. Stone, I'd like to talk to you for a minute."

"Fine, Jack. What can I do for you?"

"I want to marry Myrtle. Will you consent?"

"You know what I think of you, son. Of course, I'll consent, as you say. You're doggone right. Where's Myrt?"

"Right here listening." Myrtle appeared from behind a post.

"Aw, Jack," she said petulantly, "you promised not to give me away. Dad would have told you how to hog-tie me but he won't now."

"You need hog-tieing, young lady," said her father. "I'm glad you got you sense enough to want a man who got him some meat on his bones and brains in his head."

"I don't know when we'll get married," said Jack. "I'm quitting school at Christmas time and I'm going to work."

"That ain't so good," said Frank.

"Does it make any difference as far as Myrt is concerned?"

"Not one bit! I was thinking of what your pa and ma would say."

"I haven't told them yet, but I will."

"Whatever you're of a mind to do is your business. I hope you have you a lot of luck and my girl is lucky to have you."

"I'm lucky all right, Jack, and Dad's lucky. Suppose I had picked a boy who didn't know one end of a horse from the other. That would have been awful!" Myrtle made a face and led Jack away.

It was all of midnight before the party broke up. After the last ones had gone, and Frank had put his cows back where they belonged, he put his arm around Mary, as they walked to the house.

"It happened, Mary. Jack and Myrt asked me tonight."

"What did you say?" She stopped and faced him, her hands on his shoulders.

"I told him I was proud to have him for a son," he said simply.

"What happens now?"

"We wait and see what happens. I may be wrong."

"Frank, I hope not."

"Me, too, Mother."

CHAPTER XXIX

THE WAY WITH GREAT DECEPTIONS

The night after the impromptu Halloween party was lodge night. Frank was ready to go when he sat down to supper. He had joined the lodge years ago, and found in its membership contemporary companionship. Consequently, he seldom missed a meeting.

Frank had been pretty busy today and had not had a chance to discuss the party with the young folks. He wondered how they had liked it. There was no better way of finding out than to ask, but with four or five women running to and fro between the dining room and kitchen, he decided to wait until they had settled down at the table. Soon they were in their places. It was Calista's turn to ask the blessing, so they bowed their heads and she began.

"Dear Lord, bless this food to our use that we may do Thy will. Bless us and watch over us." She paused, looked up at her father whose eyes remained fixed in reverent pose, and then continued. "Please forgive our father for his great deception. Amen."

If he had had enough hair to do so, it would have stood on end. What in thunder had she meant? His "great deception"— was it possible she knew? He looked at Mary, who returned his gaze solemnly, and then an eye fluttered a wink in his direction. If she could wink at him it could not be so bad.

"All right, Calista, what is my 'great deception'?"

"You know," she said ominously.

"I got me so many deceptions, I don't know which one you want me forgiven for."

"Everybody's talking about it, Uncle Frank," said Blanche.

"Well, I swan!"

"Didn't you hear about Mr. Barber?" asked Myrtle.

"What is he mixed up with me for? I ain't seen him for a month." Frank was getting confused, but from the expressions it must be pretty bad.

211

"Let me tell him," said Vilas, "I'll make it good."

"It's not very funny, Vile," said Calista.

"Well, seeing as how I'm about to choke with curiosity, s'pose somebody tells me," said Frank.

"Well, Uncle Frank, last night Clara and Carrie Barber went to the party with me and Joe Wood. We had some cider and cake, and when the party broke up we heard about the barn party and came over here. Well, we ate some doughnuts and drank some more cider, and danced, and had a good time. Pretty soon Joe said to me, 'Vilas, what's wrong with Clara? She's acting awfully silly.' I looked at her and saw her hair coming loose. She was trying to dance but not doing very well. I looked over and saw Carrie pouring out another glass of cider, and she was clumsy, too."

"They were pig-eyed drunk," said Myrtle.

"Who's telling this?" Vilas wanted to know.

"You are so slow!" said Myrtle, disgustedly.

"Anyway, Joe and I tried to get the girls to go home, but they said they were having a hell of a good time, and wouldn't. When the party finally broke up, we put our arms around the girls and half carried them home." He grinned at the memory. "Joe finally picked Carrie up and lugged her a block and sat down to rest, holding her on his lap. She got affectionate and wanted to love him up, but he was thinking about what her folks would say and tried to sober her up. Clara wasn't so bad, but she was bad enough.

"When we got them home, Clara opened the door, and Joe and I sort of pushed them inside and closed it. Carrie fell over something in there and started to yell like the devil. We watched from the street until a light went on and we saw her old man come downstairs in his nightshirt. Then we ran."

"Don't know as I blame you," said Frank. "I think I'd have made me a few tracks myself."

"Oh," said Blanche, "but that's not all."

"No!" said Calista. "Mr. Barber asked the girls where they had been."

"And Carrie swore," said Blanche.

"That's not swearing," said Myrtle. "She said they had been to a damned church party."

"Anyhow," said Calista, "he got dressed and went right down to see Reverend Willard—"

"Old Cake?"

"Yes."

"Mary, I'm beginning to like this 'great deception,'" said Frank.

"And he made an awful racket to wake Mr. Willard. Finally, Mr. Willard came to the door and let him in, and he told him about his girls coming home drunk and blamed him for giving them hard cider."

"The Reverend said it tasted sweet to him, and Mr. Barber said that was because he was a man who was used to hard drink. Poor Mr. Willard apologized, but Mr. Barber said he'd have to do it from the pulpit, or he'd have the law on him," narrated Blanche.

"And all the time," said Calista, "it was you who made the girls drunk."

"Me?" asked Frank in all innocence.

"Yes, you," said Calista, pointing at him.

"Not on your tin-type," said he. "If there was anybody to blame it was your mother." He grinned delightedly, and then laughed long and loud, ending with a "Whoee!"

"What did you have to do with it, Mother?" asked Myrtle.

"Nothing," said Mary. She pointed across the table. "It was Grandma's fault."

Grandma smiled, and looked at the bewildered children. "A good drunk once in a while is good for the soul," she said.

"Damn me, if it ain't," said Frank. "Tonight I'm going to lodge and celebrate. I hope Barber is there—he'll still be blowing off steam." He excused himself from the table, stood up, and left the house almost immediately.

"I don't believe he is one bit sorry," said Calista.

"Clisty, there are some things your Dad would trade his place in heaven for. Seeing Mr. Barber quarrel with the minister is one of them."

The dishes were done, but scarcely in silence. The girls re-hashed the story and wondered how many others of their friends had been drunk, if any. They also wondered if anyone would let the secret out of the bag. Once the dishes were done, the girls disappeared next door to go over the lurid details with Effie and Ollie, leaving Mary alone for Grandma was tired and had gone to bed.

213

Mary lighted a fire in the fireplace. The nights were getting chilly now and darkness came earlier. She pulled her rocker in front of the fire and began knitting. The project was a wool sock, which with its mate, would be a Christmas present. Mary needed no additional light to see by, since her fingers had long since learned their way around.

There was a gentle knock on the door, and from where she sat Mary could make out the form of a woman. She opened the door and in the darkness failed to recognize her visitor.

"Good evening, Mrs. Stone," said the woman, "is Mr. Stone home? I'd like to speak to him."

"Why, it's Grace!" said Mary. "Grace Morrison, come in!"

"Only for a minute," said the visitor, uneasily. "You are looking well, Mary."

"Feeling well, too. Have a chair. Let me hang your wraps here."

"I mustn't stay," said Grace.

"Tonight is Frank's lodge night. He is up at the K.P. hall."

"Oh! I'm so sorry. I must be going. It was not very important anyway."

"Well," said Mary, "now that we are practically in the same family, you must come in and visit for a few minutes."

"Jack told me and his father this morning," Grace looked old, and worried. Her shoulders appeared rounded.

"What do you think about it?" Mary's eyes watched every expression on Grace's face. She led her over before the fire and gave her the rocker. She pulled up another and sat in it.

"I don't know, Mary. They are so young."

"I suppose they are."

"Clarence has his heart set on Jack becoming a doctor, and when Jack told his father he was going to quit school and had asked for Myrt's hand in marriage, it caused a dreadful row. Jack's father thinks Jack is so anxious to get married, he would throw away his medical career just to do it."

"That was why you wanted to see Frank, wasn't it?"

"In a way, yes." Grace looked uneasily at Mary.

In the silence that followed both women looked into the flames. Mary rocked back and forth, her mind in a whirl. Grace was struggling so hard to keep her secret, and was so worried about the outcome, Mary wondered if it would be better to talk to her

214

frankly and try to ease her mind. She had come to talk to Frank, but maybe it would be better this way. Finally, she reached a decision and took a deep breath. Her heart pounded within her.

"Grace," she said softly, "I know about Jack."

Grace leaped from her chair. Once on her feet she seemed to be looking wildly for a place to escape. Mary walked over to her and put her hand on Grace's cheek. Standing before Grace, Mary seemed small and like a child. Her face was calm and sympathetic whereas Grace's was pinched and distorted, as she struggled against tears.

"Please, sit down, Grace. Maybe I shouldn't have told you, but if we talk this thing out, I'm sure we'll feel better."

Grace sat down again. Her fingers picked at the seam of her dress, and her eyes stared ahead, careful to avoid Mary's.

"What must you think of me, Mary!" she finally exclaimed.

"Grace, I have always known. Frank told me about it, and I told him to give you a baby."

"Mary, you didn't!"

"Yes, Grace, I did. Most men wouldn't have told their wives. But Frank is crazy and always has been. I knew how you wanted a baby, and I'd have done the same thing you did."

"Oh, thank you, Mary, for saying so. I've always felt so wicked about it, until I looked at the baby and then I could feel no shame. I don't know why I had so much trouble having my first one. I had no trouble from then on God knows."

"That's often the way of it." The chairs rocked and squeaked. "Who would have thought that I'd have a little girl, and that the two little tykes would grow up and want to get married?"

"But why did Frank give his consent?"

"When I said he was crazy, I meant it. Sometimes there is method in his madness and he seems to be a wizard. Now, I can only hope so. Frank told me that if he tried to break up the marriage, they would only get married secretly and soon. He doesn't intend to tell the children if there is any other way out."

"Oh, my goodness, no!"

"Well, he sort of figures to give them all the rope in the world. Frank says, it's Myrt who will break it up, if it is broken. He says if he pushes her in the direction he doesn't want her to go, she'll turn around and do the opposite."

"Are women that obstinate?"

"Frank says so."

Grace considered this for a long time. There was no other plan she could advocate with any more hope of success. The more she thought about it, the better Frank's reasoning appeared.

"What does Frank think of Jack?" she asked.

"Frank and I both love him."

"You, too, Mary?"

"Yes."

"He is a wonderful boy. I'm so proud of him, but he mustn't hurt Clarence, because he loves the boy, too."

"I know. Mothers and fathers make such a mess of things when they fool with their children's love. I sometimes wonder what harm it would be if Myrt and Jack did marry. Certainly, they are half brother and sister, but—"

"That wouldn't be right, Mary."

"I suppose not, at that."

Outside a window shutter slammed, and a streetcar clanged past. The wind blew hard and it sounded wintery. Here it was warm and peaceful.

"I must tell you," said Grace, "that a load has been lifted from me tonight. More than twenty years I have been thinking about this son, and not a soul I could speak to about him, not even Frank. And then to find that you knew about it and loved my baby—" She began to cry into a handkerchief and Mary hovered over her soothingly. When she had calmed down, she said, "I must go now, Mary, but can I talk to you again? You have no idea how wonderful you are."

"Grace, we have a lot of things to worry about, but nothing that the good Lord, and that husband of mine can't figure a way around." Mary sounded far more optimistic than she really felt.

"I hope so." For the first time she smiled, and to Mary, it seemed as though Grace carried her shoulders a little straighter. Grace put on her coat and hat. In a few minutes the door closed behind her. Mary picked up her knitting and began to work, and as she worked she hummed a happy little tune.

216

Chapter XXX

JACK NEEDS ADVICE

Before Frank tore the November sheet from the calendar on the barn door, many things had happened. Jack Morrison had given Myrtle a diamond ring and they publicly announced their engagement. To the good people of the neighborhood, the announcement could scarcely have been considered news. And then it happened—on the last day of November, Clarence Morrison was injured.

He had left his office and hailed a cab.

"Where to?" asked the driver.

Mr. Morrison gave him an address on St. Clair, near Erie Street and climbed into the cab. Traffic was rather heavy close to the Public Square, but as they moved out, it thinned and the cab driver urged his horse into a trot. Near Erie Street the driver suddenly clutched at his coat lapels and fell from the seat, passing between the horse and the dashboard. The horse promptly ran away, with Clarence a helpless passenger.

A mounted policeman saw the runaway and galloped to head it off. However, as he came up alongside, the runaway horse swerved away from him and the cab crashed into a lamp post. The horse ran on with only the shafts, and the policeman in pursuit, while Mr. Morrison lay badly injured and bleeding in the wreckage. It was an hour before he was delivered to Lakeside Hospital, more dead than alive.

The physicians in charge of the patient could offer scant encouragement to Mrs. Morrison and Jack, who reached his bedside as quickly as possible. It was nearly eight o'clock in the evening before he came out of the coma long enough to recognize anyone.

"You here, Grace?"

"Yes, Clarence, I'm here."

"Where is John?"

"I'm here, Dad."

217

"Good boy." He panted and closed his eyes, until they felt he had gone back to sleep, but that was not the case. The doctor came in and felt his pulse.

"Do you hurt in the chest?" he asked as he began to listen with his stethoscope.

"No," whispered Clarence.

"Where do you hurt?"

"Nowhere. Where is my boy?"

"Here I am."

"Come close where I can see you." Jack took his father's white hand. "Promise me you'll finish school, Son. Please, promise me." Mr. Morrison opened his eyes, now so startlingly black against the white of his face.

Jack looked at his father, his whole being in turmoil. He pitied his father and wanted to promise him anything in his power, but to promise to do something which was so opposed to his own wishes was impossible. He couldn't speak.

"Yes, Clarence, Jack promises! He will do as you want! He will be a doctor—a good doctor." Grace spoke passionately and her face was nearly as white as her husband's.

"Thank you, Jack. I knew you wouldn't let your dad down," said Clarence so feebly at the last as to be almost inaudible.

"Oh, Mother, why did you do that?" Jack whispered.

"You must, dear. It means everything to him." Grace held her husband's hand in both of hers.

"I'm afraid," said the doctor, "that he is in a coma again. Both of you must go home now and get some rest. We will call you if anything happens, either good or bad."

"Will he live, Doctor?" asked Grace.

"His chances are very poor, but one never knows. He is badly injured."

"Can I stay here, tonight?" she asked. "I want to be here if he wakes or asks for me."

"We can fix you up a cot in here if you like, but you won't rest well."

"Please do." She turned to Jack and spoke quietly. "Jack, go home and take care of the girls. I'll call you in the morning."

"All right, Mother."

"Good night, dear." She kissed him, and he tiptoed out of the room. Behind, the doctor turned the light down low.

Mr. Morrison never regained consciousness and died about noon the following day.

"Mr. Stone, can I talk to you alone for a few minutes?"

"You bet your bottom dollar you can. Let's see—where can we go?" He looked around the living room. It was cluttered up with Christmas paper, and boxes. In the parlor were a pair of "lalligagers." "Let's you and me light a lantern and go see Fred."

"All right, Mr. Stone."

Frank and Jack went out through the kitchen where dishwashing was very much in progress. Frank lighted his lantern and they declined the various towels playfully being offered them. It was Saturday night before Christmas, and cold as they tramped over the frozen ground to the barn.

"Here we are," said Frank. "No matter how cold it is outside, there's always warmth in a barn where livestock is. I got Fred a dandy blanket the other day. It buckles around his neck and can't fall off him on account of this here crouper." He held the lantern up for Jack to see. The blanket showed its red and yellow plaid and bright new leather straps. "I got him a new halter, too.

"Whoa there, Boy, take it easy. Still hungry? Might spare you a bit more hay. Just a minute." Frank hung the lantern from a peg and gave the horse a small forkful of hay.

"What's on your mind, Jack?" Frank led the way over to a bale of straw and sat down. So did Jack.

"I need advice," said Jack. In the dim light, Frank noted his troubled eyes. Jack took off his cap and rubbed his head thoughtfully.

"I ain't a great hand at giving advice," said Frank, "but I'll do my durndest."

"It's about me and medical school. My dad had his heart set on me going to medical school and becoming a doctor. When I was a kid, I thought that would be fine and figured on being a doctor. Well, I went to Western Reserve and, Mr. Stone, believe me, I'm not cut out for one.

"For one thing, I am a poor hand in a chemistry laboratory, mostly I guess, because I hate the smells and fumes. In biology where we must cut things up, I'm clumsy with my fingers and I get sick to my stomach when I make a cut on anything that is alive.

219

"I'd made up my mind to quit. Honestly, I'd have quit whether I wanted to get married or not. Myrtle had nothing to do with it. When I told my dad, I couldn't make him believe it, and he raised a terrible row. He said he wasn't sending me to school to play football. He said if I'd go after my studies as hard, I could be a great doctor. I tried to tell him, but he wouldn't listen.

"Then he got hurt. Mom and I were there when he came to, and he recognized me. He asked me to promise to finish school, but I couldn't. I knew I wanted to, but I just couldn't, even if he was dying. My mother said, 'He promises, Clarence, he will finish school and be a doctor.' He smiled and passed out. The next day he was dead."

Jack and Frank sat quietly. The only noise was the grinding of the hay and its rattle as Fred filled himself. Through the windows the blue white light of a flickering trolley was reflected. The bare branches of the apple tree were momentarily traced against the sky.

"It appears to me like you got you a problem," said Frank, putting a straw in his mouth.

"I don't know what to do," said Jack. "You have always been so kind to me, sort of like a second father to me, so I thought I'd talk it over with you."

"I'm proud you did," said Frank. "There isn't any trouble that doesn't get less when you consider all its angles. Let's look this thing in the eye, and see what it gets us.

"You admit you got no points that would make you a good doctor, and you told your pa as much. If he had lived you would have quit, regardless of the racket it raised."

"Yes, I would have. Dad would have raised the devil, but I'd have quit."

"Then you still got you all the reasons for quitting you ever had." Frank saw him nod his head, but he didn't answer. "And the only reason added to the other side is your promise when the poor fellow was dying."

"Yes, that's it, and it was my mother's promise, not mine. Now, she says I am duty bound to fulfill it, because she told him I would."

Frank studied the matter for some moments. Through his mind ran all kinds of thoughts as he tried to figure the problem out, by figuring what he would have done, had he ever been placed in a like fix. This produced no tangible results.

"Let's s'pose you did go on and finish, would the school make you a doctor?"

"I suppose so, but I'd have to do better than I am doing now."

"Are you that bad?"

"I'm the worst of the lot."

"But you might make it."

"Yes."

"What kind of a doctor would you make after you got to work?"

"I'd probably make a fair horse doctor, but never a real good one."

"If you made yourself into a doctor, you'd try to be a good one, wouldn't you?"

"Yes, I'd try."

"But you would rather own you a livery stable." Frank laughed and Jack admitted it ruefully.

"Jack, would you hold it against your pa, if you finally did go on? Would the fact that you were doing something because he wanted you to do it, gall you?"

"I don't know," said Jack, "outside of this, I've never really had to do anything I didn't want to do."

"In a lifetime a fellow has to do a lot of things he might not want to do."

"I suppose so," conceded Jack hopelessly.

"Well, this is getting us nowhere fast," said Frank. "Let me mull this for a few minutes. Maybe some idee will flip out of this head of mine."

Frank walked to the door and back, paused, and did it again. At last, he stopped before Jack.

"I think I'm beginning to get some sense," he said. "Jack, I'm a father like your pa. I lived my life pretty much as I wanted to. If I made me some blunders, I paid for 'em. In a way, so did Clarence. He always wanted to be a doctor, but on account of money mostly, he didn't get the chance. Maybe if he had took the bull by the horns and tried to be a doctor, he'd have made it. Anyhow, for some reason he didn't do it, and it galled him all his life to where, by God, he was going to see that his boy made it, if he didn't. All that was wrong was that his boy didn't want to be one." Frank sat down and selected a new straw, which he chewed on.

"It's always easier on a man to do something his way and see where he was wrong, than to do something somebody else's way and find out he was right all along. A body can boot himself in the tail for being wrong, but he will never get over despising himself for not having the rind to do what he knew to be right.

"Every tub has got itself its own bottom to sit on. You got your own life to live. If you ain't made you any mistakes, it's about time you got started. Your ma would feel bad, but she ought to be reasonable."

"Then, if you were me, you would quit and do something else?" Jack sounded so hopeful.

"Yes, by Judas, I would."

"Thank you," said Jack, grasping Frank's hand and putting an arm on his shoulder. "I might have figured it out that way by myself, but I'd never have felt so sure about it, as I do when it comes from you."

"Well, Son, we all of us like to take advice when it goes with what we want to do. Advice that goes against our liking is the hardest to take."

"I know," said Jack, smiling.

"What are you going to do when you quit?"

"I have been promised a job in the steel mills."

"Is that what you want to do for a lifetime?"

"No, but I'll be getting paid, and I'll save my money and some day I'll be able to do what I want," said Jack confidently.

"Better men than Jack Morrison have said that," commented Frank, "but wives and children kept them at the wrong job. Anyway, Jack, a wrong job of your own choosing is better than a wrong job somebody else picked out, even if the result is the same in the long run."

They took down the lantern, let themselves out of the barn, and made their way to the house. Snow had been falling and there was a thin cover of it. It looked like there might be a white Christmas.

CHAPTER XXXI

MOSTLY GIVE, BUT SOME TAKE

"Hello, Mr. Stone, I wondered when you'd be coming in. I been anxious to see you." The blacksmith pumped the bellows with his left hand and stirred up his fire with the long tong in his right. When the fire glowed red, and changed to white, he put two horseshoes in it. About the shop was the strong odor of burned hoof. Lined up opposite the forge were several horses. Frank led Fred beyond them and tied him to a well gnawed post. Frank returned to the front of the shop where several grimy men were sitting on a work bench, and several others, probably customers, were seated in chairs with well worn bottoms. The smith still pumped and poked at the shoes.

"So you been anxious to see me," said Frank. "Glad to know somebody wants to see me." He tossed a few scraps of tobacco into his mouth.

"I hear your son-in-law to be is a real man. How about telling us about him?"

"What do you specially want to know?" asked Frank.

"How'd he happen to get started, and just how good is he? In fact, I'd listen to anything you can tell me about him," said the smith.

"Glad to oblige you," said Frank, picking up a box and carefully fixing it against the sliding door. He lowered his bottom to it gingerly and leaned back. The air was expectant as the little group waited for him to begin. The blacksmith was the only man present Frank knew.

"Well," said Frank, rolling his tobacco to the opposite cheek, "to begin with this boy Jack Morrison has been—"

"Jack Morrison!" exclaimed one of the dirtier men present. "You don't mean Battling Jack Morrison, the Iron Man?"

"Yes," said Frank, nodding. The smith was nodding, too.

"Well, Jack was going to school and decided to quit. He'd been quite a footballer over to the University and wasn't afraid of work where his back was concerned. He got hisself a job in the steel mill and went to work down there right after New Year's last year. Long about March the mills were having themselves quite a to-do as to which mill had the best man with his fists. Now, Jack was quite a boy, standing over six feet tall and weighing nearly two hundred and ten pounds, so the men down there sicked him onto the best man in their own mill, and Jack whipped him one noon. They weren't mad or nothing and had it out with regular box-fighter's gloves."

"So that's how he got started, was it?" asked the smith. "Wait 'til I fix these shoes, 'cause I want to hear it all."

"Go ahead," said Frank with a wave of his hand. He looked at his audience and was pleased to note that they had sidled closer. Frank loved a good story, especially if he was telling it, and a good story never lost anything with him in the driver's seat.

The smith clanged away on the hot iron, beating on the caulks and the toe plate. The sparks scattered as he worked. Driving his punch into a nail hole on the shoe, he tried each on the horse for size. One fit perfectly, but the other was too wide. He hammered it narrow and tried again. This time it was all right, so he dropped it in the tub of water to cool.

"I guess I can listen for a spell. So Jack beat the man in his own mill?"

"Yup, that's exactly what he did. Then he took on each mill's man 'til he licked 'em all. There wasn't much science to those fights, but steel mill men are mighty strong. Jack wasn't getting by too easy either. He come over to the house of a Saturday with big welts on his cheeks and black eyes, but he didn't seem to mind it none.

"Then he got old Doug Cheney, the middleweight fighter who was such a good boxer, to show him how to box and teach him how to protect hisself. Right away he began to get along better.

"Next thing you know somebody offered him a hundred dollars to boxfight a Akron fellow who was considered pretty good. Jack got hisself that money in less than a half hour and has been going like a house afire ever since."

"Does he still work in the steel mills?" asked one.

"Yup, he's been there, going on a year and a half now, and

figures there ain't no better way to keep in shape."

"Has he been beat yet? I ain't heard much about him 'til lately," said a heavy set teamster.

"In a way he has, and in another way he hasn't," said Frank after mulling the question over some seconds. "He has always had his glove raised over his head at the end of a fight, but a couple of times, he lost every round before knocking the other fellow galleywest. Once he even got a rib broke, but so far he ain't lost. He ain't scarred up, neither."

"When he meets better men, he'll probably get cut up and look like some of the rest of those old timers," offered another.

"I suppose so," said Frank. The thought had occurred to him before and he hadn't liked it then.

"Who'll he fight next?"

"In about two weeks he fights Roy Richards in Chicago for a thousand dollars, winner take all, and if he wins, he fights Cowboy Cherney here in Cleveland in August. I got me no idee what the stakes will be here."

The smith fished the shoes out of the tub and started nailing them on. However, the conversation was not over, for there was speculation as to the outcome of the fight in Chicago, discussion about the betting odds, and the dozen and one things sportsmen usually consider. By the time Fred was shod, the ground had been covered going and coming.

"In a way," concluded the blacksmith as Frank paid him and prepared to lead Fred home, "I don't like to see the young man taking on Cowboy Cherney so soon. The Cowboy is right up among the best in the game and there are a lot of good men fighting now, who could all have been champs ten years ago. He ain't Champeen, but he could give him a tussle. Jack'll get the tar beat out of him sure as hell, if he fights him."

"Jack is signing his own fights," said Frank, "and maybe he knows what he's doing. It does look like he's bitin' off a mighty big chaw in Cherney."

During the next two weeks Frank was destined to hear many diversified comments and opinions on the activities of his prospective son-in-law. Mrs. Kennedy Johnson who was a high official in an organization whose aim was to throttle the manufacture of buggy whips as a first step in the direction of kindness to animals, was particularly violent in her statements.

225

"Oh, the disgrace of it!" she railed. "Poor Clarence Morrison is scarcely cold in his grave before that hulk of a son drags the good name of his father in the gutter. When I called Grace and told her, she said she wasn't living her children's lives and hung up the phone. I called her right back and she said we had a bad connection, but she hung up and I know it." Her eyes glittered in anger and Frank tried to escape, but it was no use. "What are you going to do about it, Mr. Stone?"

"Me?" asked Frank. He sounded incredulous.

"Yes, you!" she snapped.

"I got nothing to do about what Jack does."

"Yes, you have! He's going to marry your daughter, isn't he?"

"He might and he might not. Right now they are engaged, but you know how children are—engaged one day and unengaged the next."

"They've been engaged over a year and a half, and it is your duty to protect your child from this brutality."

"You mean, I should protect Myrtle from Jack?"

"That's exactly what I mean! He's cruel and brutal."

Frank took off his hat and wiped the sweat band with his handkerchief, and then mopped the top of his head. His blue eyes looked out from under his shaggy brows and seemed to smile as he answered.

"I got me more of a job protecting Jack from Myrt."

"Just what do you mean?" she asked suspiciously.

"Well, Myrt favors her mother more'n she does me, and she just naturally is meaner'n all get out. For a fact," his eyes were wide now to emphasize his statement, "I feel sort of like she drove him into this fighting and all. He just had to take it out on somebody. No, ma'am, if Myrt is to blame, I ain't going to interfere now."

"I must say that is a very peculiar attitude for a father to take," said Mrs. Johnson, but she sounded less belligerent and Frank made his escape, before she took the offensive again.

Most people were curious and if they had an opinion, carefully concealed it. A few were openly and brazenly enthusiastic. Grandma Morrison, now old, wrinkled and toothless, was delighted. She crowed at length over Jack's feats and could quote newspaper comment, the exact round each fight had ended, and would tell you in detail the damage Jack had inflicted and sus-

226

tained in each encounter. If Jack was dragging the name of Morrison in the gutter, Grandma approved his doing so.

Jack's uncles and aunts were rather in between. If Jack received good write-ups in the press, all was well, but it did not take much of a panning to cool their enthusiasm. There was also the coolness of the clergy for them to consider. Reverend Willard frowned mightily upon the "prostitution of the manhood" of their nephew for the sake of "paltry gold."

The night before Jack left for Chicago to meet Roy Richards, he came over to see Myrtle. He was a handsome man, but tonight with his face flushed with excitement, he was more so than usual. His ash blond hair had a tendency to form a slight wave close to his forehead. Tonight it was cut closer than usual. His chin was durably built and his nose generous, while his eyes were deep-set and very blue.

"Myrt," he said when he came into the living room, "I came over for you to give me luck. I'm going to need all I can get."

He doubled up his huge fists and she planted a kiss squarely on the knuckles of each. Right before the family he pulled her to him and kissed her.

"Kneel down," said she with severity. Jack knelt. "I dub thee Battling Jack, my Knight of the Iron Cross." She pretended to lay a sword across his broad shoulders. "Fe, fie, fo, fum, I smell the blood of a Richards' son. Be he dead—"

"Myrtle!" gasped Calista. "What are you saying?"

"Sh!" said Jack. "She's giving me luck."

"Such ghastly barbarism!" Calista looked as shocked as she sounded. "I am so ashamed that you should choose pugilism as a life's work!"

"Why, Clisty!" said Mary. "It really isn't anyone's business but Jack's what he does."

"Oh, yes, it is," replied Calista. "There is honor, the honor of the name of Stone." She pulled her skirt up an inch or two off the floor and swept out of the room, her back as stiff as a ramrod.

Jack grinned at Frank. "Dad, I wouldn't say she was one of my most enthusiastic backers. She may be right at that—I may come home with a thousand Chicago dollars, or I may come home with my teeth knocked down my throat. Whatever I get besides, I hope I can rattle those cartwheels."

"I hope so, too. Don't forget though, you got you one man-sized job cut out for you."

227

"I won't," he promised. "Get on your bonnet, Myrt, and let's go to the Alhambra. I'm jittery and could listen to some good music. I don't know what is playing."

"It is Carothers Manville and Theresa Billings in *The Romance of Phyllis Ware*," said Blanche. "It's very sad."

"Good," said Jack, "I feel like crying."

CHAPTER XXXII

EVERYBODY CAN'T WIN—A FEW REASONS WHY NOT

Battling Jack Morrison, the Cleveland Iron Man, made his meeting with the experienced Roy Richards a singularly unremunerative one for the latter. The fight ended in the seventh round by a knockout. Apparently, Mr. Richards had anticipated some such climax, because from the first bell on he covered up and retreated, and when he finally did get jarred enough in the seventh to attempt retaliation, he gave Jack the chance to get a clean blow home.

The Chicago papers were exceedingly vitriolic in their comments, claiming everything from a fixed fight to charges that Rip Van Winkle could have taken both fighters at the same time. Jack was puzzled, too. In a winner-take-all fight, it is only natural to expect that there would be violent opposition, and Jack was not at all certain that it was not a fixed fight. However, he collected his money and returned to Cleveland with Doug Cheney.

In Cleveland everything was different. Richards' retreating tactics were explained as the attempt of a more experienced man to make his younger opponent carry the fight, thus laying him open to mayhem, should he ever leave an opening. That no opening ever presented itself was proof enough of the improved boxing of the Iron Man. The writers drooled over the prospects of a near championship bout in August, and wrote colorful and highly optimistic forecasts of the probable results.

The press also pointed to the stakes, as an incentive for the men. Ten thousand dollars was the amount, and the winner was to get sixty per cent of it. For a non-title match, this was a whale of a lot of money and much was made of it. The fight was to be held at the baseball park on Lexington Avenue under the arc lights. The reserved seats for the match between Jack and Cowboy Cherney were sold out completely two weeks before the fight night.

229

"Yes, siree," chortled Frank one night. He took two tickets from his wallet and held them up for all to see. "I figured, Vilas, you and me would see us a fight."

"Vilas!" cried Myrtle. "You aren't going to take Vilas to that fight. You are going to take me!"

Frank sobered, and looked puzzled. This was an angle he had overlooked. While he considered, Calista spoke.

"Myrtle Stone! Women do not go to such brawls! A lady would never be seen at a fight! Shame on you for thinking of it!" She held out one index finger and appeared to be whittling on it with the other.

"I guess a lady can go to a fight if she wants to," said Myrtle with considerable fire. "I will be there with my father, and if he can't take care of me, my fiancé can."

"Myrt, do you really want to see this fight?" asked Frank.

"Want to!" she said. "I'm going to!"

"Well, I guess, that is settled," said Vilas, "I'll get a ticket and see it from the top seat in the bleachers."

"Mother!" said Calista, "are you going to let her go?"

"I'll have to see about it."

"It's all settled," said Myrt quietly, with a spread of hands and a shrug of her shoulders. "I wouldn't miss this for anything in the world."

"Don't be too cocksure," said her mother.

But on the night of the fight, Myrtle was ready and going for certain. Jack stopped in early for his supply of luck. He was smiling and confident, although he knew that this fight was going to be a real one, for Cowboy Cherney had a wide reputation as a two-fisted slugger who would willingly trade punch for punch.

At supper neither Frank nor Myrtle could eat. Vilas had foregone his supper in favor of a position at the front of the line. The excitement had even laid hold on Grandma Parker, and she cautioned Myrtle on how to sit if the seats were off the ground, and what to say if accosted. Mary insisted that Myrtle wear her coat and flower hat, and in the near riot that followed, the entire family had a voice. Eventually, the ayes won and Myrtle left the house wearing the hat and coat, but it was evident that she did so under duress.

"Myrt, give me your hat and coat," said Frank as they rounded the corner out of sight of the porch. She skinned out of both in a hurry while her father unlocked the store door. He quickly deposited her stuff and his straw hat on the counter, locked the door, and they hurried on, lest they be caught.

"Thanks, Dad, that's much better."

"It is for a fact."

"How do I look?" She brushed a thread off her white embroidered shirtwaist. Her gay skirt barely cleared the ground.

"Pretty as a speckled pup," he assured her, smiling broadly.

Catching a streetcar was an easy matter, but it was packed and they had to stand. Apparently the majority of passengers were headed for the ball park, because there was a holiday spirit prevailing. At the entrance to the park there was a terrific crowd, pushing and shoving to get in, and Myrtle's eye was quick to note that so far as she could see, she was the only woman present. She clung a little closer to her dad.

Once inside the park they had little trouble finding their seats, and once in them, they looked around. The ring was placed squarely over home plate. For about fifty feet from the ring, towards the fields and clear to the backstops, there were rows of chairs, and close to the ring, a row of tables. Beyond the chairs, a bleachers had been set up and in the fifth or sixth row, approximately over third base, sat Frank and Myrtle.

Although it was not completely dark, and the park less than half full, one of the preliminary fights was under way. Almost no one paid attention to it, for there was a buzz of conversation and shouting.

As the place filled up, Myrtle felt all the more conspicuous, for while she had been happy to note that there were women there besides herself, they were scarcely the homebody type.

The man next to her was a provident soul who thoughtfully brought along three or four bottles of beer in a wet gunny sack, which she had trouble avoiding. Behind them were several large middle-aged gentlemen, who had apparently brought their refreshments with them, too, for they warmed up as the evening wore on.

Father and daughter kept up a steady stream of conversation about the park, its occupants and even the performers. Now two lusty heavyweights were whaling away at each other. There was no telling how much damage they might have done to one another had they been closer together, but as it was they seldom connected. If they did, the range was adjusted, and all was as before. When it came to an end, and the referee raised one of their hands in victory, practically no one was watching.

This bout was followed by one in which it became readily apparent that the two contestants were anxious to have a look at each other's insides, and were not delaying matters one bit. By the end of the first round they had done more fighting than had been done in the two previous bouts. The park was now jammed and the crowd was getting the action it had been hoping to see. Every eye was on the ring as they stepped through the remaining five rounds to a draw, which was a popular decision.

It was now time for the main event of the evening. Cowboy Cherney came through the third base gate and entered the ring first. He was followed by no less than a dozen men, carrying stools, buckets, towels and boxing gloves. Myrtle's heart fell within her as she beheld the scarred face and massive frame of the Cowboy.

"Oh, Dad," she whispered, "he looks frightening."

"Them cuts he got were give to him by men who weren't scared of him, but he has him a fierce look, and there ain't no doubt about it." Frank's heart was beating fast, too, and he was nervous.

"Those men with him have broken noses and scars."

"It appears to me that the whole kit and kaboodle in that corner been making their livings by getting their blocks knocked off." It was true. Cauliflower ears, blackeyes, and smashed features were the salient features, or motif of the group.

"Sh! Someone is going to say something," said Myrtle.

"Ladies and Gentlemen!" roared the gentleman, decked out in top hat and tails. "The next feature," long pause as he completely turned around, "is the Main bout of the evening, twenty rounds—to select a challenger—to meet the World's Champion—at a later date!"

As he had been talking, there had been a slight flurry in the corner opposite the Cowboy. Jack climbed through the ropes and sat down while Doug Cheney laced his gloves on.

"In this corner—at two hundred and five pounds—we have—Cowboy Cherney, The Texas Bad Man!" A great yell came from the crowd. Cherney stood up and skipped in a shuffle to the center of the ring and back.

"And in this corner—at two hundred and six and one-half

pounds—is Battling Jack Morrison, the Cleveland Iron Man." So far as Myrtle and Frank could tell the cheers were as loud for Jack as for the Cowboy. Jack stood up and waved his huge right fist at the crowd.

Myrtle opened her fists and looked at her hands. They were wet with perspiration and her heart thumped audibly. She looked at her father. He seemed as nervous as she was, and kept wetting his lips and wiping his face with his huge red handkerchief. The man on her left quietly emptied his second bottle of beer.

The referee called the fighters to the middle of the ring and occasionally Jack nodded. He looked so young and inexperienced compared to his opponent. His body was pink and smooth, and his muscles did not stand out in bunches like those on Cherney. Again, Myrtle was afraid, as they returned to their corners.

Before the fight could start a big man leaped up on the ring and held onto a ring post. "I am Felix Bergen, the Murdering Swede—I challenge the winner any time, any where—for love, money or marbles." A group of helmeted cops ran toward the ring, and the Murdering Swede jumped down and ran off with the police in pursuit. The crowd loved it. Then the bell rang for the first round.

The Cowboy met Jack two thirds of the way across the ring, feinting with his left. Jack crouched easily, his weight on the balls of his feet, his own left slightly extended. Feinting to the body, Cherney delivered a left jab to the face which was blocked and then brought over a whistling right. Jack slipped inside the blow and brought a left uppercut up close to his man's body, which lost its sting on Cherney's chest, but the overhand right that followed landed flush and hard on the man's chin, sending him crashing to the canvas.

The crowd roared its approval. Cherney took a count of nine, before rising, and kept out of harm's way the rest of the round. Through the second, third and fourth rounds the men boxed carefully, and Jack probably lost them all, because Cherney was an experienced hand and having learned his lesson in the first round, was careful not to take too many chances. Preferring to force the fight, Jack came out in the fifth aggressively. After a brief exchange of hard rights and lefts, Cherney saw an opening and piled four or five terrific blows into Jack, who clinched.

When they broke clear, Cherney rushed in to follow up his

233

advantage, only to run into a terrific left to the cheek. Cherney stumbled and fell. The crowd rose to its feet, yelling like maniacs, but he scrambled to his feet without a count and charged Jack again, scoring heavily.

"Kill him! Kill him! Kill him, Cowboy!" shouted the man behind Myrtle, wiping his lips with the back of his hand after a pull at his whiskey bottle. "Kill the shun of a bish!"

"Did you hear what he called Jack," yelled Myrtle in Frank's ear, pointing at the man. Frank was so busy watching the ring, he didn't hear her.

"Watch the matter, girlie?" asked the man grabbing her hand, the while teetering unsteadily. "Won't he pay no attenshun to you? What you need ish a young feller like me."

Myrtle jerked her hand away, nearly upsetting the man, who wisely sat down before he fell down. Myrtle looked around just in time to see Jack knocked down, but he was on his feet pumping away with both hands when the round ended.

Through the next five rounds the fight quieted down a bit and Jack managed to win two, or possibly three rounds. The tenth, eleventh and twelfth were all the Cowboy's way, and he seemed to get rougher and tougher as the fight went on. The thirteenth round looked like another stanza of the same song with Cherney carrying the fight to his younger opponent.

"Jush watch thish! Jush watch thish!" chanted the man behind Myrtle. He leaned over, patted her thigh, and when she turned around all indignant, pointed to the ring, "The Cowboy'sh going to kill him. I could do it myshelf." He patted her shoulder, assuring her he could do it any day in the week. He said in effect that Jack was a blankety-blank so and so and lucky to have lasted this long.

"Dad," she said, holding his arm and leaning close to him, "Do you hear what this man behind us keeps saying?"

"He'll have to do better," answered her father. "Thunderation, he'll have to do better."

Myrtle compressed her lips into two thin lines. Her jaws jutted purposefully out as she reached to her left and picked up an empty beer bottle.

There was a thump in the ring and the crowd leaped to its feet, cheering madly. Myrtle shifted the bottle to her right hand, and turned around. The man leaned forward in an effort to hoist

234

his rear off the seat, and his advice to Cherney ceased abruptly. He fell from the seat and disappeared under the bleachers, while Myrtle disposed of the evidence, Exhibit A, the lethal weapon, by tossing it after him. Myrtle turned toward the ring in time to see the Cowboy climb to his feet.

"What happened?" she yelled.

"Jack hit him like this and this," said Frank demonstrating.

The next four rounds were not particularly exciting when judged by the action in the previous rounds, but one thing was certain—barring a knockout, Jack had lost the fight. His left eye was cut and bruised, and his middle was red from the pounding it had taken.

"Jack, you're going to have to knock him out to win now," said Cheney before the eighteenth round. Jack was tired and wondered how the Cowboy was. In answer to Cheney he nodded. The bell rang for round eighteen.

Jack rushed Cherney, but was tied up in a clinch. After the break he tried again and again, and each time Cherney clinched. Evidently, knowing he had the fight won, he was going to take no chances on getting knocked out. The crowd booed him, but he retreated, covered up, and clinched.

"Where did Charley go?" asked a voice behind Frank.

"Sh!" said another, pointing to Myrtle. He whispered in his friend's ear. The friend nodded vigorously. He had to go himself.

"Oh, damn him," groaned Frank, "he won't fight!"

"Why not?" asked Myrt.

"He's taking no chances, now that he's got it won," explained Frank.

"Has Jack lost?" asked Myrtle anxiously.

"He has unless, he can knock Cowboy out."

"He can do that," said she confidently.

"Well, this is the next to the last round. Jack will have to stir himself now."

Jack came out fast and began trying again for a chance to get in one real blow, but the Cowboy was too clever. With about a minute to go, he suddenly opened up on Jack and caught him off guard. The onslaught took Jack off his feet, but he was up again, boring in at the count of seven, only to catch another blow and go down again. This time he climbed to his feet after only taking a three count and his legs were wobbling. Before Cherney could land again the round ended.

The crowd never sat between rounds. At the bell for the twentieth and last round Jack looked all right as he left his corner, but after touching gloves with Cherney, it became apparent that he was still dazed, when he didn't put up his hands. Cherney swung and Jack went down, but got right up. Doug Cheney held a towel in his hand, ready to end the fight if it looked like Jack was going to get hurt. Cherney closed again and Jack landed a light left and a hard right. However, Cherney wanted to win. A knockout would be better than a decision, so he came in again carefully, looking for a chance to land hard. The round was almost over when the Cowboy saw his opening and let drive with all he had. Jack also must have seen an opening, for his left shot out followed by a hard straight right. Just what happened is not clear, but Cherney was sitting in the center of the ring, his hands and arms behind him propping himself into an upright position. Over him the referee counted, reaching five before the bell ended the fight.

At the bell, Jack walked on uncertain legs over to Cowboy Cherney's corner and sat down. Two seconds picked Cherney off the canvas and held him between them. The referee collected the judges' ballots, and the crowd began to quiet down to see what the verdict would be. When the referee raised Cherney's glove, he had to do it in the Cowboy's corner, for that man was in no condition to come to the center of the ring.

In Jack's ears as his head cleared a voice was saying, "I'll give you ten thousand dollars for a rematch in San Francisco."

"No!" said Jack, repeating it louder and louder.

"He ain't himself yet," said Doug to the man. "See him in the morning."

236

CHAPTER XXXIII

HORSES, CARRIAGES AND HORSELESS CARRIAGES

It was Sunday morning, the morning after the fight. Grandma Parker was the only one up and about, for she had been to early Mass. Now she busied herself with breakfast, humming some ditty to herself. Above her she could hear Frank getting up to do his morning chores. Some one gave the front door bell a twist, and Grandma thought it was probably the paper boy, as she went to answer it.

"Good morning, Grandma," said a cheerfully familiar voice as she opened the door.

"Good morning, Jack," said Grandma, "come in."

"Isn't anybody up?"

"Just me," said she, catching sight of his battered face. "You didn't win." She sounded reproachful.

"Not this time," he said. When he smiled his puffed upper lip took on a decidedly sinister look. "I came over to see the family, especially Dad Stone—can I have breakfast with you?"

"Of course, you can. Frank is coming downstairs to milk, now." The heavy footsteps descended the stairs. Jack walked over to the foot of the stairs and waited for Frank, while Grandma went back to the kitchen.

"Hello, there!" said Frank catching sight of his visitor. "It looks to me like you got yourself up before breakfast."

"I couldn't sleep, so I came over to see you folks. Grandma says I can eat here."

"Good. Come on out to the barn whilst I milk and feed."

"I'll shed these duds and help you." He took off his coat, collar and tie, and hat, rolling his sleeves.

They picked up the milk pails and went out to the barns. Soon the cattle were fed and the barns cleaned. Frank took his one-legged stool down from its spot on the barn wall, sat on it and began to milk, but the cow moved away. He hitched up closer and started again. There was a terrific clatter as she kicked the bucket from between Frank's knees, tipping him over.

"All right, Blizzard, damn your ornery soul! If I have to fix you I can." He pushed her against the side of the stall and put a small chain around her hind legs and snapped its loose end in a huge staple. "Me and Blizzard have been having us a little set-to every now and again, ever since she come fresh. She may go for a couple of weeks as gentle as can be, and then she'll try to kick the wax out of me. I fixed me that chain and she can't act up." He sat down and started again to milk her.

"I suppose you wonder why I am over so early," said Jack, trying to look pleasant, but failing for reasons beyond his control.

"I figured you'd say when you was of a mind to."

"I quit my job at the steel mill yesterday."

"Is that so?" Frank felt a tremor of apprehension.

"Yes, and I was offered ten thousand dollars to meet the Cowboy in San Francisco."

"That's a lot of money," said Frank. "Do you think you can whip him the next time?"

"I don't know." Jack moved a bale of straw closer to where Frank was milking, and sat down on it. "That is what I wanted to talk to you about."

Frank continued milking, but looked at Jack out of the corner of his eye. He didn't think he had been asked for an opinion yet, so he said nothing. Finally, Jack went on.

"I told you that I quit my job at the mill. I did that because no matter what I do from now on, it won't be in the mill." Jack paused while he considered the matter, then, "Did you see the men who were with the Cowboy last night at the fight?"

"Yes, I did see them."

"What did you think of them?"

"A pretty tough bunch from their looks."

"That's what I meant. Scars, bad ears, and cuts all over them— a broken nose or two, and the Cowboy is beginning to get marked up, too." He chewed on a piece of timothy hay. Frank waited and milked. "I have been offered ten thousand dollars for a rematch in San Francisco. I have to give my answer to that today."

"Have you any idee what you are going to say?"

"I know what I want to say, but I wanted to talk to you first.

238

Do you think I'd be crazy to tell them to take a jump in the lake?"

Frank stopped milking for a moment while he considered the matter. "Jack, you would be the one who'd have to get in the ring with the Cowboy, and any reason you chose for not wanting to do it would be fine with me. From what you said earlier, I'd say those scars, ears and cuts are what you're thinking about."

"It's not so much the scars you can see that are bothering me, as the ones to their brains that you can't see. I am dumb enough to enjoy boxing, but I'm bright enough not to want to go through the rest of my life a nut."

"You got you something there."

"I've been lucky so far," said Jack, and then he added, "I think!"

"Meaning, you think you still got all your buttons?"

"Yes, and ten thousand dollars besides. Suppose I did fight in San Francisco; win or lose, I'd have to meet the next challenger, or the champ. I might go on fighting until I was over the hill and I'd end up like these other guys."

"Seems likely."

"Well now, there is the problem—right now I have my brains and some money—do I shoot for double, or quit right now?"

"It seems to me that you have made up your mind, Jack, and I agree with you. Now is the time to quit!"

"I didn't think I'd already made up my mind," said Jack, standing up and leaning against the door jamb. "But maybe I have."

It seemed to Frank as he considered the matter that Jack had been able to see past the cheers of the crowd, and the publicity and notoriety to the more sobering prospects of such a career, and that in turning back at this moment he was displaying remarkably good judgment. He told him so.

By this time Frank had finished milking, but neither was anxious to terminate the discussion, so Frank sat on the bale of straw, and Jack perched on the door sill. It was Jack who spoke, "So it is agreed that I quit fighting—and I have left the mill. I'd like to start a business of my own. I've always said that I'd like to have a livery, but do I?"

"Do I know the answer to that?" asked Frank.

"I suppose so," said Jack. "You knew I wanted to hang the gloves up. But seriously now, times change. You started in business nearly twenty-five years ago. Do you think a young man could start in business today exactly as you and Mother Stone did, and make a success of it?"

"Everything is changing in Cleveland, and we are going to have to change, too, or we will lose out the same as if we started yesterday."

"That is sort of what I meant, but suppose you tell me what you think are the most important changes in the past years, and then I'll tell you what changes I think we will see in the next twenty-five."

"Well, Jack, I think the most important change in Cleveland is taking place right in the people who live here. When I came to Cleveland, I came right off the farm. Nearly everyone else did, too, even the Bohemians, and they came here right off the boat. When Mary and I came here to Cedar and Doan, there was a lot of open country. Sure there were houses, but nearly every one had a garden, a few chickens, a horse and a cow. We were city folks on a country scale. Now look around you. Most of the cows are gone, and so will mine be any day now. It is a problem to bring hay in and feed, but the big problem is manure. When I started, I could sell the manure for gardens. When people quit gardening as much, I could at least give it away, finally I have had to give it away and haul it, too. But that isn't the end of it. Now the neighbors are complaining about the smell and the flies and that still isn't all. So many new people have moved in to the neighborhood that I couldn't begin to keep up with their milk needs. I know it's a lost cause, and one of these days we will sell the cows and the back yard dairy will be over. The big dairies are ready to take over that part of the business.

"Vegetable gardens are going out of style. People are busy, and they can get their fresh stuff cheaper from me, the farmer's markets, and the hucksters than they can raise it. It will be the same thing with chickens, and when the horse cars came along, many folks got rid of their buggy horses.

"Still folks want to be country after a fashion. They have grass lawns and grow flowers. Everybody has shade trees and back yard swings under them, same as me and Maw here. Every yard has an apple tree, or cherry tree, or a quince or something. Why, I'd bet me my bottom dollar if you was to ride over this city in a balloon, you would have a hard time seeing the houses on account of the trees."

"I know about that," said Jack. "That's why Cleveland is called the 'Forest City.'"

240

"Yup, look down Halsey Street, and you will see rows of trees clear to the end. Cedar has plenty of trees too, but now we have electric cars, and two sets of tracks. That doesn't leave much room off the tracks, so the trees will have to be chopped down and the street widened, and the city folks will think they will get rid of a lot of problems with the trees. The leaves are a darned nuisance and the roots are always clogging up the sewers."

"There is all this paving going on, too."

"I think," said Frank warming to his subject, "that at the present rate if a feller wants to see a tree, in a few years he is going to have to go over to Wade Park to see one. All the rest will be gone. The city council thinks so, too, or they wouldn't be about to buy up all the land in Doan Brook Valley, clear to Gordon Park." Frank paused for thought, then continued. "I look for Cleveland to be paved solid brick or limestone clear to the city limits."

"With streetcars everywhere, what do you think about the future of the horse?" asked Jack.

"I think people are going to have to have horses regardless. Horses are mighty useful now, but even if they weren't, I think people would have them. Dogs might have been useful once, but even though they are darn pests now, most families have one."

"Now you are getting into my department," said Jack. "I think that in the next twenty-five years the electric wagon and auto car will take the place of horses."

"Jack, you got hit harder than you thought last night."

"Am I wrong?"

"Nothing will ever take the place of a good horse."

"For racing, maybe."

"I can't imagine a city without horses," said Frank.

"Well, they are going to be here for a while at least," admitted Jack, "and when I think of what sort of business I want to get into, it always seems to be connected with horses. Suppose I was to start a business selling buggies and wagons for now, but to plan on selling automobile buggies later—do you think I'd make out?"

"I don't know why not. Would you buy and sell horses?"

"No."

"Well, maybe one of these days everybody will have a horseless carriage, but I can't imagine anyone having the fun with one

241

that I have had with Fred and the trap."

Frank was glad of one thing. Not once had Jack mentioned getting married. Perhaps, Frank thought, he was waiting until his new business was safely on its feet. Frank hoped this was the case, for time was in his favor.

"Hello, Mother Stone," said Jack when they entered the house. She regarded him critically. "You don't look too bad."

"Thank you, but I know what I look like, and I'm a sorry sight. Where's Myrtle?"

"In bed." Mary smiled at him, and pointed at the ceiling.

"Why don't you get her up?" suggested Frank to Jack.

"Why, Frank!" Mary was shocked. She glared at Frank. "Young men don't get their lady friends out of bed in the morning!"

"I don't know why not," said Frank, feigning indignation. "In Grandma's day they used to bundle."

"Only in the winter time when it was cold," snapped Grandma in her best French-American dialect.

"I'll tell you what we'll do, Jack. I'll go first and make sure the girls are decently covered up. Then you can wake 'em, or scare hell out of 'em, whichever you care to do."

"I've got three sisters at home," said Jack, "and it isn't likely I'll run into anything I don't know about."

"Jack Morrison," said Mary, "if you were my son I'd wash your mouth with soap." She shrugged her shoulders hopelessly. "That's probably as close as I could get to your mind."

Jack and Frank tramped up the stairs, and in the matter of moments there were shrieks and squeals to be heard. In a short time Frank came down alone.

"Where's Jack?" Mary asked.

"In talking to Vilas," said Frank, as Mary visibly relaxed.

"Frank, why did you do it?"

He looked around to see if they were alone. Grandma was nowhere to be seen. Putting his arm around his wife, he pulled her to him and kissed her back of the ear and on her neck.

"Just some more of my tomfoolery, Mary. It takes a lot of love to stand up to the shock of seeing your best girl in the morning, before she is dolled up. More than likely she is sleeping with her mouth open, and snoring, or her hair is done up in curlers. And when she wakes up she is probably hungry, and a hungry woman is an ugly wench. Nope, Mother, I can't think me up a better way to drive a man away than this way I just figured out."

"I didn't drive you away!"

"Of course, not—I'm different."

"So you are," she said planting a hearty kiss on his cheek.

"Yup, I am for a fact."

CHAPTER XXXIV

MYRTLE TAKES A DARE

The three girls were in the store. For the moment there were no customers and they were taking advantage of the lull, by sweeping and tidying up. Blanche who was nearest the door, suddenly motioned to the others to come over. They did, and stood peering over her shoulder.

"What is it?" asked Myrtle.

"Do you see that street car?" Blanche sounded mysterious.

"Of course, I do!"

"Can you see the motorman?"

"Not from here," said Myrtle.

"He is the most handsome thing I've ever seen," said Blanche, looking heavenward. The car rattled past, as the girls stared. No sooner had it gone than Ollie came in with Carrie Barber.

"He's gorgeous," said Carrie.

"Wonderful," echoed Ollie.

"Well, what is this gorgeous creature's name?" asked Myrtle, passing a banana to each.

"If I only knew!" exclaimed Blanche. "He has only been on this line about a week. No one knows him."

"The way to meet him," said Calista, "is to find out where he goes to church, and attend there for a while."

"How can I find that out?" asked Carrie, putting her finger neatly on the flaw in the plan.

"If we only knew someone who knew him," said Ollie, striking a thoughtful pose.

"There isn't anyone in the world that I wanted to meet," said Myrtle, flipping her weight from one foot to the other by means of an immoral roll of her hips, "that I couldn't meet in less than a day."

"Ho!" snorted Blanche, "I'd like to see you! How are you going to meet this man?"

"Who said I wanted to meet him?"

"If you did, how?"

"I'd get on the streetcar, ask him his name and get off."

"I dare you!"

"I double dare you!" chorused the others.

"You do?" asked Myrtle wide-eyed.

"Yes!" they agreed.

"Then put twenty-five cents apiece in the palm of my lily white hand, and I'll have his name for you in thirty minutes."

"It's a deal," cried Blanche, running for her pocketbook.

Soon Myrtle had four quarters in her hand, and was surrounded by the girls. She took off her apron, smoothed back her hair and walked out to the street and waited for the car to come along. She could see it just getting underway after turning around at the end of the line. In a few minutes the car jolted to a stop and she got on. Out of the corner of her eye she could see the girls watching from the doorway.

She dropped a ticket in the box, as the conductor yanked at the bellcord. She walked slowly through the almost empty car to the front. The motorman *was* handsome, she noted, as she stepped down to the front exit level.

"I am a census taker," said Myrtle sweetly, putting her left arm on the pipe rail behind the young man. "What is your name?"

"This isn't a census year," he said, impudently.

"Oh, so it isn't. How forgetful of me!" With her right hand she cupped his chin and tilted his face up. Her left held his head steady, while she planted a kiss squarely on his lips. The car skidded to a halt.

"This is where I get off," said she. The door opened and she alighted, turning demurely back toward the store. Inside the car the young motorman was a fiery red and the conductor and passengers shrieked with laughter.

The girls had been watching the car, and saw it suddenly stop before it reached a regular stopping place. Myrtle had gotten off and walked back as coolly as you please. What in the world had happened?

As she entered the store, the girls crowded around breathlessly. Reaching in her pocket, Myrtle withdrew the four quarters and gave them back.

"What happened?" asked Blanche.

"Nothing," said Myrtle.

"Did you find out his name? Did you meet him?" they asked.

"Certainly, I met him," said Myrtle.

"Well, for goodness sake, is he single? What's his name?"

"Hush, little chickadees," said Myrtle, patronizingly, "he's not for sale."

"But you already got one man," objected Carrie.

"And so have you, and you, and you, and you," pointing to each in turn. From there on, she refused to even talk about it.

The following day, at about the same time, Myrtle was busy waiting on Mrs. Kennedy Johnson, who was being difficult over a head of cabbage, claiming that none was solid. Calista and Mary were grinding coffee in the huge wheeled grinder.

Myrtle had heard a streetcar stop, but thought nothing of it until she felt herself being forcefully turned around. There stood the motorman. He pulled her to him and kissed her, holding her tight.

"Well," said Mrs. Johnson, breathing acid fumes, "what does this mean?"

Calista and Mary merely watched, flabbergasted. From inside the car, the conductor tried to see what was going on. A grin split his face wide open. The young man released Mytrle, and strode toward the door.

"Don't forget your change," Myrtle called after him.

"I won't," he assured her. The car rolled on down the street.

"Who was that man?" asked Mrs. Johnson.

"I don't know," said Myrtle, thumping a cabbage, "there are so many young men in the world."

CHAPTER XXXV

ALL'S WELL THAT ENDS! WELL?

Jack had been absent from the Stone household for better than a week. Frank assumed it was because the boy was working hard and probably tuckered out. However, he showed up one evening, and appeared to be far from tired.

"Myrtle," he said in a whisper, "I've got to see you alone for a few minutes."

"All right, Jack, let's go out in the porch swing."

"I'd rather walk, if you don't mind."

"Of course not."

They started off down Halsey Street, arm in arm.

"I'm glad you came over, Jack. There's so much I want to say to you."

"I know," he said uneasily. "Me, too."

For people who had so much to say, they were strangely quiet. They had covered the length of a full block, before they suddenly faced one another and spoke at once. "It's this way," said Jack, and "Well, suppose—" was Myrtle's offering. They laughed, but not too heartily.

"Would you care if we broke our engagement?" blurted Jack, painfully.

Myrtle stopped stock still. She looked at him and burst out laughing.

"Jack Morrison, you old sinner," she said, shaking his arm, "I was going to ask you the very same question!"

"You were, Myrt?"

"And let me tell you something, young man, no gentleman would ever break a lady's heart like you are doing. No, siree, if there is any engagement breaking, little sister is going to do it. How could I hold my head up, if the truth were known that I had been jilted?"

247

"Since when," said he, looking down at her, "did little sister begin caring what anybody thought?"

She refused to answer, striking off on a new tack.

"Is she nice, Jack?"

"You'd love her! Myrt, she's driving me crazy!"

"Isn't it wonderful to be really in love? I don't suppose we really were—we just thought so."

"I'll always love you, Myrt, but somehow it's different."

"I know. I'm gone, too."

"That's wonderful," he said, squeezing her arm.

"This is all right for us to agree to call off all bets, but what about Dad? He was sure set on having you for a son-in-law." Myrtle giggled over the idea.

"We'll have to tell him, but I hate to," admitted Jack.

"Let's go back and do it now," she suggested.

"I'd rather get punched by Cowboy Cherney," he assured her.

Retracing their steps, they entered the house. From the parlor came the crashing of fistfuls of notes on the piano, making an awful racket. Jack and Myrt looked in.

"Oh, kid!" said Calista holding up a sheet of paper in one hand and an envelope in the other, "I looked in the mailbox and found this letter from George." She kissed the letter and fluttered it at arm's length. "He's in the Philippines. He's coming back to me, after the war, and he adores me!"

They left her to her happiness, and finally found their quarry in the swing in the back yard.

"Get yourselves in and set," Frank invited. They climbed in holding hands, and sat facing the old folks.

"Dad, brace yourself for a shock," said Myrtle.

"Wait 'til I get a good brace," said Frank, picking up Mary's hand. He figured this was the moment he had been dreading. The youngsters looked so confoundedly happy. "Let her go."

"You aren't going to have Jack for a son-in-law."

"The hell you say!" He carefully eased out the lungful of air he had been holding, and felt Mary relax.

"No, Dad, we have decided to break up our engagement, and we are both very willing, since we each have an eye on somebody else."

"Is that right, Jack?"

"Yes."

"Well, it'll have to be all right with me, damn it, but only on one condition. Jack, you can shake Myrt loose, but you can't me. You come over to see me once a week, or so, or I'll be over to see you. You and me got us a lot of idees in us, and some of them ain't bad."

"I'll agree to that," said Jack, relieved that it was no worse than this.

"Why don't you children bring your new flames over to the house for supper Saturday night!" invited Mary. "We could call it an 'Unengagement Party.'"

"Fine," said Jack enthusiastically.

"And bring Grace and the girls," added Mary.

The youngsters climbed out of the swing, leaving Frank and Mary alone. Mary put his arm around her shoulders and cuddled up close, her head on his shoulder. His other hand held both of hers.

"Frank, you are wonderful," she whispered.

"Ain't I though?"

"I mean it!"

"It was the Lord's doings."

"I suppose it was."

They rocked back and forth for some few minutes, each deep in his own thoughts. The swing creaked so slightly.

"Frank," said Mary, "would you like two new daughters?"

"Two new daughters!"

"Yes, my brother Nelson's girls, Jessie and Myrtle, want to come and live with us."